The Hand Of Tæranon

Rory Haymont

The Hand Of Tæranon

(First paperback edition - March 2023)

ISBN 978-0-6456903-2-3 (Paperback)

ISBN 978-0-6456903-3-0 (eBook)

Also by Rory Haymont

The Hand Of Tæranon

Richard and Miranda sat in a brief uncomfortable silence after the greetings had been taken care of. Richard had arrived with his usual cheery greeting and Miranda had returned it with a somewhat more sombre than usual reply. Miranda liked Richard. He was personable. Always had been. On the harmless end of the personable spectrum, she thought. Completely different to some of her egocentric, but more successful authors.

'Richard. We need to talk about the next book.'

'Yes. Full of ideas and ready to start Miranda. Just waiting for the go ahead.' Said Richard. *And the advance.* He thought.

Miranda sighed. Preparing to deliver a brief history lesson. 'Richard after the success of your first two books we contracted you for three more. You've written two of those, and we're discussing the publication of the final book in the contract.'

Miranda was stating the obvious. Richard wondered why.

'Richard, I know you don't follow how your books fare in terms of reviews.'

'That's right Miranda, I believe it may stifle the creative process-es for the next project.' This was as supercilious as Richard got. Which was not very.

'As publishers of course, we need to take notice of reviews, partly because of their impact on commercial performance. We have a name for various kinds of commercial performance in the pub-lishing industry, and one describes the performance of your last two books.'

'I can imagine the need for that. Technical speak for publishers.'

'The last two books *tanked* Richard. Rather badly. We lost a lot of money. The first time we thought it might be an aberration, but after two poorly performing novels. Richard; it's a problem.'

She rolled straight on. 'Richard reviews, no matter how little we believe or respect them, can be a harbinger for the commercial per-formance of the next book, because they influence sentiment.'

'Miranda, as a writer, I found your use of the word harbinger in that context most satisfying.'

'Great…thank you.' Said Miranda. She'd hoped to raise some ire, for which she could then justify dealing a death blow. But not from Richard.

'*Oh well.*' She thought. '*He'll* have *to storm out of the place after what's coming next.*'

'You see the reviews for the most recent book are grim. Let me see.' Miranda put on her glasses and picked up a book. Turning it over to read the back.

'*Shit.*' She left a pause that she expected Richard to fill. Rather than have the word hang there in its hurtful simplicity.

'There's brevity for you. Must have been some junior reviewer from the Oklahoma Daily or something.' He smiled hopefully.

'It was the senior reviewer for the *New York Review of Books* Richard.'

Richard was dented but not deflated. 'We all get a bad review now and then.'

Miranda read from the back cover again. '*This book was so bad that I actually started to gouge my eyes out. Fortunately, my husband was able to tear the book from my hands and throw it in the fire. Thankfully I hadn't done too much damage, although I have lost my peripheral vision in one eye.*'

Richard was concerned. 'Losing peripheral vision must be awful.'

Miranda was getting annoyed at the fact that Richard wasn't. 'She was being ironic Richard. She's the reviewer for the Washington Globe. Here's another one. *I begged the newspapers Head of Literary Review to let me off on this assignment. He wouldn't budge so I went to his house and shot him rather than read any further.*' 'The Times Richard. Of London.'

Miranda could see Richard wasn't going to get angry. Only more and more deflated. She felt what she was going to say next was callous, but she wanted to prepare him, not simply drop the decision on him.

'Naturally we didn't run a first issue with those reviews on the back cover. We did indeed pay some journalists in very small towns not to read the book and provide glowing reviews. But our marketing people came up with an idea for a release over Christmas. Richard, we ran this edition of the book with those reviews and several more like them on the inside front cover, back cover, and inside back cover over the holiday period. And where there's the usual pithy review at the base of the front cover, we went for; *'Shit' New York Review of Books.*

'The use of the word *pithy* was quite apt Miranda.'

Christ thought Miranda. *'This is like beating a puppy to death.'*

'You can imagine what it's like Richard. Someone picks up your book and sees the review on the front, and so they turn it over to read the reviews on the back. Then the back inside cover and so on. Having read all of these…it's kind of funny. Everyone has a…bit of a laugh. People think it would be a fun Christmas present.' Richard saw how such a process could generate interest in his book. Which it seemed to be desperately in need of.

This it was all taking too long. She had another meeting. She had to finish the story. 'On that edition at least, we got an uptick for a while. Only lost a quarter of what we invested.'

Miranda could almost see the workings of Richard's mind as he tried to put some kind of positive spin on all of this. She thought she'd move on quickly before he succeeded.

'That brings us to the final book you're contracted to write.'

His face lit up. He could immediately see an opportunity for redemption.

'We'd like you to write the book under a different name.'

'Ah. A *Nome de Plume*.' He smiled hopefully.

'Personally, I like to say a 'different name'. Based on the reviews Richard your name is trashed, and if you ever write for another publishing house, I recommend you never use it again.'

Richard was digesting the 'another publishing house' comment when Miranda followed on. 'First of all, we'd like you to write in the fantasy genre. You're last two attempts at your Whodunit specialty, have been…' She shrugged. '…abject failures. And the genre is dying. Thank Christ. How many times can the Butler do it with some variation of 'I would have got away with it if weren't for that meddling …insert boring full time or amateur detective hero.'

Miranda could see air finally leaking out of Richard's tyres. 'It's the genre I've spent my entire writing career in.'

She had to be ruthless. 'Our research department identified that there was a gap in the market in terms of a published writer in your genre when your first two books succeeded. Now in this business alone we have two others in the stable in that genre. And their books sell. I can't for the life of me see why. I mean who really gives a crap who did what and how. Might as well go and play Cluedo to come up with plot ideas.'

Miranda had touched upon the dirty little secret of the genre, thought Richard. However, he needed to get with the program. Miranda was going to offer him a range of options, at least one might be bad.

'Fantasy.' He said. 'How hard can that be?'

'Who knows. I have the same shallow cynicism cued up for that genre but why bother saying it out loud. Personally, I'd like it if we published some actual literature now and again like we used to. Anyway. We're overloaded with crime writers, but we have a gap in fantasy. The name on the cover would be Natasha Sabre.'

Richard gave a little laugh. 'Isn't that, you know, a bit corny. Fantasy and all those swords and so on, and the author's name's Sabre.'

'It's the name Natasha was born with. The book will be written under that name. You'll also have a ghost writer.'

'A ghost writer.' This really came out of the blue. 'Someone who'll help me write the book.' He said this slowly, navigating the words like a minefield.

'Yes. In this interpretation of ghost writer, she'll be helpful to the extent that she'll write the book for you.'

'So...ah...what will I do. I'll look in and provide constructive criticism from time to time?'

'No Richard. Natasha is a well-established and successful author. Unfortunately, the publishers she's been with also thought her name was silly in the Fantasy space so she's been writing under a *Nome de plume*. She's negotiating to come across to us and use her real name. She'll be presenting her upcoming work today as it happens.'

The reality hit home at last for Richard. 'She takes the place I have for my final contracted book. The only chance I had to redeem myself.'

'We needed a no strings single book slot while we consider a multi-book deal for her. Yours was the only slot with such a…low probability of market success. There's not many options Richard. My boss had our lawyers literally, and I mean physically, tear up your contract and ask what you plan to do about it. Or you can take a deal I fought especially hard to get for you to get. Because you were in the way of Natasha finding a place here, I negotiated one half of one percent of Net Profit from whatever she writes in your slot.'

'Net profit doesn't sound like much. Half a percent of revenue might have been meaningful, but still not much I'd say.'

'Richard, I tried for one a percent of Gross Profit. No dice. They laughed at a percent of revenue. They all boil down to sweet bugger all. Your royalties for the last two books, let's not talk about them…and sales of the original two best sellers have…ah…plateaued. I really should say plummeted Richard. These days books pour onto the market and smother what went before them quickly unless they find a place in the zeitgeist or achieve cult status. Only a few author's works attract a loyal long-term following. Which yours won't. And let's face it the young people today have the attention span of an ant. Long form books will die out over the next twenty years and a saga will be twenty pages long.' Miranda wondered how far she should go with Richard and tell him it was time for him to look for a job. But that would really be kicking the puppy, and he was her brother. She had only one idea left.

'Our old IT guy embarked on this project several years back because he was a fantasy wonk and aspiring writer. Also, to be frank, a wierdo. Turns out he had absolutely no talent for writing, but he built a device that some think is a useful ideas generator for fantasy novels which are becoming overrun by tropes.'

'Except for *Natasha Sabre*.' Richard was trying to portray hurt and bitterness. He was so bad at this he could only manufacture some petulance.

'I never said tropes didn't sell Richard. I said they can get a bit thick on the ground in some genres and Fantasy is one of them. Tropes don't exist by accident or even design. And now it's a formula. Save the Cat. Beat Sheets. Whatever the fuck the latest crop of writer's self-help books proselytizes. We publish these by the millions. This formula satisfies people at a deep level no matter how much an author like you wants to write something different.'

'My advice is to stick to the age-old formula. Hero with some shitty backstory gets deeper in the shit, meets interesting people or beings, maybe develops somehow conflicted feelings for a potential happily ever after partner for life or at least a sex for a month partner. But they can't admit it for some banal reason. It's complicated. It's awkward. Things get better, whoops, then they get worse. Add a few ups and downs, maybe a tiresome comic relief, depending on the book length you want. Some top tier character gets killed somehow. Boo fucking hoo. And there's some big victory, the crowd cheers, the people in the control room do fist pumps. But hang on, the hero or his can now be revealed partner for life is killed unexpectedly at the end. But wait a minute. Wait just a Goddamn minute. They're brought back to life in any number of improbable, I don't give a shit ways. Happy forever. But wait, hang the fuck on. There's some loose end somewhere. A sequel ready to roll. Evil re-emerges. Their nemesis, or the next improbable author of destruction of the happy ending emerges Yadda Yadda Yadda.'

Richard was suddenly excited by an idea. 'Hey.' He said. As one revealing something amazing. 'I've got it. Let's bring them back to life, but *then* they get killed again. And they get brought back to life *again*. How's that for an original idea.'

'*No wonder I'm jaded.*' Miranda thought.

'Richard, why don't you give the thing this wierdo IT guy built a try. I can't explain it. He died soon after he built it, but it's simple enough to operate. So maybe see if you can drag out something original but which will also satisfy the bullshit formula we love to hate but keep churning out. It got a lot of use for four or five year or so until…there were a few issues.'

'Issues.'

'Yeah. Dissatisfied users. Legal guys sorted it out. From my perspective the quality of the writing of most users improved. Some ideas came out that some people liked to call imaginative. The quality of work in a very small minority did reduce.'

'Reduce?'

'To nothing. There were no manuscripts. But these were outriggers Richard. It's still in use, a bit less frequently now. Someone looking for yet another new angle on the Lord of the Rings or Dune or whatever fantasy classic rehash they decide on. You decide. I think it's your best shot. Take it home. Make a bit of time to be zonked out. Eat some nice food and drink a bunch of water, put a seatbelt around the porcelain rumble seat, just in case, because you're out to it for about twelve hours, though it varies I'm told. I've got it here if you want to try it. She handed over a large briefcase.

'I thought it would need a big computer.'

'The only thing I know is that this thing populates the gazillion neurones or nodes or whatever's in your brain box to recreate the world. It has the same characters each time for everyone using it as if they were already going about their business all the while. I think he called it a catalyser. People pick a bunch of fantasy type options and start at the same place and then the story has infinite possible endings. At least that's what he said before he carked it.' She looks at her watch. 'I've been talking too much Richard…' *Trying to make you storm out of here ages ago* she thought. 'Natasha's waiting. I'd been hoping to avoid… an awkward moment. But here we are.'

'Sure Miranda.' He smiled jovially. 'Once I've improved on the ideas from this formula machine, I'll drop the next best seller on your desk.' She smiled. This was the Richard she liked so much, no matter how lousy an author he was, he wouldn't know what a grudge was. You couldn't ask for a better big bother. Unless you needed someone beaten up. Then you went to her Uncle Terry.

Richard went into the waiting room expecting to see a pretentious woman with long fake fingernails, probably a fake hairpiece and fake eyelashes. Though he really had no reasonable explanation as to why he should dislike a person adorned in such a way. Dress however you want and your sexual orientation is your business had always been his motto. He wanted her to wear some recognisable badge which would allow him to immediately and permanently dislike her. However, there was nothing to purchase on. She looked like a very pleasant person, beginning a slow drift into middle age along with him. She had a frustratingly genuine smile and after getting up, rather awkwardly, he was soon shaking her hand.

She mentioned a book of his that she'd read. It seemed she'd been made aware, only after leaving her publisher, how a space had been made for her. She unexpectedly gave him a brief, tender hug, during which she said. 'We all have difficult times as writers Richard. I've read your work and I'm certain you'll come through.'

All he could manage was a 'Thanks.' As a confused Miranda called in her latest signing.

'I'll text you my address and number. Come and have a cup of tea. We can compare notes on this lot. We writers need to stick together.' Her hug had been warm, but frail. He could see by the way she walked she was in pain and probably not accustomed to walking unassisted. Natasha had managed to become the most unlike a heartless interloper someone could be.

Richard brought the briefcase home and opened it. It opened so that both halves were of equal depth and were covered in buttons. Some of the buttons were cleaner from more frequent use while some less so, but all were legible. There was a set of top tier buttons above with four more tiers below each reducing in size so that the final tier had a larger number of small buttons. The first tier included forests, rivers, oceans, cliffs, swamps, and pastures. The next tier included knights, dragons, castles, witches, wizards, princesses, elves, goblins, children and on and on. Below were language settings for different race, species types and several other settings Richard began to skip over.

The final tier was character setting. Obnoxious, kind, wise, seductive, mystical, boring, self-absorbed, pragmatic, aloof, proud, angry, lazy, and so on. There was a save sub plot button so you could pick Dragon, children, sky, cliffs, obnoxious and then choose another subplot to the story if you wanted to.

He prepared himself as his sister had suggested. He notices on the briefcase there was a small compartment at the bottom of the right lower section. It clicked open and he drew out a neural net which sat over his head. '*Shit just got real.*' He thought, tightening himself to the cistern via two joined leather belts.

It was at this point that he realised he hadn't decided what sequence of buttons he intended to press to structure his journey. He looked at the options for some time, and now that he was faced with making choices he found them rather banal. He spent some time crafting a pattern of buttons he thought might make for something more interesting and original than what had come out of the genre recently. Although he admitted to himself he couldn't really make a judgement on that because he hadn't read any.

There was a knock on the door. He was inclined to ignore it. But it got so few knocks he felt he should value each one. He could strap himself to a toilet anytime. In any event the knocks were followed up by a cheerful. 'You there lad.'

Terry still called him 'lad' which he liked.

Terry was the black sheep of the family. 'Hi Uncle Terry.' A warm hug was exchanged. Richard loved his uncle. He told stories about a side to London the average person never got to see. And Richard was the one person in the family who would lend Terry money. The other thing Richard would do is be understating when he didn't pay it back for months, or over a year on one occasion. Eventually Terry would hand over five or ten times what was owed in a big bag of cash. Hanging around Terry introduced Richard to hard men or fixers, or the dodgier people associated with sports like the dogs, horse racing and boxing.

All these people knew Terry was very fond of his nephew, and he wanted them to treat him like one of the lads. When Richard was younger, he'd sometimes set him up in a café reading a magazine. Terry told him if anyone 'interesting' came along all he had to do scratch his nose. That's all he needed to do. Everybody knew that Terry would set his nephew up to do this miles from where the job was taking place.

He hadn't seen his uncle for a few months, and it might be the first time that Richard would have to negotiate the amount of the loan because he was 'skint' this time. It might get to the point he had to ask Terry for a job.

Terry didn't want a loan, rather he said he was 'short-handed.' This made Richard a little nervous. He'd figured out the fake stakeout routine years ago. It was a bit of fun when he was younger.

Terry called a cab and said. 'We need to arrange a meeting with a punter. Ask him a few questions.' They changed from the Cab into a very tired Nissan 'My mate is on a table in small …travelling casino. He's going to cause a bit of a scene. Wants the weight and measure of the dice being used checked. He'll let the punter switch them and get legitimate dice on the table. Then he'll probably need to go to the crapper because there's another good mate of mine on the exit. He knows dice won't flush if he puts them in the loo. And there's a conveniently open window he might choose to climb through. All you need to do is use this phone with a text message ready to press in case he comes out that way. We already know where he's going. If he doesn't swallow them, which he might choose to do, you might see him throw a pair of dice away in case he's followed. Use the phone to text where. My mate on the door will take you home after a little while. Put the phone back in the plastic bag and he'll stop off at a skip bin on your way.'

It happened right as Terry said it would…almost. Shaking like a leaf Richard pressed the button as soon as he saw a hand groping for something to get hold of as a man climbed out the window. The man, in a well-cut casual suit, ran towards a car which had pulled in near the window to pick him up. The car Richard was in had a clear as it began to speed off. He saw an arm come out of the car and throw something into a stormwater drain by the road. Richard typed *'Stormwater drain. Left.'*

14

A policewoman stuck head in the window. 'You know you can't park here.' Richard was in a sudden panic and threw the phone in the air. It hit the roof of the car and came to rest in the foot well. 'Sir, you'll need to come back to the station with me and we'll show you what police brutality really looks like.'

Richard was relieved to hear a familiar voice from behind her. 'Emma, are you putting the frighteners on this lad.'

She withdrew her head from the car. 'Something I should know about Terry?'

'Nothing to see here Emma. Or there won't be soon.'

She nodded her head sideways at the car. 'Dangerous is he?'

'The worst kind Emma. Because no one expects him to be.'

'Sounds like I should keep plodding along and try to find a villain I've got a good reason to beat up.'

'It's coppers like you that keep our streets safe for the likes of me Emma.'

'We'll *fankyou*.' She said in her pronounced Essex accent. She wandered off to a police car that had been sitting unobserved around the corner the whole time.

Terry was sitting with Richard in his kitchen a few hours later. 'If there's one thing that annoys me it's taking an unfair advantage in a game of chance. When those chaps got to their hotel after we made sure they didn't have a traffic accident on the way, we found the place loaded up with the proceeds of unfair advantages.'

'But the way we work is a little different to blokes playing at hard men. We took half of a substantial pile and suggested they go and enjoy their gaming pleasures elsewhere. We even suggested a few places. These coves were surprised. They knew how others played the game. We all had a beer and left.'

Terry put a slim but substantial pile of new fifty-pound notes in front of his nephew. 'Terry I couldn't. It was exciting but…'

'Richard we all had a bit of fun this afternoon. And it was well supervised if you know what I mean.' Richard thought he did. 'You don't want this sort of money sitting about. Bury it in the garden or put it in the ceiling. And one day, a pile of cash will come in handy.'

'Sure, and it was a bit fun. I'll be honest though. Not sure I can do it again. Even though I might like to.'

'Horses for courses. But that job's a good one to learn from Richard. If there are loaded dice on the table, make sure you're in control of the game, and have a mate in charge of the door.'

Terry had gone. Richard was strapped to the toilet. He looked over the suite of buttons and every time he adjusted them, they came up with the kind of scenario he'd either read or heard of. Then he saw a lone button with a Perspex box over it at the base next to the neural net container. The cover over must have been there to avoid it being pressed accidentally. It was covered in dust and filth. Apparently never having been used. He licked his index finger and cleaned enough away to see. *'Let it Roll.'* He decided to be impulsive.

At least once in his life. He put the neural net on, opened the cover, pressed the button and in his head he heard; 'Selection Confirmed'.

He was walking beside a man on a horse. The landscape was much the same as the south of England which he found a little disappointing. It was pleasant, but he already knew it well. The man on the horse looked down and smiled. 'Richard. Good to meet you. I'm your guide. Sort of. I'm the only one in here that knows you're gathering material for a book. Though we've never had a *'Let it Roll'* Punter before, so we'll see if that remains the case.'

Richard had a great many questions in his mind, but he knew the polite question was. 'And what shall I call you?'

'That's one of the many choices you're free to make. I've been called Gilgasction. Not my favourite. Lekka wasn't too bad. Orvillius I could have done without.'

'What's your real name. At home.'

He seemed a little surprised. 'I have a wife and sixty-two children. The children call me dad of course. The wife calls me many things depending on the state of her temper. My creator called me Roger.'

'Excellent.' Said Richard. 'Rogericus it will be.'

The man on the horse showed only a flicker of disappointment. Through long experience he pretending to be pleased. Richard laughed. 'Of course it's Roger. I'm new to this fantasy stuff. Feel free to tell me if what I'm coming up with is a bunch of wank.'

Roger reflected on this. 'You'll be the first to know.'

'The second thing on my mind is, why am I walking while you're riding a horse. Do we have a master - servant relationship? Am I going to regret pressing the *Let It Roll* button from the outset?'

'Richard, I thought it would be interesting for you to see the world from a perspective no Punter before you have ever seen. They've either come to be well to do types or powerful wizards or handsome Elves; you know.'

'So, I'm a servant?'

'Not exactly. It's more a business relationship, and I'm one level above in the organisation.'

'A business relationship?'

'Yes. You're the producer and I do quality control, inventory management, market research and all the point-of-sale work. As you know it's the middlemen who make the real money and end up with greater seniority. It doesn't matter what genre. It's universal.'

'What do I produce.'

'Feminine talismans. You're an extruder. A very skilled plastics extruder.'

'I'm a plastics extruder in a fantasy world.'

'Thought you might want to try something original. Anyway, you don't need to keep that part for a book, you can replace it with being a more conventional tooth puller, herbal remedy peddler or a roving blacksmith. Which can be hard work. But wait until you see the reaction to a travelling extruder before you knock it.'

'Do we make pretty good money?'

'I do. Hence the horse. You; not so much.'

'Until I go on strike and tell you to jam your talismans up your ass.' Richard said good naturedly.

'You might have chosen a better phrase to vent your unhappiness. But since horses are cheap compared to the value of talismans, all I can say Richard, is why did it take so long for you to ask?'

They were getting a sense they would get along alright when Richard saw a Knight in shining armour. His armour was polished, so even at a distance it shone like burnished gold. And on his chest was a magnificent Sunface surcoat.

'Oh shit.' Roger was annoyed. 'A Knight.'

Richard was confused. To him it was like a big Christmas present standing by a river. 'What's wrong with Knights.'

'They're so stupid. You know how it is with the aristocracy. They only breed with each other. They get a bit loopy from that, but Knights get a double whammy. They spend most of their time while children only learning things like how to fight with a sword or joust. Most of them are halfwits.'

They had arrived to meet the Knight who was looking anxiously across a wide shallow stream. 'Hi guys.' He laughed nervously.

Richard couldn't help himself. 'That is the most beautiful suit of armour I've ever seen. And brought to such a polish. And your Sunface surcoat is so exquisitely embroidered.'

The Knight stood up to his full height and put his hands on his hips. 'If you're going to throw compliments like that around, I'll stand here all day.' They laughed. The Knight had an uncomplicated, happy laugh.

Though he quickly became forlorn. 'Unfortunately, my horse, Sparrow, is on the other side of this river. I would be heartbroken if I lost her. And I seem to have misplaced my Page Boy. He usually looks after all these things.'

Roger looked at Richard, who crossed the ankle-deep stream and led the steed back to its owner who was untroubled by how easily it had been done. 'If I fall in water, even shallow water, I can't get up.' He said simply.

Richard wanted to know about the basic Knightly duties. 'So ah, do you fellows kill dragons, rescue damsels in distress and look for Grails. Go on Crusades maybe.' For all the Knight's good nature the question struck a chord.

'All of the dragons are dead thanks to that stupid bastard St George. Went about slaying the things all over the place till there were none left. 'Georgie.' We'd say, 'Leave a breeding colony.' 'Leave a breeding colony.' No. He mucked it up for all of us. He's in an old age home for Knights now. No one visits him. The bastard. Damsels?' He sighed. 'Our wives got wind of what was going on there. There was a bit of a scandal and the girls had to get…

um… other employment instead of hanging out of the round things on the top of castles. Grails. We find it hard to get enthusiastic about. Most knights are agnostics these days. Got sick of waiting you know. And Crusades are a great deal of trouble to undertake. Hard to find someone who will commit the time to organise one let alone participate. No Punters interested in that sort of thing anymore. And there's the whole political correctness thing now. A whole bunch of people get killed while we Crusade about the place. After a ridiculously long ride. Now that I think about it, we really don't have a lot going on these days.'

The Knight looked at Roger who nodded. 'But if Roger needs some Knights, we turn up and do the job how the Punters want it done. A simple life really.'

Roger now knew that the Peoples could reveal to Richard they were characters for whatever plot was specified by a Punter. Up until Richard arrived, no one could reveal they were playing a roll, even if they wanted to. Roger gave a large sigh. It was going to be nice to be honest about who's who.

'And what do you two travellers do for a crust.' Enquired the Knight. In a language Richard was beginning to think was a little too informal.

'My friend here's an Extruder. I'm his Middleman.'

'An Extruder! An Extruder! It's seventy-three passings of the red shield of our sacred guard since we saw such a craftsman in our midst.' Said the Knight.

Richard couldn't help himself. 'How long is that? In…a solar calendar kind of way.' Richard worried that this wasn't the time measurement method used in the land of wherever he was, and things would be hard to translate.

The Knight had to do some mental arithmetic. It took quite a while. 'About five years. How much would such a Talisman cost. Christmas approaches.'

Roger smiled at Richard. 'About the price of a horse at the castle market.'

The Knight pulled a small bag from a metal pocket and handed it to Roger. 'More than enough there.'

Not wanting to unduly abuse the fellow's naiveté, Roger said there was a two for one deal on, for Knights only, and he gave him two. The Knight was delighted. With a farewell he said he was returning to the castle.

Roger tried to point out that the castle was in the opposite direction as he rode away. They could see the flags on the towers from where they stood. But he was gone.

Halfway to the castle they met a Page Boy. 'Hi chaps. Lost my Knight. Have you seen him? Very brightly burnished armour. You know how it is with these fellows.' He leaned in. 'Not the brightest. Could be halfway to anywhere by now.'

Roger said. 'He wanted to go back to the castle but galloped in the opposite direction.'

'Again. They never fight anymore, so they don't really need to ponce about in those mobile ovens anymore. But you try and tell them that. I've saved him from heat exhaustion on more than a few occasions.'

The horse market was not in the castle proper but in the hamlet in close proximity. Roger asked Richard what kind of horse he'd like and after some thought he replied. 'You know I've always liked those painted horses in the Cowboy and Indian movies. Nice coloured patches here and there on a white coat.'

'I'll ask.'

Roger returned smiling. 'They had one in stock. Lots of black stallions, white stallions, Appaloosas, Arabs. But one American Painted Horse.'

Richard was delighted to be riding a horse with striking chocolate and roan splashed over the coat. He was simply delighted that in his new temporary home, he could ride a horse. He wanted to visit the castle, but he was convinced by Roger that he should visit a castle later in his trip. 'This isn't the best example.' He said. 'Pot heads. A Punter wanted that once. And it's hard to get them clean now. That Knight was probably on speed.' They rode off and fell into a companionable silence. Roger was relieved not to be peppered with questions about what the details of the impending story were, where were the best backdrops and being asked to show the Punter cool places that no one else had been to.

'Who's that over there.' Richard said. Pointing a to figure riding a beautiful brindled mare.

Roger glanced over. 'Oh her. An Anti-Princess. Not evil, but all moody and dark. Always on some mysterious quest she doesn't even understand herself. Hence the angst I suppose. We should give her a miss. She's for a late teen female readership, which I don't imagine is your demographic.'

'Still. Nothing wrong with saying hello.'

'Anything to do with the fact she's wearing a neck to toe bespoke leather outfit suggesting to you she might be a good travelling companion.'

'It's only a hello. This is all new to me remember.' Said Richard. Not bothering to argue about his likely motivations. 'Not many of these kinds of people at home you see.'

'We'll soon know if she's a shit travelling companion. These young women can be obnoxious, self-absorbed, defensive, and hypersensitive to older men hanging around wanting to perv at them.'

'Hmm…sounds like she would fit into my new book perfectly. As a very minor character.' He laughed. Richard wanted to enjoy Roger's company, but his guide hadn't had anything good to say about anyone yet. He might need to push things along. They walked their horses though some low broken outcrops of black rock and Richard said. 'Roger, I think the language is a bit too informal for me to capture the mood.'

'Richard please don't.'

'It will make things feel and sound more authentic.'

'Richard. Anything but that.'

'I'd like us all to be speaking in Yee Olde English.'

Roger sighed. As they were approaching the leather clad rider Richard led off. 'Hail Maiden.' Hoping he wouldn't be met with a groan.

'Companions in travel I see.' She replied. 'And where goeth thou on this fair morn.' Her voice confident with a trace of haughtiness.

'Humble merchants, warrior maiden. We ridest from village to village. Our journeying never end…eth.' Richard was starting to struggle.

'My journey is one of revenge. The pieces must first be found and fitted, scattered as they were by my tormentor. Thou wouldest then see the true meaning of suffering once mine enemy rests in my merciless clutches.'

'You know what Roger; this really isn't working for me. Kind of slow and clunky.'

'Thank God. Yee Olde English; Off please.'

The young woman was holding her forehead in one hand. 'Fuuuuuck. Were you guys talking really weird or was it just me. That was trippy. Imagine talking that way all the time. I can't even remember what we said. Who are you guys?' Her smile, directed at Roger initially, was one of familiarity.

'I'm Roger, a businessman, and my friend Richard here is a manu-facturer. He's an extruder. Feminine Talisman.'

'I'm Seren. An extruder? As if I'd ever need the service of one of those.' She threw back her platinum hair looking up at the sky and laughed. She had barely brought her head back to look at them and said. 'I'll take two.'

This wasn't the Fantasy Idea Generator he'd been expecting. Certainly not consistent with his plan to market slightly off formu-la fantasy pulp fiction.

She quickly followed up. 'I've got some… girlfriends and Christmas is coming on. I think the way you've been perving at me Richard, you'd agree I've got it all going on and the last thing I need is a… 'talisman'…as you call them.'

'I wasn't perving, though that's what you might have been hoping it was.'

'Every old man is allowed to get away with it once and then…' She made the classic slice across the throat.

Richard wouldn't be out done. 'If I did perv, it was by accident. You're not my type really. Kind of leathery. And bony. And is plat-inum a natural hair colour here. I mean really. And I imagine you need the two talismans for normal wear and tear.' Richard seemed more self-assured in this world. He realised he'd gone too far how-ever, when she fluidly left her horse. Initially at least. Unfortunately, her smooth transition from horseback to throat slitting collapsed into an embarrassment. The tip of her ridiculously long sword got wedged between the saddle and the horse's rump. This left her hanging in the air. Her scabbard was strapped on at the thigh and hip surrounding her leathers. Richard wondered how she could even draw such a sword when it was nearly her own height. She was running in the air and bouncing on the tip of the wedged sword trying to dislodge it. She'd pulled out the daggers sheathed between her shoulder blades, slashing them about helplessly. It was difficult to imagine a more unlikely stealth killer.

Richard risked the two curved daggers cutting the air in frustration. He ran around to the back of her horse, and, after pinching his index finger, which would result in a nasty blood blister, he freed the sword from the gap between horse and saddle. This dropped an already very unhappy Anti Princess in a pile. She got up, as furious as Richard had ever seen anyone. He prepared to ride away, while accepting his journey to this fantasy world might be a brief one. Fortunately, she was furious at the sword. 'What kind of fucking idiot would want me to carry around a sword that's almost taller than I am. I can't even get off my fucking horse. No wonder I'm moody and dress in black.' She started to smash the sword against rocks and trees and innocent blades of grass. 'And then I've got some fucking Punter telling me I'm bony and my hairs not a natural colour. As if I don't have enough body image angst. What an asshole. And I suppose I have to go on some fucking adventure with him.'

She kept battering rocks, trying vainly to blunt or chip the blade and left cut marks in trees. She saw a rabbit which she ran after it with her sword extended. However, as she hit full speed, the weight of the heavy sword caused its tip to drive into the soft turf in front of a rock causing a windmill effect for its wielder, sending her flying over the sword, which stayed fixed in place. She landed a half dozen feet further on. When she looked up, ready to heap some more scathing vitriol on Richard, they were gone.

As they rode away Roger said. 'The problem is Richard, once they put some ridiculously long swords on the cover artwork, someone's stuck with it in here. It's what some author wanted. As with the Platinum hair.'

'It's the artists and publishers to blame Roger. You may not be aware, but we authors have virtually no control over the cover. Unless you write books and put them on the internet for free. You can have any cover art you want because no one reads them anyway. But you were right about her suitability as a travelling companion. I think all that Anti-Princess stuff would fairly quickly grow tiresome.'

'What would grow tiresome?' She said this into Richard's ear sitting on the rump of his horse, startling him. With equal stealth she was back on her horse. 'And how come I'm able to say I know Richard's a Punter Roger? And I'll need those Talisman on a payment plan by the way.' She said this as she drew her bow pointing it at Richard, though it lacked an arrow. And then she was smiling. Which caused a remarkable change in how one perceived her.

Roger advised her that that Richard was the first ever *Let It Roll* Punter and so it seemed everyone could relax and relate to him as an author. He also advised her the sale of Talismans was cash on the barrel.

This last solicited a 'Hmmff' of displeasure which was quickly forgotten. 'Can I wash my face and hands in that stream?'

She had been able to be so stealthy because she slid the sword in a loop on the saddle. This was not a permanent solution as the tip of the sheath dragged it the turf. 'Every time I want to do something I have to take the fucking thing off.' She handed the sword to Richard to hold in the form of a peace offering as she prepared the straps. He drew it from the sheath a fraction out of curiosity, and it was suddenly glowing with bright blue runes on the exposed blade and the jewel inset through the hilt began to shine bright red.

Richard was trying to be the casual one. 'Bit passé Roger. I wasn't even going to ask about a magic sword.'

'I don't have a script.' Roger smiled. 'For a *Let It Roll* there isn't one. This doesn't appear to be the sword *you were cast with* Seren.'

'Yeah. I used to tell Punters I found that one way back in the mists of time. How I pulled it out of some rock or I had to have sex with a mermaid to get hold of it. Lots of mermaids maybe. Fought a whole army of Ogres or whatever bullshit Punters would like to hear.' Seren knew what was coming.'

'Yes Seren. Not always approved narratives.'

'Sorry about that Roger. The script they give me is so boring. Anyway, I found this a few years back and exchanged it for the piece of shit I had for this slightly less shitty upgrade. You haven't been around much Roger that's why you haven't seen it.'

'All of us being aficionados of the truth, how did you come across it.' Richard said, unaware this might be taken as a slight.

'Are you suggesting I don't know what aficionados means.'

'Of course not. Didn't cross my mind. I use more complex words than I need to because…it makes me feel good about myself.'

'And that's exactly why I have platinum hair asshole.' She smiled. 'All that's behind us now and the lovers of the truth can know that I found this sword …. wait for it…. lying next to the body of a big stupid Knight.' She laughed. 'I think this sword got caught in a root, making him trip and face plant into a rock. I don't think he died straight away but all that unnecessary bright shiny, armour held him down. Boiled in his own juices probably. Poor bastard.'

'Now if he'd been wearing leather, it lets you move but can still turn a blade. It's light, supple and it breathes like…Egyptians? That's what the seamstress for Anti-Princesses said. And it's pro-duced ethically, she assured me. Which means only Fat Slag skin went into its manufacture. And who gives a shit about them.'

'Anyhow I took it out of the guy's cold dead hand because it was *slightly* shorted then the ridiculous sword I had, which was taller than me and a piece of crap. It's never done that glowing blue rune thing before. Anyway, I left my shitty, badly drawn sword with him and decided to weave this into my own mysterious journey alluding to a shrouded destiny as to why this sword chose to come to me. Perhaps one of you chaps can read this blue writing. If it makes the thing valuable, it's on sale for the price of some new leathers.'

'I can give you no assistance there myself.' Said Roger. 'I'm a humble Middleman and Richard a slightly more humble plastics extruder. What you need is a Sword Fondler.'

'Can you say that again Roger. I may have misheard you. I'd assumed it was Richard who was the sword fondler.'

The two men groaned. 'The Sword Fondler is a specialist who reads the markings on swords. Or at least the less complex swords.'

'I've had enough of this piece of shit.' She said. 'If Richard's interested in swords or any of the other magic stuff Punter's love, we could take him to Younameit city and get it read. But first, given that we're in the middle of a *Let It Roll* adventure, we could take him to Beachside on the way.'

Roger thought a moment. 'No reason why not. And great place to catch some Christmas trade rather than roaming around places like this. First time a Punter has ever gone there which is appropriate for a *Let It Roller*. I could do with a break away from the family, and since it's a work trip my wife can hardly complain about it. I should clarify that she's unbelievably uncomplaining.'

'Cool. I need to do some casual work to keep me going. Struggling Anti-Princess as I am, I don't have a big bag of high-end Talismans to keep food on the table. And then, I'll tag along to the big city depending on how much we grow to loathe each other.' It struck Richard as odd that Anti Princesses had to do casual work to make ends meet. But what else would they do for a crust. He thought.

'Younameit City?' He said.

'Most Punters want to name the city in their narrative.' Said Roger. 'We name it whatever they do. Garibaldi, Simserion, Makkitokana are examples of some of the more objectionable names.'

31

'Don't forget Blojobia.' Said Seren

Roger smiled. 'I arrange and direct things, but never intrude on the creative process.'

They rode for several hours. Richard joined in occasionally but mainly enjoyed listening to his companions talk about life in Tæranon, which he learned was the name of his temporary home. He enjoyed riding on a Painted Horse through the moors. He loved walking in wild places. After a need to relieve himself, which confirmed to him people in this world had to do that, his yet to be named Painted Horse refused to be caught for some time. He got back to his companions on a road running along a deep narrow canyon with a fast-flowing river cutting through it. The road led to a bridge.

The ornate bridge over the canyon was beautiful, with a graceful arch between the edges of the sheer cliffs dropping a few hundred feet below. There was a little house built into the supports under each side of the bridge. As Richard joined them, he saw smoke coming from the house on their side.

'Trolls under these bridges. Extortionist bastards. I'll deal with the assholes.' Said Seren. They followed behind her more cautiously, Richard taking note now, that he and Roger didn't carry weapons.

They gathered at the head of the bridge and dismounted. Seren said. 'Must have scampered once they saw me.'

A Troll came out of nowhere and had a blade to her throat and another at her back. 'Oh come on Princess, you're not quite ugly enough to make me run away.'

'You vile fiend. Let me go and I'll tear you to pieces.'

'Yes, that's why I'm not letting you go. Take some time to think about what you say in future.' The troll was ugly. But not hideous. He was like the ugliest person Richard had ever met. But still on the spectrum of ordinary ugliness. Though very large and power-ful. Standing sideways and looking in the bathroom mirror, Richard wasn't a pretty sight either. He tried not to do that anymore.

'I want to show you something Miss *I'll deal with the asshole.*' He walked her to a place on the bridge where they could look over the side.

'I try to keep them in neat piles if possible. But it is a big drop throwing all these shitheads from up here. See there's a pile a bur-nished armour, and there's some Elvin bows and the stupid shoes they wear, those smug bastards. A pile of silly Dwarf hats and a few; I wish there was more, wizard remains. And of course, my fa-vourite pile is the bespoke leather garments of the Anti-Princess. Morose tones of red, blue, green, but mostly boring black.' At the time they didn't notice. But there were no horses thrown over the edge.

'And now this one. A bit bony. And what's going on with this hair eh?'

Richard felt he should interject. Conciliatory. 'Please don't mention the hair. She's a bit sensitive about it.'

She began to struggle and kick. 'I'm not sensitive about anything you assholes.'

'I think the woman doth protest too much.' Said the Troll in a conversational manner to Richard.

'An aficionado of Shakespeare my good sir. Perhaps we could hear more later. A Sonnet maybe.'

The Troll smiled. Once this happened his ugliness really plunged right off the scale. The Troll shrugged. 'I heard a Punter say that once. So where does fate take us from here my friends?' He smiled again.

Richard often wondered what he'd do in this situation. Corny as it was, he said. 'Would you consider exchanging me for her.'

'Sure.' Said the Troll. Pushing Seren away hard in the back while she was saying, 'I might not want to be exchanged for!' The Troll held the knife at Richard's neck and said quietly. 'You know, I would take one Talisman for the three of you to cross.'

They were all laughing, having cooked up the whole scheme while Richard was off chasing his horse. The troll told him those lying dead on the rocks, didn't want to pay rather than make a fifty-mile journey around in the moors. Some thought they could sneak or fight their way across.

'Why don't these people build their own fucking bridge.' They were sitting in a large patio area connected to the house below the bridge having a drink of mead. 'Richard, I heard you're the first *Let it Roll'* Punter. In honour of someone suggesting we might have our own story, I'm giving you a free pass to cross to the other side, anytime you want *and*, believe it or not, I'm giving *you* some Ka-Ching. To reinforce to you we're the opposite of what we're painted to be. No one writes: *and then we had some mead with a very nice Troll.*'

Richard was delighted. 'Someone will now. Although all those bodies do support some of the stereotypes.'

Richard went through the process he often would when he asked for someone's name. They would run through what they thought were the best and worst names ever bestowed upon them. He usually asked what their mother had called them, and they were delighted to have someone show enough interest to find out. In this case the Troll hated the name his mother had bestowed on him as much as what the 'stupid fucking Punters' did. The Troll said although no one ever called him Benny, he'd really like to be called by that name. So they did. They made their farewells and crossed to the other side.

Twenty yards before the bridgehead a Troll jumped out and said. 'You think you can cross my bridge without payment.' He was bigger, and even uglier than Benny.

'We thought our dealings with Benny at the other end constituted payment in full.' Richard explained. 'And he suggested I got a free pass sort of arrangement. We've got some um…Ka-Ching though.' Richard was a little sad to have to hand over money to an ugly and rude Troll. He now also realised why travellers ended up at the far side of the bridge without enough to pay at each end. They were caught between two Trolls.

'That goes without saying. And I'll be taking all your Talismans and one of your number must submit to being tortured, killed, and thrown over the bridge to join the pile.'

An hour or so before, Richard had offered himself in exchange for Seren. Having captivity couched in these terms made the decision less clear cut. For her part she had undone the belt and dropped the sword with a clatter and drawn out her two long daggers. She stood in a way which may have been purely theatrical, but it gave Richard some hope they had a chance against the Troll, who started laughing. 'It's only me. Benny.' He shrank a little and his face changed to the familiar very ugly rather than the extreme ugly of the moment before. 'You dopes. Got you a good one eh? I've got a path that runs below the bridge.' He pointed to below the surface. 'Great ruse isn't it. Especially for people who want to be assholes or haggle on one side. I think that little performance was worth a Talisman wouldn't you say. I forgot to buy one for a…friend of mine… and all my money's in my other…Troll house. I thought we could do the transaction over here.' He said winningly.

'Meant to give you and extra one anyway, what with all the Ka-Ching you didn't demand and not killing us.' Said Roger.

As they rode on, Richard got a sense that very large amounts of virtual landscape could be covered in a short time if there was nothing going on to serve the plot. If Roger was working within the context of a Punter wanting a faithful timeline, journeys in different landscapes might take days to fulfil the intent and feel of the plot. Or if it suited the Punter, Roger could accelerate through the landscape and climate they traversed.

The air grew warmer, with a sea breeze. Then it grew positively balmy. Although Richard found this a little disconcerting for a while, he wasn't unhappy about it.

Seren said. 'I spent some time here when I was younger. Now I only ever come here to get some work. Though it always feels good to be back.'

Roger looked across to Richard. 'And this is the first time a Punter has ever been to Beachside. On a few occasions I've had to track down drunken characters who have important roles in narratives. I'd give Punter some sub narrative that meant they didn't need me while I found the character required.'

Richard smiled. 'I'm pleased to be the first. What happens if the person doesn't want to be the character?'

Roger and Seren looked at each other. Roger shrugged. 'They don't have to worry about that or anything else ever again. We only have one purpose here Richard. Although I'm getting a very strange sense that's starting to change.'

Roger changed the subject. 'Everyone needs a break. Even Fantasy characters. This is a resort town on the beach. Lots of different activities. Sailing, diving, beach sports, bowling, jelly wrestling, that kind of thing. Or you can sit around the pool getting smashed on beer laced with a mild psychoactive, which is what I plan to do. I've never had a break here.'

'Unfortunately, the Resort is segregated. You won't meet any Trolls, Goblins or Ogres although they do let some Rat People in for services rendered. They keep the sewers spotless. It's how things were set up from the start. The good guys and bad guys. The humans are all good guys unless they need to be cast as bad guys. But that's temporary. They run most of the businesses and are half of the holiday makers here. Otherwise there are Elves, Dwarves, Knights, the few Shape Shifters that get about the place, sometimes Witches. Even Unicorns drop in for a drink occasionally. A very small number Little People still come. They're only the outcasts though.'

They were entering a wide roadway with a few horses on it. The three beautiful horses the trio rode in on were the subject of many an admiring glance. Also at Roger accompanying a Punter. Everyone knew what the Anti-Princess was there for. But she was an impressive example of the type. On one side of the roadway were hotels advertising various prices. They boasted magnificent pools, and all of them backed onto the beach. Some touting diving reefs, others surf breaks.

'While you chaps have your big bag of Ka-Ching and an even bigger bag of Talismans, this girl has to go and get herself a job. Since you have to pay for a stable that takes up to four, could Brindlefire stable with GroundBreaker and To Be Advised.'

Roger glanced at Richard. Leaving him to make the decision. 'Of course.'

'Maybe your poor nag will come out of the stable with a name. Probably going to cry herself to sleep. I have a few excellent names.'

'I don't want to rush to give her a name and end up something silly like…'

'Like what.' Seren pretended suspicion.

'You see. I can't even think of something silly let alone anything else. She loves it, waiting for a good name to come along. It's like you can't find a good man these days Seren. You can't get a good horse's name either. The best ones are taken.'

She was mollified. 'It's true you can't find a good man these days Richard. Yet I keep looking.'

Roger ignored this last remark and was conciliatory. 'Don't worry. Halfway through a psychobeer and you'll have no idea what a horse is. After the second, no idea who you are. Three beers and horse's names will be falling like rain. Unfortunately, you won't remember any of them.'

Seren rode ahead to scope out the hotels. Once she had left Richard said. 'Thinking about this, why don't we give her one third of the Ka-Ching Benny gave me. I mean even though ostensibly he gave it to me, I assumed we'd split it three ways.'

'And we would have done, but...' Roger hesitated in a way which, during their brief experience, Richard had not seen him do. 'She has some things to do here. In her current station, before we give it to her. And I, believe it or not, don't know what they are. Some strange things are happening in here Richard. Adjustments. Things I've never seen.'

Roger chose a resort contrary to her advice. 'High end for a humble merchant and the workman.' She said. But they were now flush with Troll cash along the prospect of Christmas buyers within arm's reach. They put the horses in the hotel stable and took Seren's weapons to the armoury before going to reception.

The reception and the staff were a tiny bit Fantasy, with a few un-familiar races of humans here and there, and with more unusual and ornate fittings and furniture. But by and large, the check in experience was like it was everywhere. Roger admitted he'd been stringing out the daylight a bit, so they didn't need to camp on the way in. Richard said he'd like a nap before joining him around the resort bar. He had a pleasant afternoon siesta, setting aside, for a time, the surreal ordinariness of it all. Feeling refreshed, he went down to find Roger looking a little impatient for his first drink. They were sitting in front of a large pool with a busy poolside bar, run mainly by human looking beings, and patrons ranging from humans to Elves, some Rat People. No one sitting near them for several tables around, a small group of Dwarves and a few Knights and their Page Boys laughing away in civvies. There was a table with a couple of very haughty wizards. He saw some people at a table, very drunk and laughing, one of their number changing into an Elf another a Knight, one briefly into a unicorn and another some kind of monster with a chain around its neck. There were some women around a table, so beautiful and glamorous, Richard was sure this was illusory. He would later find out it was.

'Look at this. You two Lording it up while I'm stuck waitressing. I could hardly get my bag down and they had me out here. All the Elvin girls that usually do this shit have scarpered for some reason.'

When they looked up, they saw a person who had dragged a hotel waitress uniform, probably a size too small to begin with, roughly down over a leather suit so that the uniform was as ill-fitting as might ever be contrived. She held out a pad and paper and said. 'What'll it be?'

'Two dark ale specials please young lady.'

'Of course. If I work here for a week, I might be able to sit down and share *one* with you.' She stomped off.

'Oh, waitress.' Roger called her back right as she approached the limit of hearing. 'I see there's a hotel tasting plate. If we could get that along with some wedges it would be great.'

While she was writing this on the little pad, the pencil snapped.

'We really should give her some money.' Said Richard after she'd stomped away again.

'I like seeing her annoyed for a while to be honest. Anyway, she'd probably be too proud to take it.' They looked at each other and laughed.

She was standing with two beers in her hands. She always moved quickly and turned up without a sound thought Richard.

'What's so funny.'

'Umm.' Richard could see Roger wasn't going to help.

'My uniform.'

'No, not on this occasion. I mean, not yet. We were laughing at how thrilled you must be working as a waitress, which is not very... thrilled.'

She plonked the two beers down. Spilling a good deal of Richard's. Eyeing him off she said. 'I'm going to tell everyone in this place you have a horse called Handjob, so if you see people laughing and pointing, you'll know why.'

Meanwhile Richard had only one sip of beer and the effect was amazing. He looked up at her. 'Do you know what I'm going to do in retaliation Seren? Do you? Eh. Do you.' He didn't wait for an answer. 'Nothing. Beneath me. Too juvenile.'

She sat down with them. All forgiven it would seem. 'I'm sick of this shitty job already.' Without asking, she had a sip of Richard's beer and they surveyed the pool area. They could see that she was immediately taking particular notice of the shift change of the Lifeguards. 'Okay. can't sit around wasting time here all day.' She was soon walking back to the resort deep in conversation with the Lifeguard coming off his shift.

'Did she go off with a ...pool boy?'

'Pool Attendant is the correct nomenclature I think you'll find. Although I daresay they prefer Lifeguard.'

'I hadn't come to write that kind of Fantasy book.'

'This isn't adult fantasy Richard. In this case, as I mentioned, it's late teen chick lit Fantasy. You've chosen to team up with an Anti-Princess. They have these...dalliances...you know. Now and then. Often very heavy, deep, meaningful...dalliances, but never any details. Except emotional stuff, when they learn the fellow was an evil emissary of so and so, or was too weak to take part in her daring plan, maybe he was simply boring, smelled of garlic or whatever.'

'Or a Pool Attendant she's never met before.'

'Who knows what their backstory is Richard. Or does she really need one for your sake. You know, *any* of the buttons you might have pressed would have all led you automatically to a fairly prim and proper Tæranon. Violent though it might be. This version is where the inhabitants are more what they're really like. We've seen that with a Troll already. I had no idea he might prefer to be called Benny. And give people *money*. I've been doing this job for centuries and I'm seeing new things, real changes.'

'I feel kind of shallow now.' Said Richard.

Roger shrugged. 'Maybe you are. And maybe you'll get over it. Drink up.'

The dark ale and its special additive first helped one forget recent unhappiness, and then any unhappiness ever. But one needed to rest occasionally to avoid what might lead to strange behaviours, causing one to fail to observe social etiquettes. Seren was back with her pad. 'Been off the psychoholics for a while? Time for more. So would you like to know what I've been up to.'

Richard and Roger knew this must be a trap. They shook their heads. 'No. No. Not interested in the slightest.'

'I see. You don't give a shit about me, is that it?'

'Ah…Ah…Ah..' Richard had something good for this but it took a moment to formulate. 'We care deeply for your well-being, but we're not concerned about your whereabouts. That's your business. And we know you can…look after yourself.'

She couldn't fault that. 'I've been busy trying to understand the meaning of the mysterious quest I've been on since I was a was...' This was a reference Seren wasn't inclined to make. 'Anyway, since I discovered that sword my quest is becoming more urgent. I don't know how, but I'm finding things that will need to be in place at a critical moment in the history of Tæranon.'

Roger found tidings of a sweeping hidden purpose curious given his role in Tæranon. Yet he believed her. Richard had nothing to contribute so she started to write down an order for two drinks 'Only two? You don't want to order three by any chance.'

'Two will suffice nicely thank you.' Said Richard. She was giving him a little glare and about to make a real show of stomping off when an elf came around behind her and said. 'I was hoping to introduce myself two these two gentlemen.'

'Perhaps you could wait a fucking goddamn minute while I finish taking their order.' Barely under her breath she said. 'Fucking Elves. I hate the smug bastards.' And then at a louder than necessary volume she started to go right though the bar snack menu.

'Would you like some squid rings? No'

'How about calamari?' She shook her head. 'That was a little joke. It's the same thing as squid rings but Richard didn't know.'

'I did know.'

'Wedges and Sour Cream?' The Anti Princess went on. 'Tossed in Seasoning or not.'

Even Roger, who generally had no problem with awkward, was starting to feel uncomfortable as the Elf a few feet to the side was fuming.

Richard could see a type of being approaching. Short. Unnecessarily long nose. Stout. Could be muscular or chubby depending on the owner of the frame. Fairly ugly face however its owner would never admit to it. Eyes blacker and beadier than a Slag, which was saying a lot. Stupid hat. Purple. Oversized axe carried around in a resort. Richard supposed there might be a few reasons mixed in there for the fellow to be annoyed with fate.

'Ah Roger. Good to see you. It's been a while.'

Roger took a breath in. 'Hello, UbarkeatmouseslweeeshIhadhadenuglygirlsteadofjumpeduplilpric kwitlongsnoznevergetupduffagainincazeigetsuchshithead.'

'Ah. Roger. The full name my mother bestowed is brimming with nuance and beauty. That's what she tells me. It's in the native tongue of her people. Contrary to our custom and the courtesy we bestow on those we meet; you use the shortened version. Even after our long association stretching back a century. But I understand.'

Roger was barely apologetic. 'I've mentioned a few times over that century that the human mind was not given the capacity to remember such long names. And, the human mind, in its weakness, can also see no point in having them. I have over sixty children. My wife and I can barely remember the intentionally short names we give them. Like Ian. If we had a naming convention such as the Dwarves, we'd never get anything done.'

The Dwarf was barely listening. 'I understand there is a deficiency in capacity involved. And who is your companion? Welcome to Tæranon.'

Richard's cheerfulness had been drained away, replaced by dislike at seeing his friend being treated as an inferior. He could not even remember half of the asshole's short name version. He thought quickly. 'My name is: Ucangoandchewmydirtysandalulongnosewier dopleasepisssofffsooon.

However, and this Richard said with a severe gravity, where *I* come from, we would think that it is extremely rude, extremely rude, to use the long version of someone's name. Especially when you are a visitor or greeting a visitor. Therefore, in my culture, I would be greeted as U and you would be greeted as U.'

Some of Richard and Roger's cheerfulness returned.

'Of course…U…We appreciate that with your *Let It Roll* selection you don't want us to wait upon idiotic royalty or mine non-existent minerals. Mithril. A few Punters ago I was asked for Mithril. I wanted to tell them it was probably copyrighted. I went and bought some silver. Don't these people have an original thought in their heads? And then there's the gold and jewels. Deep in the mines. Most Dwarves hate being underground. That Tolkien's got a lot to answer for. There's no gold and jewels down there so we paint rocks and buy trinkets to break up for the coloured glass. We're getting tired of this shit.'

Richard was going to say now he knew why Santa Clause loathed Christmas, but that was for the Elves. He'd missed his chance.

'In every book we've been cast in we're these stereotypical characters. There's no nuance. Never any subtlety. And never once. Not once, is there a book which is centred around Dwarves. No matter how much we deserve it. And a great deal more interesting it would be. These days it's as likely to be centred around…' He paused as they saw Seren walk towards them in a striking new set of leathers. Midnight blue with red highlights. '…like her. An Anti-Princess. No dwarves at all needed there because those books are vapid teen romance novels, the main characters trending towards whoredom. It applies to that one in particular. Our Dwarf maidens understand modesty. They stay appropriately covered.'

Richard was about to say. *'Maybe they're so well covered because they're so fucking ugly.'*

But Seren arrived at the table quietly and was soon sitting next to Richard. 'Hello Dwarf.'

The Dwarf thought some protocol might smooth things out as, even by Dwarf standards, he'd been unforgivably rude, though only because he'd been overheard. 'Good afternoon my lady, my name is…'

'Don't give a shit. My name's Whore. Fuck off.'

The Dwarf looked to Roger. 'This is how things lie Roger?'

'You called a lady a whore U. How would it go down in Dwarfdom if Richard said that to a Dwarf maiden. Or does it apply only to humans?'

'You know Roger, things are changing. We may not be available to do your little tricks in times to come.' He looked up at the sky.

Roger didn't like being threatened. 'If anyone wants a Dwarf, and I have no idea why, I'll round up a bunch of donkeys and use their asses which would no doubt do a better job. But don't forget why we're all here Dwarf.'

'As I said Roger. Things are changing.' He said this menacingly.

The Dwarf turned and walked away but as he did, he bumped the table, as if by accident. A little harder than he'd intended, upsetting all the glasses. He hadn't taken two steps, pretending not to notice what had occurred when there was a young woman in a magnificent new leather outfit and a blade at his throat.

'Drop the Axe.' U was suddenly afraid, irrespective of all his bluster. This woman had a ruthless potential no Dwarf maiden could ever summon. She picked it up. 'I imagine this axe is really really special.'

'It was the blade delivered to my great great…'

'Too much information. What *you* need to know, is that you might be going to have to play hide and seek for it in a whole shit load of ocean. And I have friends who can make it *very* difficult to find. And I know you tiresome assholes don't like deep water. Now clean up that table Dwarf and bring out three beers personally. Don't just order them, pay for them. And we must have coasters. Are you smart enough to remember that? My friends will be here. But I won't be. I'll be ready to get on a boat, which I am going to organise right fucking now, to drop this shitty, poorly made piece of garbage in the ocean.'

She turned and walked away with the axe. U did what he was told with very bad grace but a clean table and no spillage of three beers was supplied with coasters. Seren arrived without the axe. 'It's at the front desk. Now piss off.'

'We'll meet again, and *you* won't see old age.' He said to Seren before he turned and left.

She called after him. 'And you won't see me coming next week fat boy.'

They said nothing for a while then Roger ventured. 'I was telling Richard how the really special power Dwarves have is to sap all your cheerfulness away.'

'And we damn well won't let him get away with it.' Said Seren.

'We can forget that purple hatted asshole.' Said Richard. 'And Roger and I can do what we should have been doing, which was to appreciate the magnificent purchase our friend has just made. Including the pleasant surprise as she approached.'

Seren smiled. 'Sooo, I'll get rid of these beers because they're Dwarf contaminated, and I shall, using my contacts, return with beer more suited to our tastes. That way, you will have time to prepare thoughtful and well-crafted compliments.' Once everything was in place she disappeared and came around the corner smiling all over again. It was the brilliant smile of someone who had bought something that brought unvarnished joy. They were duly appreciative, and not from politeness. They wanted to understand how such a beautiful garment could be stitched together, and in such a short period of time. Unfortunately, she was unable to vouchsafe the seamstresses arts. Because she didn't know either.

Worse for wear with the second Seren strength beer, Richard had gone off to relieve himself, and then become lost, having followed the guidance of a non-existent salamander. 'Things are changing it seems.' Seren observed.

'I've been noticing changes for some time. But the last few Punters have only wanted niche fantasies. I haven't been circulating. Now the world ain't what she used to be, in a bigger way than I realised.' Said Roger.

'And it seems our friend may have a capacity to influence things other Punters have not had.' She said in an enquiring tone.

'You think so? We'll see.' Roger wasn't in the mood for that topic of conversation.

Seren took them up to their beds, after a memorable meal at the restaurant a few hotels down. They had been drinking quantities of wine that Richard hoped, like the beer, would not lead to a hangover.

It didn't. He knew how to ride a horse, wield a sword, there were no hangovers, and he liked the people he was with. He was happy with things. He wasn't that fussed about getting a book out, he liked rolling along. The next day, when they reached the moors, Roger said on the way to the Dragon they'd stay at an Inn managed by Big People but on the edge of the Little People's domain. They might run across some of the LPs as Roger called them, but he'd rather not, he said this with no further explanation.

Richard didn't pursue the matter. He would be interested to run across some Little People on their way to visit an irritable dragon. He had met some beings he didn't like, but the interactions had been brief.

Seren asked the hotel to pack a nice lunch and they ate it next to a beautiful waterfall. She said 'Oh come on Roger, let him do it. You can see he's gagging for it.' Clearly Roger was reluctant. 'Come on. He's all excited but trying not let on. It's painful for me to watch.'

Roger sighed and gave Seren a look of 'why do I put up with you' but said. 'Why not.'

'And what am I gagging for?' Richard wished he'd not revisited Seren's phrasing.

'You want to play with your sword.' She pulled it out of its now somewhat smaller scabbard. When he took it, the writing appeared in sharp electric blue runes, and the red jewel lit up brightly.

It was a joy to watch someone get such innocent pleasure from something new and wonderful. At the end, without any ceremony Seren said. 'You want it, you carry it. I'll adjust the straps. I got my leathers so I'm glad to be rid of it.'

All Richard could manage was. 'Thanks. Thanks a lot.' Roger was going to object to the exchange, but it was Seren's to give. And she had rescued it from someone who clearly didn't want him to have it. They rode past long sections of fencing enclosing fields and orchards on their right, with only a narrow track between these and a cliff face rising on the left.

'Little People's land.' Roger said.

'Are they a bit like H…' Richard couldn't finish.

'I should have told you. Never use the H word within miles of this place. Didn't like the way they were portrayed. I have to get them to turn up and be something they're not. Which neither of us enjoy. Now, although they won't admit it, I think they're also annoyed that there isn't much call for them anymore. Usual victimhood psychology. They don't want to be involved in things but their pissed off not to be asked. You really can't win with LP's.'

Soon a whole gang of half height people turned up. No fur on top of their feet Richard noticed. They began to hurl insults at all three of them for some slight against their religious beliefs. Seren was singled out for specific attention.

'Oh.' Said Roger 'And they're fundamentalists.' Shouting above the abusive screaming from only a few meters away on the other side of the fence.

'I suppose we have quite a way to go trapped between the fence and the cliff face.'

'Yes. Either this or four days around.'

Richard had an idea. 'Do you sing to your children Roger. I know my sister does. Even though she refuses to admit it.'

To this unexpected question he answered 'Sure. One of the simple pleasures of life.'

'Why don't you pick a nice one, teach it to us, and we'll start singing it at the top of our lungs.'

Roger smiled. 'I love the idea, and I have the perfect song. It's about a *Love Monster* that makes bad things disappear.'

'Guys. I can't sing a note.' A fear of harmonies or a momentary solo creeping into Seren's voice.

'Even better.' Said Richard. It was an easy song to pick up, and they could add things that the Love Monster would make disappear and this caused the song to be interrupted with laughter time and again. They all took turns finding things, including notable features of their tormentors and other recent acquaintances, the Love Monster would make disappear. The LPs were now the ones who were being aurally tormented as the three of them rode as close to the fence as possible, singing themselves hoarse. They were delighted to see the LP's eventually give up and ride away on their cheerless ponies.

'Believe it or not, the people on the edge here are the more reasonable LP's. If you found your way into the heart of their realm, you'd probably be torn apart. They maintain this enclave of 'nicer ones' to be responsive to the needs of Punters. But with the reduced call for them, this enclave is becoming more and more like the middle.'

'All this on the way to meet an irritated Dragon.' Said Richard. Starting to wonder if anyone in the land was what he thought they would be. The night at the Inn was more straightforward. It had the charm of old England with some of the strangeness and whimsy of a fantasy world.

The barman was as typical a human as any. Roger explained that these people had large towns in many areas. In addition to playing parts in various tales for Punters, sometimes with the help of prosthetics, they were an invaluable logistics resource. 'It doesn't automatically happen Richard. I need people in the background. You won't be aware, but once you make your selection and put on the neural net, I have a week or so after you press the button to get things set up. Which often has a lot to do with these guys.' He motioned to the many drinkers now in a circle around them.

Richard hadn't thought about how much was involved in delivering a narrative. But seeing the world as it was and imaging a Punter who had ordered something up, there were a lot of collaboration required.

Roger was as animated as anyone had seen him. 'These guys are the people who save my bacon. And they don't have a problem with being who they are, who they're not, or make adjustments to portray any kind of character. Some of the time they're evil henchmen, and some of the time they're family types, warriors, or comic sidekicks.' There were man hugs and pats on the back for Roger. Partly out of understanding for the assholes he had to deal with. But also having to organise narratives that came at a terrible price for some of the Peoples. He continued, now rather excited. 'Listen everyone. Richard here has come up with the best idea ever to deal with those miserable little shits along the fence line. We all learned a song I sing to my children, about how the world is supposed to be, and then sing it at full volume at the little bastards. And Seren can't sing.'

'I have no disagreement with that.' Said Seren.

'Sounds great.' The Innkeeper was very enthusiastic. He had to listen to the reasonable, but never-ending complaints, about those *'hobbit assholes'* from his clientele 'You teach me the song and we'll teach it to merchants, cartmen; everybody. I'll put up a sign at either end. If they don't know that song, they can sing their own. The hateful pricks seem to get more insular and meaner as the years go by.'

'Strange days.' Roger said. 'I'm off to bed.' The others were not far behind.

The next day they left the boundary of the LP's land in the late afternoon and after a brief ride through a picturesque laneway arched over by oak trees, they came into fields of various kinds. Some crops were trained up on tall wires. Richard had seen them before but couldn't remember what they were. These surround-ed wheat, oats, and barley crops. All beautifully maintained. They came to a charming house with a cottage garden and a waterwheel in the river meandering by.

Then they heard a booming voice from ten stories above. 'Prepare to die humans.' The voice was incredibly loud, deep, and clear, fol-lowing by a torrent of flame which made the river boil. The thun-derous voice returned. 'How dare you come onto my land. What reason could you possibly have to stop me turning you to ash?'

Richard rode up to the Dragon who had lowered its massive head to look him in the eye. The dragon's the size of a watermelon 'I always wanted to say hello to a dragon.' Richard said. 'So…ah… hello.' The three turned their horses aside and passed around the massive beast.

'Oh all right. Come and let's catch up for a while Roger. Tell me who you friends are.'

'Thanks Andy. Richard's our first ever *Let It Roll* but he appreciates you guys have been overworked so he's not looking for any, you know, tricks. And Seren is our travelling companion.'

'Forgive my rudeness. Richard, good to meet you. Seren. I can see that your great beauty is the very least of the long list of your qualities.'

Seren wasn't accustomed to this kind of compliment and was suddenly coy, to her companion's amusement. 'Oh. You dragons.'

Richard was apologetic. 'I'm a tourist really. You're such a magnificent…I don't want to say the wrong thing…'

'Creature is okay.' Said the dragon helpfully. 'We all are. Do you like beer?'

'One of our favourite things.' Seren was quick off the mark in response to that question.

The creature shrank to the same height as they were and reached out a clawed hand in introduction.

'Now first a warning. Do not use the phrase 'home brewing' or there will be repercussions I won't be able to control. I run a Micro-Brewery.' When they went in, they could immediately see the difference. The space was set up as a magnificent bar room. The bar top made from a slab of what must have been a huge tree. Behind a glass wall at the back of the bar, all kinds of vats and beer making paraphernalia was in view. This portion of the house must have been constructed after the incredibly long, wide piece of timber was set in place. It was polished with a scented wax to a beautiful satin finished that brought out the intricate grain in the wood. Looking along the bar they counted twenty-one handles, which they would later learn were sixteen beers and five spirits. Andy was also learning the art of Micro Distilling.

He went behind the bar and ushered them to sit down at handle One. This is going to be a long night thought Richard. The beers were fantastic, each had tasting notes and some interactive discussion was expected for each style. Andy grew everything. Rye, hops, wheat, oats, and barley. Whatever he needed. He cultivated his own yeasts and had built a pipeline from a spring five miles away to use the purest water in the region. He said friends would fly in from hundreds of miles around. On a memorable night the bar might be three deep with dragons.

'All of the male persuasion unfortunately. The gentleman who created this place believed Dragons only needed to mate every century. Being such a long-lived creature, his logic was that the place might soon be overrun with us. He didn't realise that we would practice intelligent family planning like every other responsible People. Now those LP zealots breed like mean little rabbits. They're the ones who should only breed every hundred years. They're making overtures they want to extend their boundaries. Lebensraum.' Andy said darkly.

Richard was quite merry by this time, but still standing, providing the bar didn't move away on him, which it occasionally threatened to do. He held up his glass, at that moment filled with a dark ale, and said with mock authority. 'Here's to the creator of Tæranon. Well done. Well intentioned. But we've got to move with the times. Henceforth dragons may bone each other whenever they please provided appropriate family planning…um…measures are in place.' They all clinked glasses at the proclamation laughing. Then Andy and Roger shared a curious look. They excused themselves and went out into the night air. Cold air with bright stars above.

'Did you feel the setting change?' Said Andy. The two had been friends for centuries. Most peoples were much longer lived than on the Outside, but generations still passed slowly by. Including those that needed to replenish doomed armies. Dragons and the Guide were virtually immortal, or as far as they could tell.

'I believe it did.' Roger looked down and scratched his head. 'Curious chap this Richard. And it's been a while since we had any Punters out in the centre of the world. I was stuck on magical Unicorn duties for the last narrative. You can imagine how much fun those one horned schizophrenics thought that was.' They both laughed at the concept of a unicorns needing to be nice. 'Things are changing Andy, getting stranger. All the less savoury aspects of the Elves, the Dwarves and the Little People are getting more pronounced.'

'And the Anti-Princesses get better and better.' Said Andy.

'I'll let you be the judge of that, but it's true I've seen much worse. Self-absorbed, tantrum throwing, God; endlessly moody and for what reason I don't know. Weak backstories making them unhappy maybe.' Roger mused.

'Talking about me are you?' Seren could move so quietly thought Andy. Even a dragon didn't pick up her arrival.

Andy smiled. His response transparent. 'We were talking about some of the less desirable traits of some in your Sisterhood and hence all of the things you're not.'

She smiled, acknowledging a well-constructed repair job. 'Yeah. Sisterhood. Yeech.'

Richard was getting really pissed and arrived to contribute. 'This would be a great place for a beer garden. Some walls and fences with creepers to keep the wind out, nice potted plants, tables around the place, umbrellas when it's sunny. Music. Maybe some live music. You have some good local bands here? You've already got the best beer in the…where are we; Tæranon.' His eyes were swimming away from one another. 'Pig on a spit. Or whatever large animal that is culturally appropriate to roast on a big rotisserie.'

Andy's voice was full of surprise. 'Would you believe it Richard. I've been alive hundreds and hundreds of years, but never thought of drinking beer with friends in a nice garden that I'd built. I'm going to get up early to make a start. No. No. I'm going to wait 'till you guys wake up. Whenever that is. And we'll make a plan. Lay it out together.'

'Fantastic.' Richard said this in the middle of falling down face first. He had no hands out to break his fall. Completely overcome by Dragon beer. Andy and Roger were astonished that Seren could catch him, inches from a faceplant on the flagging stones. She carried him off to his room and tucked him in, just like her parents never had.

He woke up, suspicious and hopeful. Would he have a commensurate hangover to the amount of booze consumed in the real world. He felt good. No headache. No nausea. He loved Tæranon. This really was a fantasy world. And he was glad to have met someone who had a positive outlook and wasn't dreadfully insular. Elves, Dwarves, and Little People were all a bit of a disappointment. A Troll was way more fun than they were.

There was a small village nearby and they helped with the farming and brewing. He held out his claws and said. 'These aren't as good as hands for some Things. Including making breakfast.'

Which they were supplied with by a cheerful young man and his mother. 'We used to cook and clean for some Moor Elves. There's was a village not too far from here. I'd rather work for Smaug any day of the week than those…'

'Narcissistic bastards.' Put in her son helpfully. He got the look from his mother that told him he was lucky he was right.

They spent the morning planning how the beer garden should be set out. This required them to sit in various locations drinking beer. From these vantage points they could adjudicate on where there should be a rammed earth wall or a curved rendered half wall with a trellis. Where the large hearth would go to roast a pig on a spit.

As they moved about Richard said to Andy. 'You must be tired of being asked to do the same old things. Is there anything new that'd be more interesting?'

'There's been these waves of obnoxious Viking and magician children. I would rather keep getting killed by St George if I had to choose. I wish we were allowed to eat one of the tiresome brats but nope. No depth in the plots you see. If we're not being ridden on, we have to endure being saved by the sanctimonious little buggers.'

Richard thought for a moment. 'What if I put new labels on those buttons and they all said the same thing. So that when people came here, they had a new expectation of Dragons. It might even lead to some alternative material in the books they write.'

'What's our new major purpose?' Andy answered his own question. 'I think with the lifting of an irksome breeding restriction, Dragons should now be known for large scale and long-lasting sex parties.'

Roger looked across at Richard with a slight shake of the head. 'Maybe a bridge to far Andy. We need something with broad appeal but that you're going to be enthusiastic about.'

'Easy.' Said Seren. 'The Micro-Brewing Dragon.'

'Ah but that assumes I'd have the Punters visit me. Which I don't think I'd enjoy.'

'Come with me.' Said Richard and they went back into the bar. 'Look at this place. Look how beautifully finished it is. I've never seen anything quite like the detail and care when it comes to how all this is joined together.'

'You won't find a nail in this room. Though I can use 'em. And I don't use human help, I have adaptors for every tool. It's what I spend most of my day doing, but you can redo your bedroom only so many times.'

'Exactly. You're not the town burning Dragon. You're not the gold stealing Dragon. You're not the steed for tiresome children Dragon.' Richard paused for dramatic effect. 'You're the Home Renovations Dragon.'

They all looked at him for a moment and then said things like. 'Sounds great.' And 'I love it.' Andy said. 'I'd be doing what dragons want to do, help people. And working with a beautiful apprentice. Or two. Or more.' The afternoon and then the evening became a blur as they moved through the last of the beers, ate wonderful food, took a tour through the house which Andy said, 'makes the bar look like a barn' and migrated to the spirits Andy distilled. And though not as advanced as the beer, were quite passable. Richard was loving this part of Tæranon even though he couldn't imagine writing a book about micro brewing, home renovations loving dragons.

The next morning, they made their farewells and began the five-day journey to the only City in Tæranon. Roger said it was a place full of enclaves a bit like a Hollywood Studio. 'Punters have a limited suite of buttons, but we can often tailor an enclave to what they were hoping for quickly. It would get dull doing the same old things all the time so the people in the city treat it like a week of celebrations. I supply what's needed for that.' Roger was looking forward to going to the city because it had been a while. Seren had never been. The main objective was to visit the Sword Fondler.

Part of the way into the first day, the landscape they rode through changed to one of drought. The tough grasses were dying. Roger thought it would be important for Richard to meet some Moor Elves, however narcissistic. Even if they were going to put on the usual demonstrations of how they could roll, shoot an arrow, and then shoot that arrow out of the sky, and on and on. All with beautiful hair. But the village was abandoned. Almost everything had been removed suggesting the Moor Elves decided to move elsewhere. Andy always irrigated the small fields he needed for his precious beers. Not so far away land around his fields was dying. Roger looked to the sky and shook his head.

They stayed at quaint, small inns in villages of humans. The farms were gradually being abandoned as crops failed and grass for sheep and cattle disappeared. The people in the Inns feigned cheerfulness. But their trade was dwindling, and they could see no end to it. They would take what they could carry and start again where there was reliable rain.

On the third day Seren began to share what she knew of her early life. 'From what Arnall, who brought me up was told, my mother died in childbirth, and I was inconvenient to my father who already had plans to remarry before she died. There were rumours her death was not due to childbirth.'

63

'The midwives were asked to kill me, but they couldn't do it. Rather, they built a little boat out of reeds and sent me out into the river.'

'Sorry Seren, but this isn't very original material you know.' Richard had not fully appreciated the gravity of the moment, this being the first time Seren had ever told what she knew of her origins.

'Arnall found the boat at the bottom of a *waterfall*. Will you let me tell the story Richard!' After a brief death stare, she continued. 'They set me adrift above a huge waterfall because they were too spineless to kill me outright. In what can only have been a terrifying but miraculous basket ride, I ended up on the bank of the river. A pack of wolves was about to make an afternoon snack of me, I have wolf scars to prove it, but you'll never get to see them, when this woodsman came along.'

Richard was going to object again at the woodsman reference but thought better of it.

'No Richard. He wasn't the Sleeping Beauty Woodsman, thankfully. He was a misfit who preferred to live in the forest. He trapped things and sold their pelts, and yes, cut up and sold firewood. He brought me up. He was well read and liked music. It was he didn't feel comfortable around people. He's the only real father I ever had.' Her voice developed a sad tone neither of the men had heard in it before. 'When I was thirteen, he didn't come home one day. I was often out working with him, so I knew all the places to search, but I never found a trace of him. He may have fallen into the river, been a victim to bandits, consumed by wolves. I wish I knew.'

Had it been a lighter moment Richard would have said. 'Or maybe he decided to move away.'

'Anyway, I stayed in the cabin on my own for six months but eventually put together a backpack and walked out towards the town where he traded his pelts and sold the wood, although I'd never been there. I didn't know what town it was, and I was there for only a few hours when someone hit me from behind and I woke up hundreds of miles away.'

'I'd been caught by slavers and sold to the miners in the wastes of Oighir. The surface of the place was frozen, but the rock in the tunnels of the mine was baking hot once you travelled the half an hour rail trip to the face where we mined gold. Working in that mine was the worst day of my life. And not an eight-hour day. A twelve-hour day. Broke every nail on both hands.'

Roger and Richard looked at each other.

'A bit of light relief guys. I was down in the mines for four years. I kept my mind busy learning a few languages from fellow slaves, meeting shitloads of different kinds of people and figuring out how to kill guards without getting caught. Six by the way.' They started to see the Seren they were more familiar with emerge.

Roger's voice was regretful. 'I set that place up for a Punter. I updated it a couple of times for other narratives I had to deliver. Once they're built, I can't unwind them unfortunately.' Roger felt responsible but added 'It's why Tæranon keeps getting bigger and more complex.'

'I see. It was you that was responsible for what happened to me.' She moved on with a trace of a smile. 'There was no way you could walk out of that place. The hundreds of miles of frozen wasteland in every direction meant the slavers didn't need a fence. Some of us decided there would need to be enough of us willing to die in the process of killing the guards to get out of the place. Then we could take their transports to make a horse drawn convoy which had a chance of getting back. Everyone in our group was aware there was going to be a high casualty rate on the surface, but unless we came in numbers, we were all destined to die out there. It turns out our plan worked better than expected. We lost ten of our own and we killed sixty of the slavers on the surface. Sixty more surrendered, but these were slaughtered by long time slaves not in our group. They started to go through the entire tunnel system, killing every single supervisor and guard. While this was going on, we scarpered out of there, not having planned for a mass killing that wasted time. We loaded up the wagons with as much food, weapons, and warm clothing as we could find and were gone within an hour of the first slaver being strangled.'

'After few hundred miles people started jumping off at different places along the way closest to where they lived. In the end it was only me and another girl. Her family had been wealthy, and she'd visited Beachside a few times, so we headed there. Less chance of getting taken by slavers we were sure, although I was a different girl to the one slavers had crept up on in that small town.'

'I found a share house with eight other girls doing various jobs at the resorts. We pooled our money. This paid the rent and kept us in food. Then we'd buy enormous quantities of psychobeer at wholesale prices.'

'I lived that way for three years until gradually I knew I had a mission in life. Some parts of it I knew, others were concealed from me. The part I knew was that I would relentlessly track down and kill my father and stepmother for killing my mother and sending me over a waterfall. I didn't know what town I had come to when I was thirteen. And I don't know where to look. But I'll eventually find out where they are, and they will die. And it won't be an easy death.'

'The other part of what I've been seeking is shrouded in mystery, but I know it's vitally important. All of this is why I can be brooding and slightly angst ridden. I didn't join the Sisterhood of Anti-Princesses initially. I stole their look because it's cool. Then Roger needed a higher calibre of Anti-Princess. So I took the...' She let out a huge sigh and pretended to shudder. '...Vows.'

'No precisely how I remember it. But why quibble.' Said Roger.

As the trio approached the city, they crossed what was almost a neat line between drought and vibrant pasture. Roger again looked to the sky and shook his head. He thought it would be interesting for Richard to enter the city via the Wizard precinct. An area of fantasy Richard had not much interest in, though he certainly enjoyed a ride through it. Roger informed them that each Punter could only experience one part of the city. Thinking all the time it was the whole place. He said the details and ideas within Tæranon continued to grow, as Punters brought their entire consciousness into the realm. And this was especially true of Younameit. Hence in addition to the natural evolution of passing generations, new subject matter and perspectives were constantly being injected. The city was ten times the size it was in the first days of Tæranon.'

They wended their way through several themed districts and arrived at the armoury precinct. This was a medieval armour and weapons enthusiasts dream. There were outlandish fantasy swords, daggers, bows and weapons that Richard didn't recognise as weapons. There was a bewildering variety of beautifully crafted armour. Down a side street was a business that proclaimed itself as 'Shoe Repairs and Sword Fondlers.' A set of wide steps led to some very large French doors held open by massive swords their scabbards disappearing into the wooden landing.

The proprietor was small, somewhat rattish, but very friendly. He immediately asked if they could get any sword fondling jokes aired. 'Let's get it over with.' He said. 'My father thought it was funny. And it was funny. For a while. I keep the name out of respect for the old man.'

Richard shrugged. 'We ran through all the jokes before we got here. Your old man's dead so he won't care, go ahead and change it. Also, I'm having trouble with one of my shoes.' Said Richard. He thought he draw attention to his sensitivity to the name, contrary to his otherwise cheerful nature.

'I assess, trade and maintain swords. I don't repair shoes; it takes the sting out of Sword Fondling on the sign.' Said the man. He was processing what Richard had said with such confidence. He was going to try to get his sense of humour back about the name of his business. And if he couldn't, he'd change it.

'And we do wizard weaponry, although there are other places that have a larger variety of shafts. I'm the only one who has the really old stuff. I don't do wands. Find the whole wand thing a bit silly to be honest.'

'Hey.' Said Richard. 'We should get a shaft and see if I'm any good at swinging one of those things around. I might be able to beat Seren with that as well.'

'You haven't *beaten* me with a sword Richard because I haven't had one to fight you with because I was kind enough to *give* you mine.'

'Oh, yes. That time is yet to come.' He said this with less confidence now that he looked at Seren and compared her to his own physique. Entering the early stages of saggy middle-age with a small regrettable paunch concealed by loose clothing.

Roger and the shopkeeper waited for this exchange to run its course. Richard turned and said to the man. 'I was hoping for an assessment of this sword. We'd be interested if you know anything of its history.'

Richard removed it from its sheath so that it was glowing brightly as he handed it to the man. Roger and the Sword Fondler shared a glance and Roger said, in the polite way people do when they want to say, '*go away and leave us alone*'. 'Why don't you two go and look around.'

They took the hint and left. Initially Seren was making a game of it. 'That looks nice.' Richard would reply. 'Not your sword.'

Richard walked confidently down a level and passed a DO NOT ENTER sign. There were some very impressive, dust covered swords down there.

'I like this.'

'Not your sword.' Richard replied.

They went down another level and even Seren was mildly unsettled by the TRESSPASSERS DECAPITATED sign. Richard breezed past it. He was channelling Uncle Terry a little in Tæranon. 'They told us to look around.' He glanced to his left. 'That's your sword Seren.' He said casually and pointed to a sword leaning against a wall mixed with several others.

There was nothing outstanding about it. It was well crafted and tastefully ornate like dozens they'd seen. 'Take it up into the light.' He said. Immediately she picked it up a loud Bell tolled. All heard it in Tæranon and immediately knew what it meant, though it had never tolled before.

Meanwhile, the man upstairs said. 'Roger. This sword is part of a fairy tale isn't it. I didn't think it actually existed.'

'Unfortunately Ned, it is supposed to exist. I only wish it didn't.'

The man breathed out loudly. 'You'll need to go to the Consultants to get this read. This is way beyond my skills.'

'Thought so.' Said Roger. They both heard the Bell.

'So much for fairy tales.' Said the Fondler

Richard returned, very happy with himself. 'We found the sword destined for Seren. It was calling to me. Sorry about going though all those No Entry signs. I needed to look through the full range you see. And what was that Bell? Thought it might be an alarm to catch sword thieves.'

Seren went out and was sitting on the front steps trying to read the emerald flowing script revealed on the sword. It was in another language. 'You didn't give her a gimmick sword did you?' The Fondler whispered.

'What's a gimmick sword?'

'As good as any other sword to use, but when the buyer holds it, it creates a story from their memories to explain its absence. Very poignant if you go for the top of the range gimmick swords. Double the price for that style of sword.'

'Shit.' Said Richard.

Roger looked on knowingly

'Best thing is never to mention it.' Whispered the Fondler.

'But it could be genuine right.' Said Richard. 'I was so certain it was genuine, and not some kind of gimmick which I didn't even know existed. Can you turn them on and off?'

'Sure, if they have a little switch; only the Fondler or a Consultant can work, then it's a gimmick sword…'

'A what sword.' Her eyes were preparing to be murderous. 'Was I getting pulled into genuine sword ownership for the last few minutes about a made-up load of shit?'

The man took charge, held out his hand for the weapon and looked it over. 'I don't have to look for a switch. This came in a consignment a few years ago. I try not to buy consignments like that because I know they've been bought from Trolls and the Trolls probably got them from thieves who had raided castles or bought from those that did.'

'It's a dress sword, made for a young woman. If you had looked on the label attached to it, it reads NOT FOR SALE.' She took it back out from the scabbard and the sword lit up with emerald runes. He said 'Lighting up like that is begging for a Consultant to read it. I've only seen that a few times, it's a sword made specifically for you to find. Whoever made it must have had some tiny lock of hair or, yeerch, umbilical cord. Definitely yours. Get ready for a lot of Ka-Ching hitting this counter though.'

'I'll pay what's fair.' Seren said.

'I'll pay.' Said Richard, knowing the 'newly releathered' Seren would be broke and would need to work as a counter hand in a wand shop for years to pay the sword off.

'No you won't.' Said Seren.

'This again? I'll Pay.' Said Roger giving the Fondler a look that said that the Guide very rarely exercised his privileges. That was one of the reasons he was so highly regarded. But this sword was free. 'I hope I'm wrong Ned. But get ready for a run on swords.'

'Price went up fifty percent across my entire range.'

Ned looked directly at Richard and Seren. 'Your swords have stories. Their heritage written in intricate and incredibly difficult to read runes. Unnecessarily so in my opinion. This is because the Consultants who oversee the making of these rather special swords, also have control of the scribing that's engraved on them. And later, they get paid to read them. And they'll read any sword, including gimmick swords. It's a racket. Some of the stories can be quite long and boring and fortunately there's usually a scrolling feature and you can ask them to skip some of the padding. You're always polite to a Consultant of course but you need to be firm. It's their main source of income although they wouldn't admit it. Also make sure you have plenty of Ka-Ching. They often charge more than the sword itself is worth.'

'We have no choice but to visit them, as we really need to know what's on both swords.' Said Roger. Who seemed to be taking the whole thing rather too seriously Richard believed. He thought that he and Seren both having magical swords was pretty cool. They didn't need to visit any Consultants. He was happy having runes and a jewel that lit up.'

Roger had no more business in the city, and they were soon heading directly towards the foothills below the mountains. There seemed to be no shortage of rain in the area around the city. The crops included corn, pumpkins, tobacco, and potatoes. As they rode along however, the land became more and more drought stricken and they were eventually riding though crops that were failing. Near the foothills of the mountain range Richard looked off to his left and saw smoke. 'What's that over there?'

Roger looked across. He had an inkling of what it was. 'I don't think you'd enjoy a visit there Richard. Not at the moment.'

Richard smiled and said. 'Let's go.'

He'd assumed that when someone died in Tæranon, they came back to life to be part of the next Punter's story. But on the way, Roger explained that if you were killed you were dead. Like anywhere. The Punter might want a battle, an assassination, a plague, or a ritual suicide. Roger had to make it happen, and the populations had to bear it. Elves and Dwarves lost very few. Goblins and Ogres on the other hand had to have large families in response to the attrition.

Richard was now sombre. 'Are they less…sentient?

'I'll let you judge that for yourself Richard.' Said Roger.

Near the town, the pastures were all dry and the grass crisp. Sheep and cattle tried to sustain themselves on crops that had failed. They rode into the main street. Richard expected to be met with suspicion, but the greeting was warm and friendly. The Goblin who was the head of the town remarked on the long absence since Roger visited, and the pleasure and respect they had for Richard's *Let It Roll* decision. He said this was his first encounter with an Anti-Princess and they were 'Honoured to have her visit.' He told them the horses they were riding were magnificent and he wished he could ride a horse having seen theirs.

After this well rounded greeting the Goblin introduced himself as Gordon. He was apologetic. 'A bad time to visit I'm afraid. We're getting some fires under control and trying to put some supports under buildings to stop them falling. I can take you on the path around the far edges of the buildings and you'll be able to see a typical Goblin town. And we have some great bars.'

Before Roger could get a word in Richard said. 'How can we help. Perhaps you could let us help put out the fires, or with the buildings.' It took Gordon only a moment to process this. 'Of course. If you could join the bucket line, we'll get the water there faster.' Seren wandered off and found some Goblins struggling to hold up buildings weakened by the flames which had be put out in those areas. Rather than helping those holding the first storey up, she began running at full speed finding supports to add to the stability of the building. When one building was stable, they all began to do the same thing until they were all held in place. Passing along buckets, Richard looked around at the extensive damage. A quarter of the town had been badly damaged or destroyed. 'This would be a good project for Andy.' Richard said to Roger.

After an hour all the fires were finally out, and the building were shored up. Richard heard a sound coming from what he assumed would be the town square. 'Let's get to a bar the other side of town and really show you guys some Goblin hospitality. And gratitude.' Said Gordon.

'What's happening over there.' Said Richard.

'Nothing to see.' Said Roger

Richard was becoming more and more self-assured in Tæranon. More like his Uncle Terry when the circumstance called for it. 'I want to go over there.'

In the town square there were a hundred or so bodies laid out neatly in two lines. Many children. He saw a pregnant woman. Richard stood in disbelief. Richard had never been confronted with death in real life. He said. 'Why?'

It was some time before Gordon answered. 'They used to come and demonstrate how they could dive and roll, shoot trees and then split the arrows, all with perfect hair. But recently they've become more violent, demanding. They want stores we don't have. So they burn a few houses. This time they burned houses and went through the town shooting at random. We're used to having men fulfil the requirements of the Punter's stories. But we never once lose our children. We've never had a Punter who would want such a thing.'

A huge black shadow passed over the town. Several shadows. Andy and three female Dragons landed at full size and then shrank. 'I can see a bit of home renovation is required here.'

'How did you get here so fast.' Said Richard.

Andy's voice had a trace of condensation. 'We're magical Richard. We heard your request yesterday. We talked about it and thought, hey, Goblin architecture is a brand-new experience for us. Myself and these three delightful apprentices decided to come.'

He saw the dead laid out. 'Elves? The bastards.' He looked at them for a long time. 'We have long memories.' Soon they were busy planning a 'renewal' for the burned or damaged parts of the town. The Goblins, never having seen Dragons up close, were encouraged to come and watch the work. They planned to have a large beerhall session with the Goblins that night. Richard, Roger and Seren made their farewells and left.

The travellers were subdued the following day, winding their way through the foothills on tracks through summer pastures and in some cases fields of wildflowers. All at once the terrain was bare of vegetation. Above was a landscape that grew steeper and steeper. They climbed the track which began to pass along a chasm with a river far below. They came to a sign which read in large bold red letters. **Pass This Point and Die**. In smaller letters in green it read. '*Sword consultations welcome. Business hours only please.*'

A hideous Witch appeared from within a dense black cloud. She laughed. 'You fools believed that nonsense about sword consultation. Your death will be painful beyond what you could ever imagine.'

Seren was reaching for her knives. Roger said. 'Hi Tina. Can we skip this part?'

'Oh Roger. It's you. Good to see you. It's been a while.'

Roger's answer was a study in being unenthusiastic. 'Unicorns.' He sighed. 'And Witches have, as you know, had a bit of a lull in literature. Bit parts.'

'We like being forgotten by Punters. We can get on with the things we really like doing.' She smiled hideously at Seren. 'Now you must introduce me to your friends.'

Roger gave the basic introductions, highlighting Richard's trade and said they would like to have the sword owners confirmed and the swords script read.

'I assume you have large quantities of Ka-Ching? Or we can do business with gold, slaves, and expert certified heirlooms.' Tina was hideous and her smile alarming. 'Or…' She winked at Seren.

'I'm recalling a few things I forgot on your behalf Tina.' Said Roger enigmatically. 'Maybe I could unforget them'

'Three talisman and two Ka Ching.'

'Sounds fair.' Said Roger

'It's called extortion.' The Witch said, hurt to be put in a position which so undervalued her craft.

She had barely said this when Richard interrupted. 'Is that the way you really look.' He was a bit unsure why he was saying things like this now. The Witch transformed into a young woman, alluring and walking towards him as a seductress.

'Um…how you really look.' Said Richard. The figure morphed a handsome middle-aged woman. Apparently a little anxious about the reaction she would get. Richard was sincere. 'The real you is way better than those other two.' She knew he meant it as Richard had never been good at concealing anything. In this case sincerity.

They went into a little house not far from the sign which had two rooms, one with only a wooden table surrounded by chairs. Its sole purpose being sword readings. 'Show me your swords.'

She looked around to those assembled as she read the runes on Richards. 'Oh. And save your laughing for the end. I didn't come up with this stuff.' She warned.

'The only Goddess of Tæranon, whose name is lost in time, gave birth to twin boys before she became the forces of nature. One boy was evil to his very core and would care nothing for the Peoples and how they suffered. The other child would be easy going, friendly, liked people and hoped they had a good life. A personable fellow.'

Tina broke her recital. 'Famous text this one.' She was scrolling by flicking her finger like a phone. 'Don't remember it going on and on. We were paid by the word back then, so this is what happens.'

The others in the room shared a silent conviction that she should stop the commentary and continue. 'The First Mothers of all the Peoples had been called to be midwives to the boys birthing and they convened a meeting before going to usher forth their People into the new world of Tæranon.'

'My great great great grandmother was there as the First Mother of Witches. I may have left out a great or two if anyone's interested.' No one was.

'Some who convened that day said the evil child should be killed before he could spread a blight across the land. Ultimately though, as Mothers, they couldn't kill a newborn. They settled for a strategy in which they concentrated all the boy's powers in their hands. They exchanged the left hand of the twins. Having one personable hand on the evil child was expected to result in him being a very unpleasant person, maybe nasty sometimes. But not evil. The other child was expected to be much like he was until somebody pressed his buttons. Then look out. The children were assigned to ordinary families to live out their days as a farmer and a craftsman. The immortality problem was a difficult nut to crack so the First Mothers ignored it. They all agreed they'd done as well as they could and left to get on with their usherings.'

'But the connection of the evil right hand with its bearer restored his original nature. He learned who his Mother had been and that he was immortal. Now that he fully understood his powers, he became Wizard King of the Invincible Hand, he insisted everyone call him that, even though it was a mouthful when having a conversation with him. He killed people who tried to turn it into an acronym. His power began growing, spreading, and taking over the Peoples in his region as his Vassals. He built a magnificent castle looking west towards the mountains and east across the wide plains of Geopor. He forged the mighty Sword of Anon. Have you had enough detail, or shall we skip to the end. My scrolling finger's tired.' She laughed.

Richard had a simple, pleasant smile. 'I'm new here so it's interesting. We can take a break till your finger is rested.'

She continued. 'Meanwhile, a mysterious group of wizards, shaman, holy men and the Guardsman Challengers, the only people who can pass through the Citadel Guards, forged the Sword of Tær for the easy going twin. They bestowed upon him his own long name; The Wizard King of the Personable Hand. But he would only answer to his first name. They failed to advise him that he had to pay the costs for the sword as shaman, wizards, Citadel Guards, and holy men aren't loaded. He said he would have preferred it if they'd told him that up front, but said it was okay and he'd work the sword off on a payment plan. He never earned enough to pay it off however and so the fate of the sword was shrouded in the mists of time.'

'Didn't have a middleman you see.' Said Roger.'

Tina glared at him. 'This is a sacred calling you know. Anyway, not written on the sword, but the real story is he sold it to a big stupid Knight, and it became a family heirloom. The Personable King wanted to live debt free.'

'He was a reluctant monarch. He made his living as a humble craftsman. The details of what he produced being shrouded in the mists of time.'

'Hah.' Said Tina. 'My ancestors used to be such prudes when it came to sword inscribing. The Wizard King of the Invincible Hand knew his adversary didn't have the kind of money to build a castle like his, so he built one at the very far end of the Geopor Plain, so the two castles, on a clear day, could be seen from each other's parapets. It was not hard to divine they were constructed awaiting the day when a massive battle would decide the fate of Tæranon on the plain between them.'

'The craftsman sent a polite note, thanking his adversary for the castle, but he couldn't move in as, it was larger than his needs, too ostentatious for his tastes and a little draughty. He'd also never be able to afford the upkeep.' He again thanked the Wizard King for his kindness and said perhaps he could recoup some of his investment by renting it out. Possibly by the room, like a hotel.'

'The Wizard King of the Invincible Hand was annoyed by this for a few reasons. Partly because he'd called him the 'Wizard King' which caught on and he couldn't kill that many people. Later, a more well healed group of mysterious supporters set the craftsman up in a small kingdom so that when the time came, he would at least have some experience at being a King, albeit a very modest one.'

'And that's it.'

Richard laughed. 'Lucky that wasn't on a magic ring. You'd be dizzy Tina. The chap whose sword this is sounds like he wasn't ever really interested in the whole King thing from the start. Got dumped on him by some well-meaning über midwives. But it gives him a nice excuse to go on a noble quest to find his sword. And maybe help a damsel in distress. Find a queen. Who knows.'

Roger introduced a less esoteric explanation. 'Richard the man who created Tæranon wanted it to evolve with the beings he created, and with the new ideas and the mini creations of Punters. He wanted to see what the various Peoples became without being held in what you might call characterhood. They played their part as actors but weren't bound to behave that way in their day to day lives. As we've seen, there's been some surprises in the tangents different Peoples have taken. For us at least. The creator of Tæranon expected a Punter arrive at some point who would help him fulfil his grand design.'

'I suspect the Wizard King has been grooming and slowly marshalling his forces. Dwarves, Elves, The Pegasus and Little People for some time. Knights who may not know what they're being led to. Your arrival, like it or not, has stimulated preparations for war. And now the Alliance of the King, formerly known as the Wizard King of the Personable Hand, will need to be built.'

'My arrival? Alliance?'

'Pull up your sleeves and show us your forearms would you Richard. I imagine you've been a bit curious about that.'

Richard pulled up his sleeves and revealed marks four inches up from his wrist. Rough stitch marks around four inches up from the wrist of his left hand. 'The Wizard King has similar stitch marks on his left hand. He's the man who created this world, and he lives in a big black castle on Mt Anon.'

'The man who built the briefcase. The man I thought had died of cancer?'

'It was a convenient story. He chooses to live in Tæranon nearly full time. I believe he has to leave from time to time. I suspect on some of these occasions he can make time stand still so he simply re-joins the narrative. At other times I suspect he's as happy have a more involved Tæranon to return to. I met him only a few times. He established my role. Way back then I could see the castles being built and heard of the swords being forged, I was very busy with my set piece productions for the Punters, and they weren't per-mitted to be anywhere near Geopor. Gradually I began to see the slow shifts in alignments and attitudes of the Peoples. And now the sword is recovered.'

'But me being a one-time Punter means…?'

'You're the King, and from the moment you used the sword, a process was set in train. When you first began to use the sword on the moors do you recall hearing a soft bell.'

'I heard it.' Said Seren. 'Richard was playing with his sword as usual.'

'Do you ever get tired of your predictable double entendres.'

'No.'

'I heard it also. Over a week ago.' Said Tina. 'And then there was the big clanger a few days ago.'

'Yes.' Said Roger, providing no more details about that bell and why it tolled when it did. I increased the rate of travel somewhat to get here. Which I will now need to do a great deal of. Contrary to the rules I was to abide by. There is a month between the loud Bell and the Horn that marks the moment when battle will be joined.' There was a pause.

Richard thought he'd provide some conversational fill while he processed this. 'Ah…would that be a calendar month, or the straight twenty-eight days.'

'I expect you'll be receiving emissaries about that issue and more.'

'Emissaries.' Richard could not help but be impressed. 'But what if I'd rather go home to a very modest flat outside of London. Emphasis on very modest.'

'Richard, it would mean there would be no battle.' Richard brightened a little. It didn't last long. 'All of the Peoples you've met that you've liked the best would be attacked village by village, home by home, person by person.'

'That's rather grim. Why me?'

'Because he thinks he can beat you. And...' Roger smiled enigmatically. '...I think he's greatly underestimated you.'

Richard thought this would be a good occasion to look around saying nothing. That was everyone else's strategy until things got awkward and Tina said. 'There's another sword left to read. Seren is it?' Seren nodded. 'How about you come with me into the coven...ah... lounge room as the newly minted King considers his position.'

Seren and Tina were soon settled into a very pleasant lounge room that might accommodate a dozen people to talk, get a drink from the bar or play pool. It was empty when Seren walked in.

'Hope there's not as much on this sword. Interpreting those ridiculous runes into the common tongue is fiendishly difficult. That's why we make them that way, no one else can. Naturally we make money being paid to cast spells and do potions. All complete bullshit of course. Thank God for the placebo effect. I mean really, as if a newt's anus and the eyeball of a porpoise are ever going to have a meaningful impact.'

Seren could tell Tina had some pitch to make before reading the sword and she wished she'd get on with it instead. 'You know we're always recruiting new members of our Unholy Sisterhood. But we are very discerning as to who might join us. I would need to consult within the coven but I'm confident you'd be able to walk straight into the role of Apprentice Witch. That's only for a year. Then you get all the privileges and your own flying broom.'

Seren imagined one needed to be careful rejecting an offer from a Witch. She went with the. 'I'm honoured. Thank you. I'll need to give it some serious thought.'

'Sure.' Tina smiled knowingly. 'We also have a 'Witch for a Weekend' program. That might also be of interest. But let's have a look at the sword that found you.'

'Richard found it and said it was mine.'

'Yes.' Said the witch. Giving nothing away. 'Let's get rid of this hideous camouflage shall we.' Tina took out something reminiscent of a tuning fork, tapped it on the table and put it on the end on the hilt of the sword. A paint like substances fell away from all over the scabbard and hilt revealing a beautiful sword with a tasteful silver and gold hilt and a scabbard with a golden filigree encrusted with emeralds on one side and rubies on the other. 'The Sword Fondler can't do that. You see when someone sends out a sword like this, they are hoping to have found, they don't want it to end up in some rich assholes collection. It needs to circulate. I'd say this one circulated a few years longer than the sender would have liked.' She drew it from the scabbard and asked Seren to hold it. Immediately emerald runes appeared. By the time Tina had finished interpreting the sword, Seren was looking into space.

She asked if she could wait a while before joining her companions. Tina understood. They had a cup of tea. 'Just normal tea.' Tina said.

'What's was on the sword.' Richard ventured as they started riding down to the foothills.

Seren let out a big huffing sigh. 'Sword stuff.' Which conveyed 'don't ask again'.

'And where to from here Roger?' Richard was tentative, trying to sound like someone without a care in world.

Roger slowed to a stop and then turned his horse so that they could face each other. 'It depends if you want to build and lead an Army Richard. Otherwise, most of the parts Tæranon you've liked most will be overrun within a year. Our friends the Witches think themselves immune. But no one will be, and all must decide. The cities and towns of human must remain neutral and can give no help to either side. The creator wants his world to function in the long term. I don't think he'll be so interested in Punters anymore. He still comes and goes via his briefcase. Your briefcase will be re-possessed. I think I'll be out of a job. So, I'm going to side with…'

Richard sighed, the enormity of it still sinking in. 'Me?'

Roger smiled. 'The Wizard King of the Personable Hand.'

Richard nodded. 'The acronym would even be bit of a mouthful. Let's go with Ricard.'

Seren said nothing so they turned and continued.

'Roger, from what I can tell there will only be a few Peoples who would stand up directly to be counted for a battle on the Geopor Plains. The key will be to get some of the others to change their minds and be, either directly involved, providing support at least not participating as part the enemy's army.'

'It sounds like I'm your man for liaison and logistics.'

'The other main role I'm going to need to fill soon is, what might one call it? I like Battlemaster. Someone to turn the various troops into an army. A formidable fighting force.' Richard starting to at least appear grave.

'You've picked the formal name the Wizard King…ha…I mean your brother uses. A Battlemaster would need to have nerves of steel. Able to discipline Companies of Peoples of all kinds. Able to both command while also reach consensus where necessary.'

Richard nodded. 'Ruthless when necessary but merciful when such an approach is in the best interests of the Alliance. And able to communicate with Captains and identify weaknesses and remedies in battles. We'd need an outstanding horseman, easily able to defend themselves in the absence of any guard.'

'Surely Richard, all this doesn't exist in one individual?' Wondered Roger aloud.

'It does Roger. But will she be too humble to accept, or…or will she have other more important things going on in her life at the moment. And will we have to go through the no, yes, thankyou process.'

Seren now joined in. 'You're offering me the job to put together an army, co-ordinate it and lead it into the biggest battle in the history of Tæranon. A battle on which the future of all of the good guys depends.'

'That's about the size of it.' Said Richard.

'Easy. I'm in.'

'Not to diminish your choosing process. But I think the Bell got the jump on you when a certain person of immense talent had a sword bestowed by her King which she'd carry into battle.'

'Bit like king Arthur really, except we pulled it out of a dusty store-room.' Richard smiled. 'The three of us combining our formidable talents, though I haven't yet figured out what mine are, will defeat our evil foe and his huge army of experienced and well-armed soldiers. We have a lot of riding to do.'

'Unable to reveal its existence due to the assurances I gave on the first day I met the Wizard King, there exists a 'magic' door which I use for logistics in preparing a Punters selection into reality and getting them to the starting point, all unawares. I can in fact set it to turn up anywhere. Which will now be somewhat of a necessity in order to conduct diplomacy and then hopefully marshal the troops to where you want them. It'll save everyone rather a lot of riding and foot slogging.'

'Roger won't the Wizard King be a bit peeved at you helping our side.'

'Yes. He certainly will. But I don't want to live in a world where all his assholes have the upper hand. Look at what they did to the children at the Goblin town. Over the next few days, I'll move my family to somewhere he's never been. You see the place grows when the Punters want something we don't have. Like a mine in the frozen wastes. Tæranon is twenty times bigger than when it started.'

'When they arrive, I meet everyone at the same place I met you Richard, but I they walk straight through the door. Over the years, I've suggested a few ideas to some of the Punters which has allowed me to create some very pleasant, very had to get to places.' Roger switched to strategy. 'One of the first things you'll need to do is to meet one of your major allies. They live in the huge delta of the Nadi River and places like it around the coast.'

'Downstream of where Seren grew up.' Said Richard.

'What did you say?'

'In the story you told us. You grew up on the Nadi. Near the head waters.' He said matter of factly.

'I didn't tell you where I grew up because I didn't know.'

'Ah. You know. A writer's mind.' He said with slight superiority. 'Comes up with its own stories. Especially where yours wasn't very…ah…internally coherent on all occasions.'

Seren let it pass. 'And what else has your writer's mind come up with?'

'There was no Stepmother in the wings when your mother passed away. Your mother died in childbirth. Your father loved your mother so much he made it clear he would never marry again. You were the apple of your father's eye. He'd spend hours playing with you. Contrary to the local customs of fatherhood.'

'But your father had an enemy. He paid the midwife to poison as soon as you were delivered. Then his enemy was waiting until your father had deeply bonded to his daughter for nearly three years. The enemy had the same woman who poisoned her mother take you and throw her off a bridge. The father eventually found out who had done both deeds, and although generally mild and merciful, he ensured the woman suffered an awful death.'

Richard broke into his narrative. 'Can a three-year old baby swim?' He wanted feedback as to the plausibility for this part of the story.

'I can't say they can or can't.' Said Roger unhelpfully. Richard was going to reply that Roger had had so many damn three-year-olds he should have some idea.

'Is there more.' Said Seren flatly.

'Yes, there was a wolf appearance. The Wolf was a bit of a hero really. Pulled you out of the river before you went under permanently. He gave you a good shake, presumably to dry you off before dinner, when an arrow whistled…do they whistle…I'll have to look that up. Stories should be accurate to at least some degree. I'm not much good at the research side of things and it shows. It's something my sister Miranda is only too quick to point out.'

Richard had forgotten what he was talking about.

'Well.' Seren was a little teste because she knew there was more.

'Oh. Yes. The woodsman you thought you were saved by was mainly a poacher who did legitimate wood selling as a front. The day you'd gone missing from the castle emissaries were sent saying the King had lost his daughter and that he would pay a huge reward to have her returned. Your father assumed you must have drowned. But he still sent people out. However, so did his enemy. They told a story that a child was lost, and her father was trying to kill her to please his new wife.'

'Your guardian, Arnall. He didn't know who to believe. So he kept you hidden.'

'How did you know his name?'

'I'm certain you mentioned him earlier. As a child, when you began to be able to talk, he told you your name was Seren, because that's what both groups of emissaries had said. And your father told everyone it was your mother who had chosen such a beautiful name because she knew you would be such a beautiful child. Anyway, Arnall said if you ever met a stranger, you were to give them the name 'Gör' which is a little ironic because that happens to mean brat in German.' Richard added quickly. 'But of course, I'm sure Arnall had never heard of Germany. As a writer, this string of made-up aspects to your early life is interesting and might, with further development, reveal more of the characters past hardships and mysterious quest. Though not wildly original.'

Seren ignored that. 'There is no way you could know that. I never needed to use that name.'

'And that is, all I know...sort of.' Richard was a little afraid of Seren now.

'Keep going.' Her voice conveyed his life was not in danger.

'Your father heard about a girl living in the woods about the age his daughter would be. He led a search through the forest and they came upon an old abandoned poachers camp. They went to the Sheriff who said there was a man working off his crimes as a poacher in a quarry and had been doing so for four years. He interviewed the man, who introduced himself As Arnall and was deeply grateful to the man who'd been a father to you. After their adventures together, your father put him in charge of all the forest and made it be known he could take what he wanted and run tours for sports hunters. Which he found very profitable, but Arnall never recovered from the loss of the girl who was a daughter to him and who had disappeared without a trace.'

'Once Arnall was freed, he and your father immediately made enquiries in the town. Eventually, they came up with a ruse to let it be known that your father wanted to buy a girl. An approach came from a slaver soon after. He didn't have one but said if The King described what he father wanted he could catch one to order.'

'The man was treated very roughly. Another time your father diverged from his generally easy-going nature. The slaver had no knowledge of what happened to you, but he had information that helped them find the one who originally took you from the town. It was early winter and the paths through the tundra and icefields were difficult to find. Eventually they arrived at a deep mine with massive workings far underground including a rail system and with underground living quarters so that most slaves never returned to the surface. When they arrived, they were shocked at the carnage. Everyone was dead, either brutally murdered or through the process of slow starvation There were hundreds of dead, only partly decomposing in summer, and re freezing each winter.

They rode home. Your father had given up hope. But Arnall had heard of homing swords and so your father thought he would have one made as his last act in trying to find you. He commissioned one of the most beautiful swords ever forged. A dress sword for a young woman though as effective in battle. The sword was camouflaged and Arnall got it into the hands of a petty thief in the city which is the way homing swords are generally circulated. Both your father and Arnall have always held onto the slim hope you would find it and return to them.'

Seren seemed resigned. 'And now I have it, where do I take it.'

'To the castle, at the headwaters of the Nadi. The castle of the... ah...never mind.'

'What was the castle called Richard.'

He paused as if trying to remember. 'What was it? Hmmm. The Castle of the...um...Wizard King of the Personable Hand. Silly name.' Richard thought he'd add something diversionary. 'Much less ostentatious than the castle on Mt Anon. This whole thing is all a bit like Star Wars really, two whole trilogies with same underlying key plot element if you ask me. Luke, I'm your father. And then Rey is Luke's daughter in the big reveal. I mean, these are big budget movies. Can't they come up with something original.'

Richard hoped he had swung attention from Seren's saga, via another one.

Seren didn't know what to feel or say first so she started with. 'What the fuck is Star Wars. And how the fuck can this be happening when I was certain killing my asshole father was half of my purpose in life.'

'Now that's enough of that kind of language from you young lady.' There was an extended silence when Richard said. 'A little joke. Lighten the mood. Things are a bit heavy.'

After twenty minutes of plodding in silence Seren said. 'Have you been able to 'find' the door yet Roger.'

'Oh. Here it is, right as you brought it up.' He didn't want to break into the story with something he could have done an hour before. 'We'll be arriving in the Nadi Delta near the largest Ogre colony. How these People mature as individuals is a little unusual. I'll let you experience it rather than explain it myself.'

They went through the door and were soon in a tall grassland on a built-up path running though wide shallow waterbodies which drained east, sluggishly now. It was clear from the pathways that the water was perhaps a quarter of its usual depth. The grass was turning brown and dying. Not accustomed to the water level being so low. Roger looked up at the sky as he'd done so many times. When Seren and Richard joined him, they could see tiny black dots moving about.

'Rain miners. Or should I say rain relocators. Thieves. Do you know the Dwarves are afraid of being underground? Not so in the sky. Supported by those asshole Pegasus People. I've brought us in a little out of the Ogre town so as not to startle them.'

At that moment they came upon a large figure standing in the middle of the track. He was fourteen feet tall. His skin was grey, and looked greasy and he was fantastically muscular with arms, legs and chest designed for amazing power. He had an uncomplicated smile. 'Hi. You'll never pronounce my name so the Youngers said you should call me Bruce. What are your names?'

Bruce was cheerful. Pleased that he'd been the one to encounter them. They were expected, and on each of the tracks leading to town an ogre was waiting. Richard was now expected to lead any conversation. 'Hello Bruce. I'm Richard and these are my good friends Roger and Seren.'

'Hello Richard, Roger and Seren. The Youngers asked me to take you to them as soon as possible.'

They started moving off when Bruce said. 'Try to ride as fast as you can if you want.'

They were happy to oblige, and Bruce loping along beside them running straight over all the smaller plants, deep pools, and wide sections of grass. It was clear that to him he was barely ambling. He laughed. 'We love to lope. I could go more than twice as fast.' He was laughing like a child.

They came to a large town built from the local material which was mud huts with grass roofs but soundly built and beautiful. An Ogre the size of a human was waiting for them outside of what appeared to be a communal building but turned out to be the Tæranon equivalent of a high-tech workshop.

'Hi. I've picked Fergus to be my human name.' The others introduced themselves and Fergus got down to business.

'Roger may have told you that it's the young Ogres that are the adults intellectually and that we have the greatest store of knowledge and maturity. Our people revert slowly to a more infantile state as they age, hence the quintessential ogre in a Punter's story appears unintelligent, but it's really because they're intellectually young and immature. It breaks our hearts to see them go to the activities specified by Punters. All they're allowed is nothing but a near useless chain to swing fastened to a ring our around their neck. And I know Roger you're unable to tell Punters about this. I also know this part of your work is the least palatable.'

Roger's eyes were downcast.

Interesting and important as the conversation was, Richard was looking over the Younger's shoulder at the very large room full of Ogres, all young in age, sitting and workbenches with soldering equipment, cutting tools, and bending and grinding equipment for different kinds of metals. They were making simple devices for use around town such as gardening and various other tools, but a few were winding copper around coils and making rudimentary radios. With ogres at various workbenches chatting away to someone else in the workshop.

'This is amazing' He turned to Fergus, excited. 'You're on the cusp of the microchip, and all here in low tech Tæranon.

Fergus smiled. 'Microchips?'

'I'd love to get together with your key people doing metallurgy and technologies. I'd like to understand what you're up to. This could be vital. I suspect you're trying to crack the code of a certain device.'

Fergus looked uncomfortable. He changed the subject. 'Sadly, we can't eat technology Richard. The fish are dying or migrating permanently to the ocean, half of our crops have failed. Some of our brothers and sisters ask if they can move here. We tell them we have no more than they do.' He tried to be more upbeat. 'I thought your focus would be on warfare. These technologies would be useful for weapons development. But we're only allowed to use a length of chain attached to a ring around our neck.'

Richard was making Kingly decisions already. 'There will be no limit to what weapons you choose. Your technologies may be the most powerful weapon you've ever had. There is one thing you *will not* be allowed to have. A ring around your neck with a chain attached to it'.

Fergus was enthusiastic 'We may get the better of some Dwarves and Elves before we go down in the end. With some freedom and dignity at last.' Yet still absolutely resigned to the outcome.

Richard was still Richard, but parts of him were either metamorphosing and breaking through a slightly above average insecurity without disturbing a native geniality. All at once a completely novel battle strategy leapt into his head. Too ridiculous to be taken seriously. Which was one of its strengths. 'Not one Ogre shall die Fergus. Not one. If that occurs my plan has failed. You must make your people believe they will never be used by me or anyone else as cannon fodder. Remember this for now. Loping is a primary characteristic of Ogres which will contribute to success. The leadership of all the other Ogre colonies need to come together for a meeting about strategy and interacting with the other Peoples. When can you bring those nominated to represent the other Ogre colonies together?'

Fergus was pleased. 'Two days. Those coming will be excited. There needs to be a good reason for a Younger to lope. Ogres all look forward to our childhood days later in life as Olders and we can lope for the pure pleasure of it.'

Richard then spent two hours in the workshop having animated conversations with the Youngers, most around his height. The Ogres were mesmerised, partly with new information, but also with excitement to at least attempt a victory rather than be victims of inevitable defeat and slaughter.'

Richard said farewell to the Ogres and asked Roger to take him to the Goblin town which the Elves had attacked. They arrived to find five dragons, Andy and four 'apprentices' putting the finishing touches on a repair to what was damaged, plus a general upgrade and modernisation of the town. Gordon came running out to welcome them. Seren was surprised at how delightful Goblins could be when they were happy. They weren't accustomed to being hugged but that's what they got from the trio. He spoke of the magnificent work the Dragons had chosen to do for them. 'We offered them our small treasury of Ka Ching, but the Dragons said they do it for the pleasure if the 'booze was free'. They are a bit noisy at night.' Gordon said quietly. 'We try to blot it out with our own noise.' His smile suggested the renovation was a good thing all around. He was laughing, but everyone could see the land around them was dead. The townsfolk were skin and bone. Andy knew he was refurbishing a town people would soon have to leave. But he would be watching over it until they could return, and anyone messing with his renovations would be cinders.

Andy was fitting some trusses, helped by a beautiful forest dragon, when Richard approached.

'I know what you're going to ask, and sadly the answer's no Richard. Dragons aren't allowed to fight on either side. That Invincible Wizard King or whatever. The bastard. Wants things to *appear* to be an even playing field.'

One of the traits Richard had that people loved, was the unfeigned pleasure he showed when reconnecting. He smiled. 'I wasn't going to ask you to fight. I thought you could deliver a message though.'

Richard explained what he wanted, and Andy rubbed his chin with his clawed paw. 'Now that would be funny, and I think allowable.' He slapped Richard on the back. 'These poor sods living here have really shit lives. It'd like to help get them back their pastures at least.'

Richard told Gordon they'd like to use the door to visit the other Goblin towns to see who wanted to be involved. Gordon said there were seven. He would be glad to visit six and suggested a unified Goblin block would be easy to achieve. Goblins were autonomous but were always on good terms with one another. He said he would not visit the seventh.

Roger made the door ready. He knew all the towns well for his own bitter reasons.

'And why not the seventh?' Said Richard. Gordon shrugged. 'I don't like them.'

Richard smiled. 'We'll do the other six first.'

The towns varied in size, one very large. The responses were all the same. 'We're dying. If we die in battle against the People turning our children into skeletons so much the better.' They said they would nominate a Captain from each town. They needed no coordinating Goblin Commander unless the Battlemaster wanted on. The Captains would report to the Battlemaster so she could deploy them as required. Like the Ogres, they assumed their role would primarily be cannon fodder. Expecting to charge in lines in the front to catch the Elven arrows, swords of the knight and axes of the dwarves as they ran headlong into a well-armed and armoured enemy. Richard told that no matter how unlikely it sounded, his objective that not one, *not one* of them, would die. He told them they would go to the Ogre town which was now the HQ. They would train initially on short distance bows then build a smaller group of longbow archers. They were also developing weapons only Goblins could operate. The Ogres were building prototypes.

He'd spoken to Andy, who agreed to send dragons with stomach loads of water to keep the vegetable plots of the Goblin towns going. He advised Goblins to centralise forces in the largest town. 'Roger will use the door to bring what food could be acquired to support the Goblin forces as they built up. Roger knew some far flung communities who would like to make donations or sell surpluses at a fair price.

They went to the final Goblin town. It was large. The whole feel was different to the other towns. It was a martial place. A military fetish pervaded. They were greeted by the Commander of the Garrison. 'Your arrival in Nargate has been expected. The resources we need for life dwindle and we look forward to the day we can make our foes of old pay dearly. As Roger can confirm, we have the largest contingent under arms in the Goblin population and we have been called upon more frequently than others to pay the heavy price of the battles to satisfy the fantasists.' Roger stiffened at this description as it wasn't accurate. 'We have the finest troops and leaders. If you have not selected a Battlemaster and Generals for each of the Peoples myself and my Captains stand ready to serve.'

Richard looked at the Goblin for a little longer such that for those standing around it began to feel awkward. He said. 'It was useful to meet you. I'll take my leave.' He turned away. The others following. His companions were not accustomed to this approach from Richard who was evolving before their eyes.

The creature was all at once between Richard and door. 'What's this. We are superior warriors to any Peoples. *Any*. And you would not bring us to the centre of the Army you're trying to build. You would cast aside three hundred swords ready to fight to the death.'

'Your swords coordinate with none but themselves or those they can master. You cannot collaborate, but neither could you *moderate* you action. I require both to meet my ends. Move aside.'

Richards's answer was mild in response to the escalating stringency in the Goblin's.

'And so, what kind of King is this. With a child, and a female for a Battlemaster, and a collaborator in the mass murder of Goblins on your staff. If we were wanting purely to fight it would be for the Wizard King, our master of old.' The Garrison Commander of Nargate was incredulous.

'If you're so monumentally stupid to fight for a King who is turning your children to skeletons, you're as stupid as you sound with respect to how you would conduct a battle.' The Goblin started to draw a blade. Richard pulled his sword out. The blade was alive with fire along its length. 'I could have everyone dead in this village before the tip leaves the scabbard of your sword. I won't use this on the field of battle but watch how you speak of my companions. You're a witless fool compared to them. You should be careful not to be anywhere near Geopor on the day. Move aside and may we never meet again.'

When they stepped out of the door Gordon was waiting. Trying to supress his curiosity. Richard smiled and said. 'I didn't like them either.'

Seren and Roger were seriously starting to flag. It had been a big day. Full of some strange and significant revelations and reunions with mixed emotions for Roger. Richard seemed fresh and had several ideas for Peoples he'd like to canvass. But Roger's eyes told him that those who weren't newly minted Kings were exhausted. He asked Roger to take them to one last place.

They arrived near a comfortable cottage in the garden of a pleasant castle on a river. There was a man coming out to get another armload of firewood. Seren was off her horse and running as soon as they came out of the door. 'Arnall! It's me Seren.' Richard looked at Roger and they watched as the two embraced, then laughed, embraced again, followed by brief stories of what had happened. Then Arnall came to Richard and gave him a bear hug. 'My King never gave up. Always hoped. He believed if his sword was good enough, it would find you and you would find him.'

Richard thought he'd sidestep all the confusion and improbability surrounding the whole issue. 'We thought it would be good if you'd like to come to a nice resort and stay the night.' There was momentary uncertainty, but Seren returned to her breezy self. 'Ever been to a resort Arnall.' He shook his head and smiled. Roger, having a good bag of Ka Ching, said they'd all go to one of the best hotels on the strip.

It was indeed a pleasant place with the three men drinking psychobeer and Seren having disappeared. Returning with what later turned out to be Head of the Dining Room. He had asked if he could meet Richard and see his sword. He was in awe of the craftsmanship and the beautiful runes.

Seren looked across and squeezed the young man's arm with a message 'Now get lost'. She brought four new beers even though they had only half-finished a round. 'You've been getting watered down shit.' She put the half-finished beers on the table of some Rat People she knew were skint. 'There's no one appreciates you guys until the bogs start overflowing.'

'Ain't that the truth Sister.' The Rat People were a simple race. They were nice to people who were nice to them. And mean to people who were mean to them.

Arnall saw Richard, the man drinking now heavily spiked psychobeer, seamlessly as the man who had found him, pardoned him, and then shared a journey over the Oighir wasteland where they nearly perished. The Richard who had the most beautiful sword ever made sent to find his daughter if she still lived. The Richard who engaged him to manage the grounds of the castle and game keeper in all the forests. Arnall showed high end sports hunters where to hunt, while managing game populations. The shooters often didn't want what they killed so he gave it to the poorest families in the town.

Seren and Arnall were deep in conversation while Richard quizzed Roger on what other allies he might call upon. The Rat People were quickly discounted. They were ungovernable and, it should be mentioned, smelled really bad. That was evidenced by the fact no one was sitting three table deep around them. Richard wanted to at least introduce himself. He also wanted to go and see Benny at his bridge. Roger said Trolls never fought in wars, but Richard wanted to visit anyway. That appeared to be the end of the list. But Richard knew Roger was holding something back.

'Who else.' He said.

'They've never been engaged in any Punter's fantasy; they were part of the ecology the Wizard King created. I utilise giant spiders but those are small in number and unpleasant on the cusp of being irredeemably mean and dangerous. But their smaller cousins subsist in the forest in their thousands. Tens of thousands probably. In a forest not that far from your castle. Much smaller spiders. About plate sized.'

Richard shuddered slightly. 'Would that be a bread-and-butter plate?'

'Dinner plate.'

Richard shuddered again. 'I'd like to meet with them tomorrow. And see Tina again.'

'Sure Richard. But Witches don't help anybody.'

'Then we'll have to help them.' Richard paused briefly, changing subject. 'Roger would it be right to say that the usual amount of time a Punter is here will elapse around the time of the battle.'

Roger made a face that said he should have thought of this before and said. 'Yes. The time of the battle will occur sometime after you'd be scheduled to leave. The departure is signalled by bells in the Punter's head. I can hold off a little if there's a final part of a story that hasn't been tied up. But for a few hours only. Eventually the bells start to drive a Punter mad, and they simply have to go.'

'If I leave now and return in what would be a week for you here, that will get me back in plenty of time.'

'Yes, though you'd be away for quite a bit of the preparation.'

'We have a few days to set things in train. The Ogres will be ready to meet the day after tomorrow, during which we'll be busy with

Spiders, Trolls, and Witches and yes, Rat People, whom I intend to go and introduce myself to. Never thought I'd say a sentence like that. You and Seren will be very busy with your logistics and her Captains. I'll need to spend time with the Ogre Youngers before I leave.'

He could not hide some trepidation. He worried his stomach contents would win the fight to get up and move out when he walked over to introduce himself to the Rat People sitting nearby. They were polite, but on the front foot. Johnathan was their Leader, who happened to be at the Resort doing 'quality control' with his supervising shit engineers and shit technologists working there. 'Good afternoon King. We anticipated your approach, and we admire your aspirations. But we decline your kind offer inviting us to join your ranks in the impending battle.' Jonathan had been quietly whispering with his companions on versions of this small speech to polish up something impressive for Richard's arrival. They were intelligent, and wanted to be polite to a King who at least came to see them in person. And Seren had given them some free booze. A precedent of consideration for their People.

But Richard, who had done some research, explained his battle would give them something they wanted. Two things perhaps. And at no risk to themselves any of their kind. None. They listened. And were interested.

That night, as usual, the Psychobeer caused dreaming about things huge and implausible and left no trace of a hangover. Richard advised Seren of the day's activity. Arnall asked if he might come along and received a polite no from Richard.

At the Troll Bridge, Richard conducted his interview out of ear-shot of the others. Benny laughed. The mere concept of Trolls helping anybody was funny, let alone join in a battle. Richard cast around for what Trolls loved most to see if a battle could some-how give them something. Giving it some thought, Benny realised there was something they would very much desire from a battle. When Benny told him what they wanted Richard winced. But it achieved something Richard wanted to achieve as soon as possible in the field, uncomfortable as it was. Benny was going to get in touch with the rest of his People and start the design process.

'Make it quick and painless.' The others only barely heard Richard say this as the two walked back to where they waited near the 'Throwing Off Place'.

Benny laughed. 'We'll be ready well before the armies muster at the line. Trolls can withstand hardship for days.' He smiled which was always a little disturbing. 'If it's worth our while.'

The Witches supplied a polite 'no' before Richard had taken his first sip of tea and been able to ask for anything. Roger had grown used to Richard having conversations out of their hearing. Seren grew more and more incensed. 'I'm supposed to be the Battlemaster, and I'm kept in the dark.'

Roger laughed. 'I think Richard is keeping all of this on a need-to-know basis. And you don't. You're the Battlemaster now. A high value kidnapping target. But you should also remember who you report to now.' Roger smiled and Seren thought about it. Richard was no longer someone who they'd befriended. Yet the relation-ships hadn't changed much. But she knew it had to. At least a little.

Inside the comfortable high roller consultation room next to the sword reading room, he said. 'You haven't heard what I was going to ask.'

'We're not going to do it.'

'Rolling in Ka-Ching are you? Laughing. *Actually* rolling in it.'

'Our pile isn't deep enough to roll in, but we get by.'

'What about a few thousand swords all in one place. Peoples waiting around days before mustering. A lot would love a consultation. A bit of poetic licence on how amazing the sword was, destined for great things in the coming battle wouldn't hurt. Once the Peoples hear some favourable sword readings are coming out, you'll be swamped with Ka Ching.'

'What if it's an unfavourable reading.'

'Tell them the truth. We'll get them a better sword. But tell me. In all your years of Consulting how many unfavourable readings have you arrived at. Like a birthday card I imagine. Vacuous crap saying the same thing a hundred different ways.' Had he crossed the line, he belatedly thought.

'I would be outraged at how you demean our art with such talk.' She sighed. 'If it wasn't so close to the mark. There are some very special swords. Like the one you had made for your daughter. But most of the swords this crew will have are gimmick swords. We can say what we like because it's a bullshit piece of steel with a handle. Yes, I can see how we'll make a tidy amount. I know what you want in exchange.'

He told her. 'Is it so much to ask? Bit of a lark really. And your customer base would grow a great deal in the potions and lotions business. Oh, and there would be a few new customers. I've given them the rights to enemy weapon salvage. Real collectors. They'll want them read before they go up on the wall.'

'If you want us to do what you've asked, your people will need to supply fuckloads of newt's tails and grasshopper eyeballs and all that other crap we'll have to have. And yes it is real. I tell people it's the placebo effect because the truth makes us stereotypes instead of the diverse, free spirited and adorable characters we really are.'

As Richard laughed as he walked out, he said. 'Who knows. Could be a bit of recruiting potential depending on who turns up.'

Tina nodded thoughtfully. 'I'm going to keep working on Seren. That one would be a great ass…et to the coven. My next offer is part time Witch. Sort of Witch at Large.' Richard smiled in a 'good luck with that' kind of way and left.

The Spider People were different. And Richard didn't anticipate a tête-à-tête would be so uncomfortable. Roger said they must leave the horses behind and they may experience quite some discomfort when first interacting with the spider colony. 'Stand still; whatever happens.'

They did. Shortly after stepping through the Door, they were covered in plate size spiders. Three or four deep, but none on their faces thankfully. A spider only slightly larger than the others hung disconcertingly from an invisible strand of web a few feet from Richard's face. Richard was much less concerned than his

110

companions, even though he had never been a big fan of spiders. 'Greetings. How should I address you Sir?'

Richard got the jump on the spider with introductions. 'My names Bertolt, for your purposes. For your information we nominate a Leader by acclimation, which are in fact a series of local informal elections. Leader of the Spiders is the usual title. Very little need for this role however as we are a harmonious people. We don't interact with other Peoples except to liquefy and eat them when they are foolish enough to come into our forest.'

'We all need to live somehow.' Said Richard with unfeigned understanding and good humour.

'And I know you are the Wizard King of the Personable Hand. How shall we refer to you.'

'Richard is what I like. Some children in the school I went to tried to call me Ricky and get it to stick. But I wouldn't have it and they grew tired of the project.'

The spider was put off balance. But then Richard unwound all his good work so badly it didn't really matter. The spiders had been gradually walking off their bodies and they felt every tiny little footfall.

'I'm sure being the Master of all of the Insect World is a heavy burden, but I come to ask for what help you can spare in the coming battle.' All the spiders returned to where they'd been. There was a long pause, which felt much longer due to the spider cladding.

This was awkward for Richard. Bertold was deeply affronted. 'It's basic Taxonomy. Do I need to ask you to count my legs Richard, or my eyes? Not only are we in a different Class to insects we're in a completely different Subphylum; Chelicerates.'

Before Bertolt could complain further Richard abased himself. 'This was an unforgivable lack of basic knowledge on my part and the reasonable expectation that I might become appropriately informed prior to a meeting between two, Heads of State, as it were. I hope you and your colony can forgive me.' For some reason he added. 'Now I know how Canadians feel.'

Bertold had been cut off by a heartfelt apology. But he had to put his argument in context. 'You're very genuine apology is accepted. And I might make the same about my fastidiousness concerning taxonomy.' But what he said next indicated he was unapologetic about his taxonomic fastidiousness. 'Worth remembering Richard, is that there were five other species in Homo, Neanderthals being your closest relatives. To move only a Class, is to meet our good friend Australopithecus. And he's no oil painting.'

'When you put it that way it does give one pause for thought. I expect, without knowing this, that the spider is a much more ancient creature and so has a longer lasting and secure place in the Animal Kingdom.'

'It does, and yet the footprints of the other Peoples are now everywhere.' It now become a competition in praise to settle the matter. Which had become tiresome.

'Indeed. Yet spiders go where they will among them. Even as res-
idents of the greatest castles.' Richard hoped they had exchanged
sufficient pleasantries and he had gone some way to erasing his
faux pas from earlier.

Bertolt sighed. 'Now outsider's footprints grow heavy on us for
the first time. The Goblins and Ogres we catch, and the humans,
tastiest of all, tell us of the bleak times ahead. We assumed they
exaggerated, to try and make us feel as guilty as possible while we
eat them. But it's happening right around us now. Rivers are barely
streams, trees we danced and made love in sicken and die.' Seren
tried not to imagine spider lovemaking. 'And the witless insects,
you thought we were related to, who make up most of our diet, fall
in numbers not by the year now, but by the month.'

'You're never going to let me forget me calling you the Master of
Insects are you Bertolt.'

'Now that you reminded me you called us the *master* of the insects,
I find it less offensive. Yes. Let's forget about it.'

'I've come to ask you to join our army. Intent on defeating those
wreaking havoc on your forest and force them to restore the natural order.'

'We're courageous, but small compared to the beasts we'd fight
against. I dislike pointing out our deficiencies in anything, but we
are also slow by comparison and our bodies are fragile. A blow by
the hand of most creatures would kill us, or as good as, injured
on some huge field. Our bites are painful, and several could take
a dwarf down for instance, but he would fall incapacitated for an

hour. Our venom is designed to liquefy our prey once inside a web. With many, many bites. It's not that we don't want to fight those destroying our homes, rather we see no point in throwing out lives away for nothing.'

'I would find that completely unacceptable also. But your web, how fast can you spin it and to what degree could you incapacitate a humanoid without killing them.' Richard had barely finished speaking when he heard Seren calling out.

'Hey. What the fuck…' She was surrounded in web, but it was so fine all the details under the web were visible.

Bertolt spoke directly to her. 'If you would like to give a demonstration, try as hard as you might to break free. You're a powerful human.' Bertold turned back to Richard. 'It was I that spun that web. I could do so to each of you five times over. Given a supply of water and nutrients I could spin webs all day. My hobby is geometric shapes and famous arachnid statues.'

'Bertold, would it be impolitic if you and I discuss some opportunities for collaboration in our common cause. The key message to all arachnids is that in this battle, not one spider fatality will be acceptable. Not one. If we don't believe this can be achieved, we won't bring you into battle.'

Richard and Bertolt were going to a small nearby cave when Seren, who had been struggling mightily against what appeared to be only a thin layer of web, called out. 'Hello there. Yes, you've made your point. Grade A webs.'

Bertolt looked back. 'Would you be our Battlemaster? I know a lot about how much web it takes for a human to extricate themselves from. You're not trying hard enough.' He went into the cave while Richard looked back at her with a disingenuous. *'What can I do Seren?'*

This all did in fact create motivations for Seren to fight her way out. The sounds the hundreds of spiders were making with their legs might have been cheering. Might have been laughter.

Bertolt and Richard emerged from a small cave.

Bertolt said. 'We're going into battle against those that can only destroy and ruin. We go to battle with brothers in arms we can trust.'

Richard said. 'The arachnids who join our cause will be *the most important weapon* in our arsenal. By far.' They both said 'farewell', not having intended to choose the same word, but it worked out.

They were back in the Goblin town. Andy and his 'apprentices' had left. Leaving the town in mint condition, and stylish. Gordon was there when they returned. While Richard had been cloistered with Tina and Bertolt, Roger had been taking short trips with the door to the other Goblin towns and assembled the chosen leader from each town. Richard arrived from his meeting with Bertolt, and discussions were about to commence when Gordon advised the King there was an uninvited attendee. The leader of Nargate sat at the table. Chairs vacant either side.

'I've ridden hard to humbly take my place at a meeting to be directed by you and your Battlemaster as you see fit.' All could see he was struggling to offer unconditional service. Richard nodded and strode over to the table before him. 'Here's my direction.' He pulled out the sword, burning bright with a blue flame. He slashed the sword down and cut the table in half, leaving the Goblin exposed. 'Leave here, and never trouble my army again.' It was Richard's eyes that had the Goblin on his feet and leaving as much as the sword confronting him.

For Richard the moment had passed before the Goblin had left the room. 'Good old Trip Hazard.' He said. Only two people in the room knowing what he was talking about. 'Now, as I advised earlier, I'd prefer my Battlemaster to command your contingent through an overall Commander you choose. When it suits her, your Commander will manage your Captains based on an agreed plan, however without notice, she may dictate any strategy and tactics directly to your Captains individually. Have you reached a decision on an overall Commander?'

Richard could sense some discomfort in the room. He shrugged and said. 'Who.'

Gordon felt some explanation needed to be given. 'Unlike Nargate, we came to our decision via consensus on criteria including proficiency with weapons, study of tactics, durability, maturity and capacity to navigate difficult strategic situations.'

'Quite so.' Said Roger.

'Sounds perfect.' Said Richard.

What appeared to be a sixteen-year-old Goblin boy stepped forward. Gordon continued. 'Jackobie could best anyone of us at what's described, we believe we should be humble enough to choose the finest. No matter how strange the choice may seem.'

'I think it's great.' As always Richard asked. 'Is there no way we could try to say your Goblin name instead.'

Jackobie replied. 'Sadly, you would mangle it so badly it would make us very sad.'

'I see.' Said Richard moving along. 'Tomorrow the Ogres will have assembled their leaders in the Ogre town which will be our Head Quarters. We'll meet with them in the morning and then meet as a group with the leaders of all Peoples in the afternoon. Be prepared to be asked to collaborate with strange allies, learn new skills, help the Ogre Youngers to produce new weapons and shields. But most of all, be prepared to know absolutely *nothing* about the battlefield strategy. It must not leak out. The only person who knows the strategy is me. Your leaders will learn of it only shortly before the battle. And the main troop, only minutes before it must be executed.'

Richard left the room. He told Roger he was shagged out and wanted a psychobeer. Soon they were sitting at the same upper end resort. Being a Wizard King didn't involve any salary it seemed, so Richard and Roger knew they would need to downgrade next time, they may even have to ask the Goblins or Ogres for a loan, which felt wrong for those suffering Peoples. Tina perhaps, but there would always be strings attached with her, even for a repayable loan. And Roger said it would be unseemly for them to ply their original trade.

They were all delighted to see that Arnall had decided to stay on. He was about to buy a round for the trio when Seren came over to Roger and said. 'Give me the bag.' Once he realised what she wanted he handed over a bag that was full of the female Talismans.

'I guess this bag merely tops itself up magically from time to time.'

'Yes.' Said the King and plastics extruder. 'I'd hate to have to deal with the different moulds and the dyes to make the various colours and shapes. And now it's not Kingly anyway.'

'Wish you hadn't described that. I'll go and do some hard sell. Yes, that was a joke and I expect to see you still laughing when I get back.'

She was gone for over half an hour and came back with a much-reduced bag of merchandise, and a very impressive bag of Ka-Ching. 'Did I mention fifty percent commission on sales. It was tough going out there. I had to do a demonstration on more than a few occasions to seal the deal.' She looked around at them. 'What. Have you lost your sense of humour? Lucky a Battlemaster is allowed to do stuff a King can't. Ever since he found all his virtues resides in his right hand.'

She disappeared to get a money bag to split the Ka-Ching and brought back her legendary spiked beers and told them two house tasting plates were on their way. She split the Ka-Ching into four money bags and sauntered off.

'Where did I go wrong with her.' Richard mused.

The tasting plates made them full, the beer made them high, so they went off to bed shortly after sunset. On the way, Seren was at the bar with a gardener at the resort. She dashed over and gave Richard a hug. 'Night daddy.' This was followed by a trail of laughter as she returned to her companion at the bar.

The next day was spent at the Ogre town, with more and more of the Youngers flowing in and taking up Richards full attention most of the day. This was after an early meeting with the nominated battle Captains from each settlement. An Ogress was nominated as Commander for her People. Jacinta was very large in early middle aged, for Ogres. She immediately took a liking to Seren as they had very similar temperaments. As with the Goblins, they would be directed via the Commander or Captain by Captain should Seren require it. Richard worked quickly through what he thought were the key points. They all agreed swinging a chain was shit. Richard said he had been watching some of the old Ogres throwing stones at targets and was impressed by the accuracy, force, and distance. They laughed that it was one of the diversions of the Olders, but it was also the traditional way they hunted. If you looked like an Ogre, you needed to kill something from a long way off.

'And you could carry a large number of these stones?' Asked Richard.

Jacinta, her name for human purposes, laughed. 'A Middle Age in their prime could carry half their weight. An Older perhaps equal.'

Richard met with Roger. 'Could we get all the Commanders and Captains of the Ogres and the Goblins to the Land of the Spiders for familiarisation session. Or is it Kingdom of Spiders? Forest of the Arachnids? He's a bit easy to offend. We should find out.'

They started with the Commanders. The visitors weren't treated to the spider coverage which Roger, Seren and Richard had. The spiders knew that Orgs and Goblin would have killed as many as possible immediately.

Before anyone could speak Bertolt, a note of apology in his voice, which surprised Richard said. 'Okay guys, sorry, I know we've eaten a lot of your friends and family over the years.'

Jacinta shook her head. She should have accepted the apology the Leader of the Spiders gave and left it at that. 'How many of our people have been turned to liquid and then devoured.'

Bertold was now less conciliatory. 'A spiders got to eat. And … ah…it is called Forest of the Spiders for a reason you know. Ogres vegans are they?'

'It's for me to apologise. You offer an apology you need not have made. I'm a guest in your land only to insulted you.'

'I think we can move past it. And what shall I call you.' The introductions were made, and Richard described what he wanted. Although all the creatures had a vague notion of what might be expected, the reality of it was uncomfortable. Some had thought that a small troupe of spiders would be following along behind an Ogre or a Goblin company, ready to disperse and take cover when some danger required it. But that each and every Goblin would have a spider on their shoulder was not what they'd expected.

There was foot shuffling. And the arachnids had a lot of feet, so it was soft foot shuffling but an awful lot of it. Goblins were looking down the barrel of having the fangs to deliver a debilitating bite an inch from their neck. The spiders thought it would be easy to get swotted in retaliation for a lost brother, in an incident later claimed to be an accident.

Richard knew there was going to need to be bridges built quickly. 'I have some ideas about changing the dynamic with respect to things getting eaten in the forest. However, for the upcoming battle we need to build trust quickly if we're going to function as allies. I propose that we build this over the next week, every solider has a spider on their shoulder, and every Captain comes here and gets the all over treatment. The spiders will show the visitors how the forest is dying, and the soldiers how their land can no longer support their families.'

The farewells of the Commanders were slightly warmer than the greetings. But with an undertone of anxiety.

Richard spent another day with the Youngers exploring how armour could be designed for the Ogres and the Goblins that deflects all but the heaviest blows and would repel arrows. Both Peoples had always gone bareheaded, as they were disorderly cannon fodder in most narratives. It was very difficult to get through the skin of an Ogre anywhere on their body except by a heavy blow with a sharp axe or sword. They were generally brought down with wounds to the head and neck, especially the eyes. This is where Elves and Dwarves aimed. Richard wanted something that would repel or significantly lessen the impact around the head and upper face. A group of Youngers were designated to this task. Never having been allowed to protect their people except for an antiquated neck chain, they were immediately galvanised. The helm they devised was very strong, comfortable, and didn't limit movement with only modest impact on peripheral vision.

The Goblins would be giving up the short sword which was useless against long swords and bows. They would be carrying a shield that covered much of their body, too heavy for any of their adversaries to hold. They would carry lighter, longer swords which could be slid though slots in the shield such that they could push swords into an enemy without exposing themselves. Only an arrow shot from a bow in close proximity would pierce it. If the most sensible approach for a certain point in the battle was to temporarily retreat, the shield was made to hook over the shoulders. Richard came back again and again; not one Goblin, Spider or Ogre is to die.

Some of the Goblins were starting to become proficient with the short bow. The material used for the bows was light, based on a honeycomb design. The best ten percent of the archers in a proficiency trial would focus on longbows. Neither of these were to be used for what Richard saw as the wasteful arc shooting at the enemy. These were for closer range. During preparation thirty percent of all troops would cycle through to help the Younger Ogres, already helped by a large group of non-combatants, with the fabrication of the helms, breast plates and armour designed to protect the Spiders.

For the Ogres, they had to gather a massive pile of rocks so that the Middle Agers could practice with targets at a range of distances. They also had large amounts of ore to carry in from the mines. Roger accelerated this process hugely with the door.

He called a final meeting before leaving Tæranon. He told Seren that from that point forward she'd be giving all the briefings and direction. She'd be fielding all questions at any gathering.

Seren knew Richard had dealings with the Trolls. Roger had advised her Richard had visited the Rat People a few times and provided no details of the outcome as usual other than that the Rat People had been given the 'Rights' to what was the sometimes-overflowing latrines at the Head Quarters. Moving this to where they wanted it via the door was not Roger's favourite task. They had also been given the 'Rights' to something else, which got them nearly as excited as having access to so much shit.

Everyone had their tasks to do for the week Richard would be away. He made it clear that all authority he had rested with Seren. When he put it in those terms, it was both daunting but also made her realise how much faith he had in her. She rode through the door to say goodbye at the place Punters arrived and left. Roger had seen it hundreds of times, but to Seren it was a little disconcerting to see Richard fade away.

For him, it was very odd to be conscious suddenly in the peace of his own lavatory. Especially after being a Wizard King only a moment before. He made an inspection and was pleased to see there was nothing odious to clean up. He started to untie himself from the cistern when he heard noises from within his flat. He lived alone and had not invited any callers, especially the kind who let themselves in.

There was a voice at the door. 'Cup of tea Richard. From what I can gather it's white and one.' Instead of saying. 'Who are you?' His native politeness caused him to say. 'Yes Please.'

'Amazing job Richard.' The voice continued. 'I would never believe someone could pull together such a coherent Alliance of the, shall we say, unsavoury populations of Tæranon. I must admit I haven't examined the evolution of those populations in over a century. Roger provides for the Punters needs while my needs are met by mainly humans and elves.' The voice was disconcerting. 'The days of Punters are finished Richard, and so is my need for Roger, whom you also seem to have co-opted.'

Richard knew he had to move and take the briefcase out with him. 'Quite a mess in here unfortunately. I'm going to have to take a quick shower. Sorry about the tea. I'll be down as quickly as I can and make a fresh one. Naturally I'd like to learn about how all this got started. I got a sense while I was there that my involvement was…temporary, but I feel lucky to have seen and experienced what I have.'

He said this as he went around the corner. He saw the back of a man with white hair filling the kettle. Richard went into the bathroom and turned the shower on. Then went to his bedroom and started to climb out the window. He was about to jump when he realised his wallet was on the kitchen bench. He went to raid the largess from his outing with his uncle which was only yesterday and removed half of the money temporarily sequestered in a slipper. He was on a ground floor, yet it was still a jump of six feet, which he was only barely able to execute without rolling an ankle while carrying the case. He estimated it was mid-morning while he ran to the most likely place a taxi would be passing and waved down the typical London Cab driven by a typical London Cabbie. He hadn't picked up the piece of paper with her address and phone number.

He'd considered his sister. She lived too far away. And it would take too long for her to get though the cynicism phase alone. He could go to a hotel, but he didn't have his wallet for the Credit Card they all wanted these days. He also hoped he could be with someone who would understand what was going on so they would be there when he got back, again and maybe again and help with the basics to support his metabolism, now that his flat was 'compromised'. And he remembered the warmth of the embrace she'd given. He knew she would find all this fascinating. It was her genre. He knew the suburb and was reasonably sure about the street. 'Shit.' He said. The Cabbie enquired what the problem was. He said he'd lost his 'girlfriend's' street number. He gave the Cabbie her name, and the man made a few calls. 'Probably not supposed to tell you. But it's not hard to find out because she gets a special Cab for her wheelchair.'

Richard nearly said. 'She's in a wheelchair?' But that would give away the girlfriend extreme exaggeration. He was dropped at the street address and told the flat number.

Knocking at the door there was no response for some time, and he thought he should have held the Cab and tried to get into a cheap hotel with a sob story about a stolen wallet. He was turning to go when he heard. 'Richard? Good to see you. Come in and have a cup of tea.' Stepping inside, she looked up and smiled. She walked slowly to the kitchen, trying to look steady on her feet.

'Would you like to sit down, and I'll make it.' He said. 'I don't mean to suggest...'

'I'd like that Richard. And if you want to suggest I'm not able to do things without a crutch or a wheelchair that's fine. I can't.'

'I'm very sad to hear it.' He said the words softly. Richard could see she'd been a dynamic and energetic person. There was evidence of that on the walls and on mantelpieces.

'Twelve to eighteen months, inoperable, refusing some of the more drastic treatments after being on them for years.'

'What are we going to talk about for the next hour. I was planning to tease all that information out over time.'

She looked at him severely and spoke sharply. 'You're planning to stay that long?' He felt the kettle to see how far along the boiling process it was.

She laughed now with a genuine warmth. 'Stay all day Richard. I don't have much going on.'

He finished making the tea and brought it to the table. 'I thought you would be working on...'

'No. During my second meeting with the publishers, I got the same treatment you did Richard. The people running the meeting had looked over my ideas. Your sister hadn't been involved in the 'qualification process' which they had only finished before the meeting. I'd proposed a trilogy and a few stand-alone works, and they said they weren't interested. Said the ideas I had were stale. All been done before.'

'The great challenge in any genre.' Said Richard. 'The bastards. They lure you from your publisher and then cut you lose. Even worse than what they did to me. Told me my last two books were shit and I could get lost. Even if Miranda was right, it did sting a bit.'

Natasha laughed. 'It was Miranda, on reflection, I had the most respect for. Once she knew the score, while the others tried to work around the inevitable for a while to make it a longer meeting as if I deserved that much, Miranda told it like it was. She was right. Nobody knows this, but I haven't written a book in ten years. The most recent release was written twelve years ago. I think that's what they realised. I really don't have something fresh to offer. Which, ironically, my more recent books had. Even though they were over a decade old. I still write. Ghost writing mainly. I think I can write good prose. But I seem to have run out of ideas. And after the meeting I made some calls and found out that my publishers had orchestrated the offer from your publisher. They didn't want to do the coup de grâce themselves and thought it would better for all, including me, if it came from strangers.'

Richard reflected on this. 'I think I have the reverse problem. My writing is lousy, but I like to think I have interesting plots, and sub plots and aspects that are at least a little bit original. While I've been in Tæranon I've been working on some ideas in the evening. Then I asked the Younger Ogres if there was any chance of getting the notes back. They believed they could tattoo it onto my skin, and it might come back with me. When they read out what I wanted written on my back the little bastards had come up with several improvements.' Richard felt awkward to be asking. 'If I could go into a bathroom with a mirror I'll go and see...'

Natasha, who had understood absolutely nothing of what Richard had been saying laughed. 'How about you pull the back of your shirt up Richard. 'Oh my.' He'd pulled the shirt up and she saw what initially looked like dots, but was in fact very neat, tiny writing. She could see it was a detailed book summary. She reached out and touched the skin and wasn't sure, but thought she saw a brief shimmer of electric blue flow to her finger from the text. 'It's here Richard.' She said slowly. 'It's tiny writing. It's a story.'

Richard looked at the time and was at once distracted. 'Yes. A few some ideas. Not specifically about Tæranon but picking up some concepts and noting down what I had come up with. Which is what these Ogres are supposed to do.' Pointing to the briefcase he changed the subject. 'Natasha are there any hotels nearby. The Wizard King of the Invincible Hand was waiting for me outside my lavatory, and I had to jump out of a window. I thought I would have plenty of time to study silicon chips and motherboards etc, but I'm running out of time. I'm getting the Younger Ogres to build something which might do the job is essential to my battle plan. Eventually. And do you have a tablet I can borrow.'

Natasha thought she'd work on the simplest aspect of the few sentences he'd shared with her first. 'And why do you need a hotel Richard?'

'When you get plugged into what's in this briefcase, you go into a kind of trance. I'll probably be in it for ten hours, so it's best to be...um...safe rather than sorry.'

128

'I have the littlest room in the house, and you get in via the laundry. You'd be welcome to stay here if that would save time.'

Richard gave a sigh of relief. 'That would mean a lot. Now that I know what the Wizard King's been planning it's more important than ever I get back.'

'And what part do you play, or I should have said who are you in ...Taer...'

'I had thought I was a humble plastics extruder who made...plastic things. But it turned out I was the Wizard King the Personable Hand. One of my hands had been chopped off when I was a little baby and exchanged with the other fellow. Now he's preparing for the battle he's always wanted, so I've been working with the Rats, Spiders, Ogres, Dragons, Trolls, and Goblins. All of whom are very pleasant, unless you want to cross a bridge with no money or walk through a forest.'

Richard was becoming agitated as time passed by. Natasha said. 'I'll leave it to you to prepare. I did want to ask if I could photograph your back and I could have it written out for you when you get back.'

'That would be great. Thanks. It would give me some space to have more written down if they can do that. They have this psychobeer there that gives you fantastic ideas. Sadly, you can remember only a small fraction of them.' He was drinking tap water and about to ask where the lavatory was, when he had a thought. 'Oh. I'll need some rope. To tie myself to the cistern. Damn. Maybe I could use a sheet if I could borrow one.'

She disappeared and returned a few moments later with a role of material. 'This is soft cord for tying up tomatoes. Which I can't eat anymore. Use four or five lengths together to wrap around and it will be very strong, but also soft.'

She quickly photographed his back as he said. 'I can't thank you enough.'

She smiled and said. 'Bon Voyage.' Having no real idea what he'd been talking about.

Richards best character trait was simple sincerity. 'I'm looking forward to seeing you when I get back.'

Seren sat at the bar of a Tavern. Roger had dropped her there with the door, reluctantly, while he went and caught up with his large family. She had wanted to be far away from Dwarves and Elves and Spiders and Ogres and all the rest of them for a few hours. She was pouring in everything she had to earn the title of Battlemaster. To do that she knew she needed to get away now and again. Another Anti-Princess, Grainia had been sending messages wanting to catch up so Seren asked her to come to this Tavern. Seren set the time for Grainia to visit an hour after she'd arrived so she could have a few Psychobeers in peace. However the Anti-Princess walked in shortly after she'd arrived. 'Hail Sister. The ride was easier than I thought, so I came straight in.'

Seren provided the less formal. 'Hi Grainia.'

'Doesn't look like you think much of your calling.' Said Grainia in one-part good humour and one reproof.

'Only the pompous self-aggrandizing garbage. Otherwise, I love it. Wander the countryside on a mysterious quest, no master to bow down to. About the opposite of what you're stuck with.'

'No master until now.' Grainia said blithely. 'The Wizard King of the Bland Hand I hear.'

'Bland Hand'. Richard would like that. What's your business *Shape Shifter?*'

'I wanted to ask if you would consider moving across to the winning side. The only thing the Peoples you're leading are good at is getting slaughtered. And Seren, losing isn't a pleasant experience when you lose to the Wizard King of The Invincible Hand.'

'I think if an Anti-Princess crossed the line, she wouldn't be having a good time win or lose.'

The Shape Shifter ignored this. 'Seren, you know things we'd like to know. There are lots of ways to extract information.'

'Hold that thought Shape Shifter.' In a blur of explosive movement Seren raced through the tavern. Three throats were cut, two casual drinkers disembowelled and a powerful, driving blow to the heart of a sixth. This resulted in an anticlimactic moment when Seren was unable to dislodge the dagger until she put one foot on the dead creature's chest and pulled back. It came out suddenly and she barely avoided sprawling backwards and hitting a table.

She returned to the bar. Now Grainia was gone and a tall, very handsome elf, stood in her place. 'Thought you might like this better.' His voice could not conceal irritation building towards anger.

'Don't give a fuck.'

'Or maybe this. Or this.' He turned into a Lifeguard and then a Gardener, then an Armourer.

'Wow. You're not getting any if you need to follow me around like a pathetic little voyeur. I do whatever I want in my spare time. I bet you can't. I am impressed though that you can hold five assholes in a Shape Shift.'

'Only in close proximity.' The Shifter was honest enough to admit. Despite his anger, he appreciated the compliment. 'No other Shifter can do more than two.'

'But there's a character dimension. Bad character.' Said Seren. 'Even though they looked like men, the Dwarfs were such assholes and the Elves so supercilious. You can't Shape Shift that away.' She was relaxed and friendly now. 'Sorry your little scheme failed. But if you look over there.' She pointed. 'You'll see I had some protection of my own.' There was no one over there. But as the Shape Shifter turned to look in response to the simplest of ruses, her dagger flashed and left a deep cut on his cheek. 'My little way of saying thanks for trying to kidnap me.'

Even though it was on a false Elf's cheek, as no one had ever seen the Shape Shifters true form, the blood was real. She expected retaliation. However, the Shape Shifter's tone changed to one of grudging respect.

'I'll see you on the field of Geopor Battlemaster.' The cut on his cheek disappeared.

'I'm sure it will be an interesting day Battlemaster.' She returned his smile of respectful parting.

Seren looked at the Inn Keeper. 'Would a half a Ka-Ching cover the clean-up.' She had to economise because as with the King, there was no remuneration for the role of Battlemaster. 'You can have the weapons.'

The man beamed. 'If I can keep the weapons.' Which had been concealed behind the imposter's backs. 'You can keep your half Ka-Ching and have free drinks for you and any companions all night. They'll look great on my walls. Genuine Dwarf axes and Elvin Bows and swords. They'll become family heirlooms.'

Seren was glad for the man. She would never take money for a weapon of a foe she'd killed. Saving a half Ka-Ching squeaked through the moral equation.

Grainia arrived with a 'Hail Sister.' And Seren groaned inwards. Who comes up with this shit she thought 'Good to see you Grainia. Can I get you a beer?'

'Oh, it's the month of *Jessoni*. We only drink water and eat a small meal before sunrise.' Grainia said this in the fashion of one stating the obvious to someone who should be making this small observance.

Seren wanted to yell at her. *These days Anti Princesses are a bunch of idiots bent on turning a good lifestyle into a shit lifestyle.* 'Instead she said. 'I forgot.' And ordered another beer.

Grainia continued, but in a more sisterly manner. 'There are those among us who see the day approaching and know what's at stake, for all not co-opted by the Wizard King. Many of us would like to offer our services to the King. There are twenty or so who would come and another twenty still giving it consideration.'

Seren had no idea there was that many Anti Princesses floating around. The uncharitable side of her thought a good war might thin the self-righteous bitches out a bit. A thought she was immediately ashamed of. Seren was surprised at the difficulty she had in coming up with an answer straight away. Grainia noticed this. Seren eventually said. 'I'll consult with the King. He's only days away and we can get a message to you. It's likely you'd come to the Ogre Towns which is our Head Quarters to meet him.'

Grainia had expected more enthusiasm from her Sister. 'We had thought as Battlemaster you could give us some conception as to how a group of us might serve. It might sway those yet undecided.'

'I understand.' Said Seren. 'Let me put it like this. If you'd like an answer tonight. Fuck off. If you'd like to wait until I consult with the King, he may see a place for you. But beware, I suspect many in our Alliance may be asked to do what is uncomfortable for them. Very uncomfortable. And this applies to me as much as to any. So if you do choose to serve, be ready to serve however you are commanded to or don't come.' She drained her glass. A kidnapper and a whiney fucking Anti-Princess had managed to spoil what was supposed to be a quiet drink away from the demands of her job.

She was about to say her goodbyes when Grainia said. 'I know you have no respect for us Seren. But we have respect for you.' This brought her up short from her planned brief farewell. At first she had no answer.

Seren was honest. 'It's not disrespect for the Anti-Princesses as people. It's this growing cancer of meaningless observances and rules. Ours is a simple life. A beautiful life. I'm very sorry I was rude. A Shape Shifter tried to kidnap me before you arrived.' Seren nodded to the dead Dwarves and Elves which Grainia had not looked around to see.

They both laughed. Grainia a little nervously 'I'm sure that can put you on edge.' She said. 'The little observances make many of us feel good, and closer, and perhaps bolster some who's sense of mission is… not as strong. Maybe our Punter's original backstories were not so interesting. And yet the absence of observances makes *you* feel good. We'll need to make sure not to turn our Sisterhood into a religion that excludes those who don't want to conform.'

They gave each other a warm hug at the door. Seren was emotionally exhausted and Roger physically and emotionally exhausted through entertaining and being entertained by so many children. Although some were nearly eighty years old. The Creator gave Roger and his wife virtual immortality, but that meant they had begun the heart wrenching process of burying some of their children who had reached a great age.

The next day was the first day they waited. He should have been back. Roger said that the fact that Richard was going to be away and back so quickly meant that the signal he usually got may not work because it would have to happen in the past. Seren decided to not ask about that.

She kept performing her duties as Battlemaster. Roger stayed at the pickup point except for essential logistics trips. And both waited and waited and waited. Seren had all in readiness and her Captains and Commanders continued to train and prepare. Finally, they got a signal. It was not the usual week's notice. Only two days.

Richard made himself ready to go. He had skimmed over all the diagrams and pictures they'd recommended on his 'information places' which was their name for the internet. He's sprayed some pre-emptive air freshener around and finished some left-over spaghetti bolognaise from Natasha's refrigerator. He punched in the words into the LED screen he hadn't noticed last time. The Youngers told him what to write. It allowed for some more nu-anced requests then the buttons.

He hit *Let It Roll* and immediately found himself walking slowly by a man on a horse. It was Roger. At first he thought the world had reset and he was a plastics extruder again. But things were different. The horse Roger was riding was a bony old nag. 'Welcome back at last Richard.' Said Roger. Obviously pleased to see his friend, but with a tone that said he wished the greeting could be in better circumstances.

Richard wanted to stave off any unpleasant truths. 'Am I an extruder again?'

Roger laughed. 'No, this time you're a leather tooler.'

Richard kept hoping things were not too different. 'Leather costumes for Anti-Princesses I suppose.'

Roger said. 'No. Not much call for that anymore. You're a leather craftsman in dungeonware. Speaking of Anti-Princesses, it looks like they've let an old friend out to come and see you.'

The caped figure was riding an even older nag. Below the cape she was wearing the wimple of some religious order. She coughed. 'Richard. It's so good to see you again. It's been so long.' She coughed again.

Richard was broken hearted. He had made some mistake and arrived years too late. 'The battle...?' He wished he hadn't raised it. He found himself wondering about how he would eventually broach the subject of going back home and then he was immediately ashamed he'd thought about it. So soon.

'There was never any Battle. I never got to be a Battlemaster. Our Alliance fell into disorder and there was no one to face the forces of the Wizard King of the Invincible Hand that day on Geopor. They rolled like a tide through the lands of our friends. Sent me off to a Convent for my sins. The first five years I struggled against what I thought was stupidity. But as the years have passed, I've seen the truth that hides behind their ridiculous rules and observances. Although every now and then...' Seren started to pull the cape away. 'I have to teach those fucking bitches to get out and *party*. Yeah.' Once her cape and wimple were thrown back it revealed the same laughing Seren he had left only hours before.

Roger beside him said. 'Two weeks. It was supposed be six days. We thought a bit of punishment was in order. After I got a belated notification of your arrival time.'

Richard was relieved. The others dismounted and each handed out a welcome hug. 'Two weeks.' He said. 'Less then a week left. He was in my house you see. Trapped me in the lavatory offering tea. I had to jump out of a window and go to a friend's place. Not really a friend as such. We're only starting to get to know one another. But I think it's fair to say friendship is not out of the question.'

Roger knew which part of the story to home in on. 'Who was in your house Richard?'

'The Invincible...fellow said he thought we'd done a better job than he expected. And that was the end of it for me. Getting away with the briefcase and getting to Natasha's flat took up some time.'

'Natasha eh? Friendship not out of the question.'

'Seren, keep up. I have King stuff to focus on. How's everything going.'

'Things are going well. I'll take you straight to the Ogre Town which is now a huge multi–Peoples Garrison and Head Quarters. But first a few friends.' Jackobie brought out GroundBreaker, Brindlefire and TBA, which had become imbedded as a name, no matter how much the horse disliked it. Seren said the poor nags they were riding on were plough horses bought from the 'asshole'

Little People by an adjoining human settlement and they were going to rehabilitate them.

Barely a minute later they were through the door and into the Ogre town, which was now nearly a city. There was a large encampment of Goblins. Richard was soon greeting many of the Ogre Youngers and Goblin leaders. Having had a break in a London suburb, it made him realise how many people he now knew and liked, no matter how strange they'd appear to a Londoner. After a few moments he turned to Seren and said. 'Where's the spiders?'

She was uncomfortable and said. 'Bertold said they would join the battle, but he didn't see the need for the daily perils of riding on the Goblin's shoulder until then. There was an incident during one of the 'familiarisation' sessions. A Goblin Captain reacted by reflex when a spider landed on him.' Richard looked alarmed but Seren added. 'Bosco's fine, well, he has four broken legs, but they splint them up and generally the spiders are able to walk again. I mean crawl.'

Seren had barely finished when Richard was asking for Roger to advise Tina and Bertolt he'd like to see them.

'I'm sorry Richard. I should have tried to resolve it. Bertold has made himself hard to get hold of.'

'Don't worry. It's my fault. The was no need to have that close up experience training for the Captains. I should have seen this coming. If the Goblin feels bad get him to come and see me.'

He was heading for the Younger's workshop. Seren was beside him and had wanted to get her most difficult issue out of the way so she could focus on the training and find out what Richard wanted her to do as they approached the day of the battle.

'There's one other thing I wanted to talk to you about.' Said Seren. Richard pulled up at the threshold of the workshop. He gave her the feeling that she was far more interesting than whatever he was doing which she appreciated. 'I've been approached by some Anti-Princesses who want to participate. I told them I'd let you consider it, but I made no commitment. I told them that what they were involved in might be unpleasant for them.'

Richard smiled. 'A perfect answer. I'll give you a response to take to them tomorrow. Can they, a bow with a few hundred yards at a moving target.'

'Sure. Keeps us in meat when we're out travelling around brooding or selling feminine talismans.' She smiled.

'Good.' He went into the workshop alone as she knew she was to know nothing about anything until he told her. The experiences with the Wizard King's Shape Shifting Battlemaster had taught her the wisdom of that. And the folly of traveling away from her forces alone.

The workshop Youngers gave Richard a big welcome. He loved the interest they took in him. And Richard made them understand they were essential to the effort. He pulled his hair back at the side of his head and there was a plug to insert a jack into. He'd specified it in on the LED request section of the briefcase. There was all kinds of diagrams and schematics, with some pictures of mother boards, computers, laptops, and tablets streaming onto the rudimentary computers of the Youngers. The room was filled with exclamations of excitement and then astonishment. The chatter across desks became a blanket of sound. Richard left hoping he could visit Tina soon and then Bertolt.

Roger has transported him to Tina who presented herself as the young, smoking hot version, which Richard had no problem with. He asked his question and she said. 'Sure I could fix him. Placebo effect remember. With some potions and incantations, we can have that little critter all fixed up and ready to drop into a cauldron before you know it.'

'Maybe we could go easy on the Cauldron jokes.'

'Why. Bertold has a big sense of humour. Laugh a minute that guy.'

Richard hoped he wasn't about to make things worse. Once they were in front of Bertold Richard asked if he could apologise to Bosco. He said the initiative he'd suggested was stupid and had harmed the Alliance.

Bosco thrived on attention, so he didn't need an apology. 'I really appreciate your apology King. I can accept that for the sake of the Alliance I'll only ever be able to crawl from now on.'

Tina couldn't help herself. 'Isn't that what spiders do. I mean crawl.'

'Boom.' Said Bosco. 'Your beautiful and smart. I meant to say I can only crawl in *circles* from now on. Can I take you home to meet my mother?'

Tina smiled. 'Maybe once I've healed up those legs.' She got to work.

'Hey Tina. Will I be able to play the piano after you've fixed my legs up?'

'Do we have to go through this Bosco?'

'Yep.'

'Bosco, yes you'll be able to play the piano.'

'Wow Tina. I could never play the piano before.' Bosco looked around the small patch of forest for some appreciation. He got some indulgent smiles.

'The problem you'll have is, the legs I've healed will be so powerful you may indeed spend your life crawling in circles. But in the other direction.'

'Hey Tina. Is there any chance of a spider taking you out to dinner? I imagine you could turn me into some handsome guy or, whatever you want, we have a nice meal, some wine, see where things go to from there.'

'Maybe. But I'd find it hard to not talk about all the spider body parts we use to make spells and incantations, including the one I'd need to make you human.'

'I could imagine that recipe could be a chiller on the conversation.' He said

'And it goes without saying you'd be a gorgeous lady human. It's all I know how to make.' She smiled at him to see if he was still interested now knowing all of this. 'To be honest we *never* use spider parts for anything. Too hairy. It's the web we need. It binds the incantations together, blah, blah, blah. But it's not easy to get any because the spiders believe we sing stupid songs and chop them up and throw the spiders bits and God knows what else into a cauldron.'

'If I give you a lifetime supply of web there's a chance for us.'

Tina shrugged. 'Sure. Only casual remember.' She leaned down and said. 'We'll talk later.'

Bertolt wanted to return to protocol. 'I appreciate the effort you've gone to, to heal Bosco.'

'And maybe share the opportunity of a lifetime with an outrageously beautiful Witch.' Bosco felt he should add.

'Only something casual.' Tina reinforced.

Bertolt said. 'If we could get back to what I was saying. Richard, I know why you've come here, I appreciate your point of view, but we'll turn up for the battle, and that's all. It's too perilous for us to be going around on a Goblin's shoulder for a week.'

Richard was pleading. 'It's many more times perilous to only ride in battle. The Goblins move in a certain way. They will be running, turning, and trusting their weapons. The Spiders will need to shoot their web at real targets, moving in relationship to how your mount is moving. To reduce the peril, we're making strengthened small spaces in the back of the armour which will turn arrows and bend only with a heavy direct blow from a sword or axe in that location.

Spiders can get into these and come out as soon as their mount calls them. I'm begging you to reconsider Bertolt.'

Bertold thought it strange that a King would beg in front of Bosco and Tina. He had also presented a strong case. 'I'd like to stage the return in case it fails. One third of your force will get spider companions each day, starting tomorrow. I know we both hope there are no injuries or loss of life.'

'You know getting injured hasn't been so bad.' Interrupted Bosco.

Bertold was growing irritated. 'Yes. Thank you for you input Bosco. You can return to the Cluster. And yes, it's also sometimes known as a Clutter before anyone tries to jump in and correct me...or be pedantic.' He looked around. 'Or more pedantic than me that is.' The Clutter were given more assurance by that that they had the right Leader.

'Sure Boss.'

'I think I should walk Bosco back to the whatever it's called to make sure the healing has succeeded.' Said Tina

Bosco made a loud cat purring sound. Roger appeared with the door and was provided with a potted summary. They then stood around, somewhat awkwardly, until Tina returned. Beaming.

'Eight hands.' Was all she would say.

The next day, a third of the assembled army had companion Spiders. Richard called all the Commanders and Captains together. It was a large gathering. The Battlemaster was giving a report on progress. A tenth of the Goblins were now bowman, all were practicing running, turning, making a feint, finding cover, and waiting for a target. The Ogres were throwing rocks with deadly power and accuracy. Seren was trying to convince them there was a place for Older Ogres in the battle provided it was safe. She told the assembly there would be a squadron of Anti Princesses joining them and they would be practicing bow skills.

She added there was another task to include. Although it didn't seem difficult, the fastest runners needed to be nominated and trained to run down the line with a short message. The army would be receiving orders minutes before the engagement, and they needed to respond to them *exactly* as instructed.

The King invited anyone to ask a question.

A Goblin said that they were pulling in food and water from every Goblin town via the door. But whether they won or lost they'd return to gradual starvation with their families. In many places the grain stores and larder would not feed the towns for more than a month.

Richard said that he knew for a certainty the Wizard King planned to roll through and raze every Goblin and Ogre village to the ground and run down all the of Allies. And this was his plan whether they turned up to fight or not. But Richard would not condone sacking the stores of their enemies. No matter how much they might deserve it.

An Ogress said many found it hard to believe that they could survive such a battle with no casualties. They or their Olders had only been in battles where most were slaughtered. They now had new weapons and armour and good leadership in their Battlemaster, who convinced them they could win. But people were cynical about the suggestion that there would be no casualties. She worried this would erode confidence if people felt they couldn't say what they believed.

Richard appreciated the fact that even though she was a giant and powerful Ogress, these People were hierarchical in nature. To question a King from her rank took courage. 'I understand it sounds impossible. But it's possible and we can do it. But tell people I understand if they don't believe it, and that's okay, if they believe they can win. But they must be willing to follow the instructions the runners bring down the ranks on the day and follow them to the letter. They may be unusual.'

The preparations went on as days passed. The runners practiced. Many Ogre workshops were turning out what were like Viking helms for both types of People as they protected the head and some of the face but didn't obstruct vision. Elders were hauling ore and coal day and night, the workshops working the same. They called in each soldier to make their helmets individual. It took a few moments but might make all the difference.

The Army was given a day of rest. Roger was going to walk the entire army onto the field ready to marshal. Richard was certain there would be no forgiveness from the Wizard King for him. He'd told him what the man had said. That the days of the Punter had gone. It became clear to Richard and Roger that the Wizard King, to his credit, had given himself no special powers. He believed the army he wielded would be sufficient. And a magnificent battle, with two great armies in play, is what he'd always wanted. And then he would reconfigure Tæranon to meet some new vision.

That evening Richard revealed his plan to Seren.

'We're going to do *WHAT?*'

'Run away.'

'*Run away.*' She repeated.

'Yes; but we're going to run away in a very strategic manner. I told you it would be surprising.'

'Richard. If you're joking let me know. If not, I need a minute to digest this.'

'Let me describe the running away process Seren. We're assembled as an army in good order. As the runners give the message to the Squad Leaders, our army will leave formation and form hundreds of huddles with a message passed on ten minutes before the battle is joined. They will then return to formation. Soon after that they begin to turn and run in the other direction from the back moving forward. This will look like groups of disorderly deserters, but it will be a strategic redeployment of troops.

'The objective is not to attack, but rather to exhaust them in the chase. Each battle company will have an Older Ogre for cover and several Goblins with shields hanging behind them. The troops will stay in the squadrons of their battle companies and listen to their Captain. No one must die. Friend or foe. All must survive. As the enemy becomes disconnected the Spiders will be brought out to do their job. As they progressively leave the rear, Goblins are to drop their swords and bows and run. The Ogres will carry their bags of rocks and can hit the legs only of any enemy soldiers close enough to bring them down. Get your mind in the right place and this could be fun.'

'I thought it could go either way if it was a head on contest, but I could never understand the concept of no casualties.'

Seren sounded more open to the strategy, but still doubtful. Richard continued. 'There are two initiatives which we have between the enemy and ourselves on our side of the dead ground. I won't reveal them even now. They'll get through these after we've cleared the field and repositioned our troops. I've convinced the Youngers to allow the Elder Ogres to lope within arrow shot to get the Elves to waste some arrows. The Spider companions will tell their Goblin to run faster or slower. There will be no confrontation until the enemy are close enough and exhausted or have a broken leg.'

'The Dwarves are poor runners after a time and their heavy weapons depends on battlefield proximity. Elvin horsemen are lost without a horse. The Little People mainly carry meanness as a weapon. They have short swords, metal shields and helms that cover much of their face. Like the others, they aren't designed for a long combat running in a chase. In this case trotting away on short little legs exposed to the merciless stone throwing of Ogres.'

Richard was sombre. 'I know the Anti-Princesses would be disappointed with the role of only supporting the Witches. Although Tina was delighted with the arrangement.' He paused. 'If they want an active role, it would be to take down the horse from beneath every rider and any riderless horse. Sadly, horses won't count as casualties. Other initiatives should have taken a proportion of the horses out of circulation before the Anti-Princesses would be needed. If you don't think they'll be able to do it, best not to ask. We can have a few squadrons of Goblins keep their bows rather than cast them away. But they'll be more in harm's way as their bowmanship is comparatively poor.'

'I won't ask them. I'll tell them. They came here to give us support with knowledge some of the tasks will be unpleasant. If they leave, it will be in disgrace. I'm becoming attuned to your plan and can see the merits. But our soldiers must understand and accept this in a few minutes.'

Richard agreed this was essential. 'As they come out of the door tomorrow, we'll be saying get ready for a big surprise. Unusual. Follow the new orders. You and I will be at the door taking turns saying it. We'll be hoarse but they should be ready. The people will be walking straight onto the field and cannot be susceptible to spying or giving the plan away because even then they have no idea what the plan is.'

Seren nodded. 'I understand why I'll be under heavy guard until we leave. All the Commanders and Captains for the Goblins, Ogres and Spiders and the messengers are in a barracks now. The Anti-Princesses are in a large house built by the dragons.'

'I'll say nothing more in these briefings.' Said Richard. 'The Army is now handed over to you and you can brief the Peoples at any interval before to the battle you think best. As an exception

I can brief the Anti-Princesses if you believe it would be better coming from me.'

Seren realised what a responsibility it was having control of an entire army hours away from the biggest battle in the history of Tæranon. And to execute such an unusual strategy. But as time went by, she believed this was the only way to capitalise on her army's strengths and bring out the weaknesses of the enemy. 'I'll brief them.' She said.

It was the senior Goblins briefed first. There was surprise that they were to drop their brand-new weapons and run. They would keep their shields, which protected their backs and most of their legs. Dispersing they would give the appearance of a rout; however, they would stay loosely in their battle squadrons, though it wasn't to look that way. They would be issued with maps for each squad that would direct them either to ambush their enemy or draw them further away from their line. Every Goblin squadron would have an Ogre in the group to further protect them from bowmen and deal with horsemen. The former could exhaust themselves shoot-ing arrows at an Ogre's back. And an Ogre's stones would break a rider or horse's legs from a long way away. When they come to attack in close proximity, they'd be wrapped up in Spider web. The aim was to exhaust the foe. 'You are faster than any in their army on foot, even the Elves. That is our advantage. Never attack head on and *none* of the enemy are to be killed – not one.' Seren said the night before the battle.

The Ogre's briefing had the same messages. The Ogres would not drop their bags of rocks. They would turn and run with the

Goblin squads and would set the pace within bow range to waste Elvin arrows.

The briefing for the Anti Princesses was short but hard. They were given their assignment. In response to the instructions Grainia said. 'We'll do what's required of us.'

After an initial briefing with Bertolt who gave some feedback that led to improvement to the approach, the entire spider army was given the briefing that night. No spy could penetrate their Cluster. They liked the Plan. They had Ranger Spiders who now knew where to be and crawl to remain safe. The Companion spiders knew what guidance they had to give, and they were given strategies to escape safely if, as a last resort, they needed to jettison their ride.'

Seren, was surprised at how readily they adopted it. Bertolt sensed this and said. 'We've always feared that a weaker force would take on a stronger one head on.'

All the spiders would be through the door at the Head Quarters an hour before muster. The Ranger spiders would go to wait at the locations Seren positioned them. They would run along the rocks at the base of the cliff face after the Horn. The main body of the spider force formed a long rank in the right order to join their companions as they walked through the door.

The entire army had been brought to the Head Quarters at Ogre town by the door operating through the night so that they could file out as a complete force, fresh, fed and rested. They stopped briefly for Companion Spiders to climb aboard. Either Seren or the

King would say to a Squad as they passed. 'Prepare for some very unusual instructions. Listen carefully to your Squad Leaders and Captains. We will win this battle, with no one killed, on either side. Do what's asked of you.'

They'd said it about thirty times each, so they decided to start to hold up three Squads at a time. The Anti-Princesses received a 'Good luck Sisters.' From Seren. She didn't like calling them that, but it was a small concession to a participation they didn't need to offer, and she would be loath to fulfil herself.

The Alliance army martialled very quickly. The battle ground had been crafted centuries before. The ranks were constrained by an escarpment on one side and on the other by a deep, fast flowing river, which none could use with craft for attack or even wade if or the battle was forfeit. There was a downward gradient below Seren's first rank for a mile or so. This favoured their opposing forces who fought downhill in the battle. There was a mark defining where each rank was to stand, unheard of compared to un-co-ordinated rabble Goblins and Orcs were usually forced to fight in. Now their marshalling area was made of a long series of dots. These markings, put on laboriously by rubbing clay into the turf by hand, were unhelpfully rained on, exactly at their side of the dead ground and had to be redone; twice. This made the hundreds of people supporting the army want even more to take back control of the rain and make it as it always had been.

All the ranks were in their lines and in the right position within five minutes of the last Squad coming through the door. The opposing force had been marshalling nearly two hours. Many had ridden through the night or arrived late the night beforehand to take a short briefing from their Battlemaster. He advised them to expect bloody battle. However, they were 'only' outnumbered by a few hundred, and these would fight against Elves and Dwarves, trained for battle as a lifestyle, the Little People aggressive and merciless. The Knights, even though they were stupid, were also highly trained and would be directed by his best Elvin Captains.

Looking across the field Seren noted that all their enemy had expended considerable resources on how they looked for this great battle. Each distinct group of Elves and Dwarves caparisoned in their own colours in fine cloth. One colour and cut of breastplate and fabric was immediately familiar. It was Nargate.

The entire army of the Alliance were all dressed the same. No clothing other than a loin cloth below. A grey tunic over armour except for the Ogres who needed none. The Anti Princesses wore a long grey tunic over the leather. The enemies Battlemaster had begun the processes of riding up and down the front line calling out what a historic battle they were privileged to take part in. Seren in her turn walked Brindlefire up and down, much more slowly saying things like. 'What a dickhead. His people can't hear even a whole sentence as he rides along to say what a great idea it is for them to die. For what. A tyrant and an asshole.'

Literally out of the blue Andy arrived. There were three dragons with him in the distance. He bore the quintessential loose scale of Smaug showing itself invitingly. The Battlemaster called to his troops to spread the message and remind all that if anyone takes a shot or swings a blade before the Horn their battle forfeit.

By this time Andy was floating low over the Knights. *We aren't participating in the battle. We're visiting some old friends* he'd told his apprentices 'Hello chaps. Thought we were all extinct didn't you. All because of that bastard St George. All the stories you've heard that he's now living in an old Knight's home are lies. I ate him and shat out his armour. Which I display proudly on my wall.' The truth was that Andy, human size, would visit St George at a little cottage he built for his friend a few miles up the river from his own house. They had let bygones be bygones long ago and enjoyed each other's company and tales. And Andy's beer. St George kept his identity a secret and had a wide range of friends. But not Knights. 'Unfortunately, they really are intractably stupid.' He would say to Andy. 'And no one wants to confront the fact that there's a real drug addiction problem out there.'

Andy was lying in the air as if on a chaise lounge. 'There are hundreds of us dragon still about. We had a rest for a few decades. Now we're back because everything is in such a mess this place is going to be easy pickings.'

'We've kicked things off with a major discovery. The castle of Blarney is currently under siege by ten dragons with more set to arrive as word gets out. It seems the place had a very special role. A religious order of Damsels has been protecting a Grail for a century now. There are literally dozens of Damsels leaning out of windows, offering up a Grail to anyone who'll help them. I came to make sure that you have a really shit day, wasting your time against stupid stinking Goblins and Ogres any idiot could kill. We would have liked to have had some battles with you fellows. Like the old days. Mano o mano. Instead, I'm going to come back later and show you the Damsel pieces still stuck between my teeth. And a stupid cup I'll use at home when I need to do a crap.'

The Knights were now restive. Their leader, Rasputin the eleventh, could feel their attention shifting and didn't need to consult. 'Those who must answer our enduring quest follow me!' He knew all would come. A Knight rode up beside Rasputin. 'Do you know the whereabouts of the Castle Blarney sir?'

'No.' Said the Knight. 'But I have faith the call of the Grail will take us there.'

The Knights departed through the far Western ranks of the Wizard King's army causing chaos and then the need to reorder the front rank. Horsemen from the Elvin regiments of bowmen were required to spread across the Knight's sector of the battlefront in a thinner line. Which didn't please them.

Seren began to ride up and down the line calling for them to take orders. The runners ran up from the rear ranks, and others from the front giving orders and maps then running to the next rank. One squad went into to a huddle and others quickly followed. Soon the entire army were in circles of twenty listening to the Squad Leader. Their battle Captain riding past saying things like 'Cannon fodder no more' or 'We do what we're good at, and what they're poor at.' They were told to follow instruction and they would win. They were also told *not one* of their enemies must die. 'Exhaust them, confuse them, ambush them. It doesn't matter how far they run. They'll tire in the end and there is nowhere for them to run forward to except where we await. The Ogres will take care of the arrows, Spiders give them notice and the Goblins take safety behind their shields. Kill the horses and break their enemy's legs. Get the Spiders in range when it's safe. They will put most of the foe down.'

The troops returned to their rank position. But now it was untidy. Soldiers could be seen having side conversations. Seren lifted her sword. In that moment she was to appear supremely confident. Her army array for what could only be interpreted as the traditional head-to-head confrontation so many Punters who wanted a battle had specified. She stood on the stirrups and Brindlefire stood back dramatically, her front legs pawing the air. *'Get Ready to Let It Fucking Roll.'* But the back ranks of Goblins started to peel from the army like sand from a windy dune. They turned and ran. Flinging down their bows and the longer swords they now carried, both of which they had been practicing with for more than two weeks. But they were running at only a quarter of their potential speed. Spreading, weaving, and taking instruction from Spiders so their retreat appeared to be a rout. These rows had the farthest to run. Into hiding for ambush. One minute out from the Horn to engage battle more and more of the army disappeared behind Seren, who looked discomfited.

The Squads, each with an Ogre began to drift away. Seren was left with a thin line comprised of two lines of Goblins and one of Ogres across the entire front line. These had pushed through the ranks to appear they were the few who would not retreat. Behind them were hundreds upon hundreds of weapons which had been cast down.

She could hear the laughter from her opponents. The confidence and the excitement about slaying an army in rout and then, rolling on through every settlement. She looked at Nargate's Company and could feel his desire for revenge. But she knew the Shape Shifter would never allow then to be in front of his main army, no matter how much he'd like to. Seren knew the Ogres and Goblins would hold their place and only at her command lope a pace equal the Elves.

The Horn sounded. The horses leapt forward, and a flight of arrows came across. They landed harmlessly on the Ogres back and the Goblin shields. Contrary to Richard's explicit command Seren sat on Brindlefire, in the front and centre of the remaining troops. She was an irresistible target. However, Seren's mind was unusually sharp. She could watch the flight of arrows come in and know which individual arrow she needed to move aside from or a little further to find a gap. She wore a light suit of armour, Viking style helm with Brindlefire having light armour on the upper part of her head and fanned across her neck and rump.

The thin line was standing, against an army racing towards them. Richard said they needed to hold the line, so the oncoming army maintained its speed. Suddenly horses began to go down in large numbers. It was difficult for Seren to see why.

The most prized food, even better than a human for a Troll, is horsemeat. Specifically, horsemeat that is converted to jerky. A horse from the bridge can last months as they savour small pieces. That's why those trying to cross the bridge with horses had such a hard time making it over. No matter how much they paid. They were often told to offer up one horse and they could pass. Of course, Benny would get another one on the other side A haul from this battle would last years. And Elvin horse was almost unattainable for the Trolls, as the bastards know how it works and pay at each end. And if the Elves don't come home from crossing the bridge, the Trolls often had to deal with hundreds of the supercilious shits turning up wanting revenge.

The horses were being killed by a simple rocker system in the ground. Two green flensing knives were slid into place at the sound of the Horn. They were mounted on what was like a child's seesaw on wood under turf. No matter where the horse stood the forward or back flensing knife would come up instantly. The front knife slicing the neck, the back knife eviscerating the horse. Once the task was done, the springs would rebalance, so it again looked like turf.

Two thirds of the army's horses lay dead, dying or running unhinged through the troops whinnying in pain. Some riders sat beside their mounts of a lifetime heedlessly crying. Bowshots were coming from everywhere now. Seren retreated to safety behind an Ogres back.

Seren said. 'Three will lope behind the reformed squads of Goblins when I call the line to retreat.'

Richard said to hold the line until they hit a second surprise. He wanted the foe to regain their speed. And be angry. Very angry. The Wizard King's Battlemaster did what Richard had predicted. He screamed at them to stop and reform the line and fight in the sequence of Peoples he'd decided on. This took more time than the army, spoiling for vengeance, wanted to spend. But bowman moved back from the front as there were too few targets and a depleted supply of arrows. The remaining cavalry moved back for the same reasons. The Little People, the Dwarves, Elvin infantry and Nargate's Company were selected to cut the main body of the army to pieces as they retreated still well within striking range. The Battlemaster released their formed troops as the vanguard. The forward group began to build pace. Benny and his compatriots locked up the horse traps of those still in front of the army. These Peoples increased their speed as the thin front line of the enemy, holding its place, was close now. The Dwarves and the Little People could put on an impressive turn of speed, but only briefly. The Commander of the Nargate garrison had to shout and threaten those who wanted to streak ahead. Seren looked at the advancing line. Now able to see the faces of the killers coming towards her. And then all at once they disappeared.

No one else can quite see the appeal, but the Rat People love shit. It's said that Eskimos have fourteen different words for snow and about the same for icesheets. Rats have thirty-two for the colour of shit, fifty for the different shades and hues of those colours, eleven for the texture and three hundred and nine for the taste of shit. They love the stuff and literally bathe in it. What they also love is trophies on their walls, particularly the war trophies of other Peoples.

To be allowed to both play with a large variety of shit from different Peoples, some they can never usually get near like Troll shit and collect any of the enemy's weapons cast away along the line of the shit trench, was an offer from the King, too good to refuse. They had to build a small tunnel and from that build a larger tunnel with some supports, across the entire field where the King wanted it until they hit rock on the one side or river on the other. It could be no deeper than four feet, so a Little Person or Dwarf would not drown in shit. But the walls of the trench needed to be three feet above the surface of the shit to make it very difficult to get out of. The Rat People's Shit Engineers said they could only manage two feet of freeboard. The time they needed to get the shit in there limited how much they could excavate. And they were also helping the Trolls with their projects. Roger had to work night shift while they ferried shit from the latrine. The Door opening right into the tunnel. 'Give me an obnoxious Punter any day.' he said to Richard of his clandestine mission.

When the enemy hit the trench not far from Seren's line, the first four ranks of the enemy, in a tight formation, fell headlong as a roof of crusted shit on light sticks holding up the watered virgin turf gave way beneath. Their speed and the depth of the fall made sure their heads went under at least once. This led to screams of disgust and frustration. The army behind them had momentum and knew nothing of the need to stop. No matter how much the individuals on the edge of the trench pushed back and shouted, they were driven in ones and twos. A call went back. 'Stop running. Stop pushing. There's a trench.' The Battlemaster arrived and screamed in rage. They'd brought no ladders to attack castles because even though there was one with a sprawling town all around it, it remained empty. There was only one solution he could see. Fill the trench with soldiers to the extent the remainder of the army could walk across on their shoulders and leave a small squad to pull them out once the main force had passed. The people nominated to tighten up the packed shit bathers began to slide themselves reluctantly into the viscous liquid. Several of the People being asked to undertake this task demonstrably lacked enthusiasm. The Battlemaster picked up one of the Little People and smashed him across the face with his sword hilt. 'You go into the trench willingly, or I will drown you in there myself.' One of the unfortunate side effects of the trench being filled up with people was that the overall level of the shit rose. This created real peril for the Little People and the Dwarves of smaller stature.

At the very back ranks of the army the Ranger Spiders had reached the rear and were starting their work. Two Dwarves were talking about how they were going to make the enemy pay for these indignities in ways contrary to the accepted codes of war. Suddenly one would be wrapped up neck to ankle in an unbreakable web. There was a way to get it off, but you needed a spider to do it. And they would only do so at the direction of the Battlemaster.

The Spiders could not see far in distance, less in this brightness. They were accustomed to the filtered daylight out of their forest but could see up close and feel vibration such that it was like seeing. They could scurry up to a likely target, wrap him up, and be gone in under thirty seconds. The back ranks were now populated by those fruitlessly trying to find and kill Spiders who had crawled there from along the rock face after the Horn.

The trench was slightly narrower at the far edge against the rock face. And this was intentional. The horseman inspected it and thought they could jump the distance. Soon the horses and riders were assembled in a loose group as one after the other began the process of jumping across. There were twenty Anti Princesses spread throughout the rock faces. They were instructed to let five cross, and so establish some confidence. Then kill or slow down those horses who made it across while as many of those waiting were killed as quickly as possible from the rock faces they had crawled across to after the Horn.

Tears were rolling down Grainia's cheeks as she let the first arrow fly killing a horse from under the rider after they'd cleared the trench. They all had their target areas. The heaviest rain of arrows was now on the waiting horses and specifically on those that turned and fled. Tree escaped the arrows and fled the field. Grainia knew the Trolls were waiting to come in with large carts they drew with their own phenomenal strength, cutting the horses into lumps and dragging them away. Over three hundred horses dead. Jerky. The Anti-Princesses were eager to join their Sisters on their next assignment. With a few left to mop up any horse in range of their arrows.

His army was now crossing the trench in substantial number. The Battlemaster could see no value in a formation march, and even if he had, once clear of the trench his army ran forward in a blind rage. However, he knew now their enemy would be content to let them run for a hundred miles if they chose to. The supplies his army carried in water and food were for ten hours. Far longer than he'd expected them to fight. There was no prospect of an organised retreat. He loathed the very thought of it. They'd have to re-cross a trench. And run the risks of flensing knives coming from nowhere in the turf. Would-be deserters were already dissuaded by the sight of Trolls, completely indifferent to the Army, butchering horses and putting them into carts. The Battlemaster didn't even know about the Spiders at that time. But he did know what would happen should the Wizard King of the Invincible Hand's Battlemaster call for a retreat.

Richard and Seren sat on a high point. She had runners come in with intelligence and take back instructions or a question. The biggest problem much of the army had was that there was nothing to do for an hour or so. The runners relayed how successful the first initiatives had been, including the Ranger spiders and the Anti Princesses. The Captains were sent to reenforce the message that this was part of the strategy and every minute of it tired the enemy while they rested, ate, and were hydrated as Roger and the door worked constantly to keep the army ready for battle. There must be *no* enemy casualties. The King sat saying nothing now as Seren managed the battle. When she arrived from the front line at the rough platform made for an obsidian mine which were all along the escarpment, he merely said. 'Many enemy arrows were wasted.'

They were in two and threes. Hundreds of groupings of the Wizard King's soldiers. The far west of the field began to fill with marauders, seething with rage. The advice to the Alliance squads was that if there was any way they could let them pass do so. They can run for miles and so much the easier to capture. If they were near the Ogres, legs would be broken, those left could chase after the Ogre into one of the specially designated ambush areas, loaded with spiders and some Ogres blending into the rocks beside them. If in the open, the squads were to keep moving back, as if exhausted, to make the rout look as real as possible. They could run in big lazy circles if they wanted. Dwarves, Little People, and unhorsed Elves were not used to running constantly for any distance. The deception of the rout began to become obvious to the Wizard King's forces. To have an enemy running around, the Olders laughing, as they couldn't help but do, was infuriating. Miles were travelled, legs were broken, and webs encased them.

Back at the trench, all the army had passed and there were soldiers left behind to pull the bridge of the shit dwellers out so they could join the fray, which they intended to do with a vengeance. Several Ogres had crept to the trench after the Horn, the attention of the enemy solely on the front. Progressively going forward and then squatting silently as boulders, thanks to the tattooing of their Youngers. Once the main army was some distance away in pursuit of the Alliance Army and the first few shit encrusted individuals had been pulled out of the filth, several Ogres emerged. They were loping along the trench, massive arms with a bunched fist held out, reaching halfway across the trench, knocking every single individual standing near into the shit, which was already standing room only. And there was no one to get them out. Their army had moved forward.

Jackobie sat on a horse, an innovation for the Goblins, partly because usually no horse would carry them. He took the same approach as Seren which was to have runners come and go. With directions, messages and receiving intelligence. He was staring intently at one part of the battlefield and had been doing so for ten minutes. Giving only the briefest reply to the runners. Then he rode forward calling out. 'Dwarf in the Blue cap. Stare at him.' Almost immediately the Dwarf became an Ogre and many saw it. 'Light skinned Ogre near that wrapped up Elf.' He called.

'We see him.' Came the reply. Goblins, Ogres, and spider started to form a circle. 'Riderless horse charging to get out. Block the path, it's not a horse. Deploy webs, ten, twentyfold more than normal. The horse was brought down but began to shrink to a Younger Ogre, then a Goblin youth. 'Keep spinning it to the ground where it's lying. It can't shrink more than its actual size, but I think it's going to be small. Keep going and leave only the head free.'

'An impressive achievement.' said the King from their vantage.

This event coincided with those hinge points that often occur in life and war. The Wizard King's army was tired and saw scores of their comrades with broken legs or wrapped up wherever they looked. There was barely a horse and rider anywhere. Some knew they were running around in big circles and if they came too close to any creature they had no hope of killing it. A rock the size of their fist would shatter a bone in their leg. Their Battlemaster was captured and now there was a large enemy force behind them, as they'd been encouraged to run past. This including countless Spiders. Simply resting and watching to counter any retreat. Joined now by Ogres and Trolls who thought it was a bit of fun to frighten any deserters into heedlessly running back to the army, but not to fight.

The capitulations began, in ones and twos, then groups came together. Hoping that the evil creatures they had fought since time out of mind might give them some clemency for surrender, or at the least a quick death. Seren commanded that every single individual must be wrapped up so there could be no chance of treachery, which might cause the casualties the King promised they could avoid. She also had to decide who to send to manage the Wizard King's hold outs. Once things were in hand, Richard said he would like to visit the 'Tent of Healing' as Tina called it.

Before leaving he suggested there may no longer be any need to kill riderless horses. Seren gave a piercing whistle, which was returned. 'Impressive signalling methodology.' He said. An Anti-Princess arriving within minutes.

'Anti Princess stuff.' The King left it to his Battlemaster to oversee the surrender.

Richard went through the door to the medical centre a few miles to the rear. There was a stream of Spider web wrapped bodies being carried through the door. Most with a splash of blue paint. Some red. Some injured Ogres and Goblins also went through or injured Spiders on the shoulder of the Goblin. Richard was anxious. 'Has anyone been killed. Have you seen any bodies?' They all smiled. 'No Richard.' Which is all he would allow anyone to call him. Even enemy soldiers with whom he struck up conversations.

The Witches, all in the flower of youth, were now being support-ed by young leather clad women, fetching, and carrying anything required, moving people from one part of the tent to another. Spiders were on hand to dissolve the part of the binding web to reveal the injury. This was not what any of the enemy Peoples had expected. Their wounds were generally completely healed, and they were given food and drink. Everywhere in the tents spirits were high and one Dwarf thought he saw Witches and their helpers going into a back room and coming out wiping their lips, as one does after drinking psychobeer. Goblins and Ogres had a similar side door, for the same purpose. Once rewrapped in that section, the injured were all taken and laid on a large shallow grassy hollow that wrapped around a flat bottom at the edge of the lake the river discharged into. The Ogres had excavated it for a purpose and laid fresh turf on the large area of gentle slopes not far from the Castle of Tær. Hundreds were brought in and were laid out in what was a huge amphitheatre.

The Alliance was now in control of the trench. Peoples were pulled out, wrapped up, and loped to the place the rest of their comrades were. They were not a welcome prisoner to lay next to. They were given water and a few pieces of sweet moist cake which was easy to swallow. The only recalcitrant now was Nargate's Commander and half of his Company. Holed up in a cave but difficult to capture without killing at least some of them. Their Commander would not negotiate. The Ogres merely laughed and began to play a complicated game using multifaceted coloured stones. Those guarding the cave were soon lost in the game. They knew these Goblins, who had made such fools of themselves, ultimately had no options. The Oath taking on the field would take a long time so there was no hurry. Then the Company broke with their Leader and began to ask to be removed and bound. Soon it was only the Nargate Commander. The Ogres left him to himself, but the Goblins were unhappy. He had disgraced them by fighting for their enemy of old. They asked to borrow a cart from a Troll, lined it with spider's web and filled it with shit. They carried it in buckets and poured it into cracks and holes in the cave and went back for more. The Ogres had enjoyed building a dam in front of the cave scooping earth with their powerful hands. When Nargate's Commander was knee deep he agreed to unconditional surrender. He was soon loped to the place where all the enemy where bound and dumped on the grass amphitheatre.

Grainia rode up to the small HQ beside the medical tents with six handsome Elvin horses in train. A unique breed. She came to Seren and congratulated her and said she was looking forward to having beer with her as soon as their duties allowed it. She went to join the rest of her Sisterhood assisting the Witches. There was some Troll's grumbling about the fact that the Knight's horses had been taken out of play by the Dragons and a few of the Elven breed had been left to live. 'You got double what you expected. Stop pretending to whine and come and have a beer with us.' Was Richard's reply to Benny

Richard had been through the hospital wards asking the Witches to now focus on the serious cases only. He wanted to start a Ceremony as soon as possible as there was a whole army to deal with. Even some serious cases, if they could be dosed up with some sort of joyfulness potion, they could be attended to after. Any of the Allied armies injured had already been healed.

Seren hadn't been to the hospital and walked through the tents. The Witches, young and beautiful were wearing low-cut leather nurse's uniforms with high cut skirts. Grainia said to Seren as she worked beside Tina. 'Tina's been telling us about their 'Witch for a Weekend' program and how great it is.'

'It's great if you like wall to wall...' Tina glared at her. 'Witch stuff.'

'Tina said you've done it lots of times and you get right into it.' Said Grainia.

It was Seren's turn to glare at a Witch who returned a cheeky smile. 'Only do what you're comfortable doing Grainia. I only go there for *actual potions and incantations and shit.*' Seren only had to walk a short distance into the amphitheatre which was why the area had been excavated near the medical facilities. Now the wounded coming in were only given pain killing spells or placebos. From Richard's computer surfing, the Younger Ogres had developed a crude Public Address system.

Richard wanted it to be very short and sharp. Partly because he was tired and wanted a beer. But also; who remembers long speeches? Once all the enemy were laid out in place he came before them and spoke calmly, and without the triumphalism they expected.

'We've been victorious in the field of battle.' A huge cheer arose from the Alliance Peoples and, after a moment he encouraged it to subside. 'Where we could have been cruel, we've been merciful. Where we could have been vicious and cared nothing for the lives of our enemies, we've cared for them as much as we have for our own lives and I'm hoping that all those who were injured will leave this field healed.' Another cheer from the Alliance soldiers. Intoxicated with unhoped for victory. 'Comrades. After years of being misrepresented you have taught the whole of Tæranon the meaning of Benevolence.'

'But that benevolence now must be earned. All we ever wanted was what was rightfully ours. Our lands, the peace to raise our families and our rains as they have always been. Remember that we have never once attacked other People's towns, never once tried to steal their land, and never once tried to interfere with their rain or rivers.'

The Alliance People were relieved to see that their King was not endlessly charitable. 'To leave this amphitheatre you will swear an oath to never, ever attack or participate in armed combat against any member of our Alliance. You will return the land which all agree is rightfully yours. And you will direct rainfall until, as quickly as possible, the fields, deltas and forest of the Alliance People are returned to their former state. And then restore it to its natural patterns for all time. You must do this at the cost to your Peoples until it is achieved. To any People who wish to send food and stores stolen via the shameless drought imposed on the Alliance Peoples, it will be gratefully received. Our children starve. But we will sack no one's stores, although we could. Finally, you will swear that you have heard our offer that *your Peoples* can become Allies and cease pointless battles. You will communicate this to your leaders. Even if the probability of such an Alliance may appear low. You must remember that it is we that hold out the hand of friendship, and for all time.'

Richard read out a short sharp version of the Oath. '*I will never fight as soldier, a mercenary or bandit against any Alliance Peoples or my life is forfeit. I acknowledge the Alliance Peoples stand ready for friendship.*' 'Those willing to swear will be released immediately and in groups will be transported to within a mile of your home.' It would have taken an awfully long time for them all to swear to him, so he deputised the leader in each People, including Bertold on a fine marble pillar. Seren was also deployed. Lines began to form.

Those who refused to take the oath had a splash of black paint on the webbing. Now Richard raised the fate of those who would not take the Oath. It was harsh. 'We have shown benevolence in battle. And we ask for a promise that what is ours will not again be taken or attacked. If this great generosity has not been appreciated, once we have had the last Oath, for those unwilling to take it, and have packed our things we'll never return to this place. The bodies of the prideful and stupid can rot here and be fodder for the animals that would eat such poor fare.'

He turned to the Alliance forces assembled behind and on either side. 'Please disassemble everything, in an orderly way so that it can be returned to those who donated it. Ensure those badly hurt are healed, even those foolish with the black mark so they can die only of ignorance.' Richard was relieved. They had been his last words as King. He was going to sneak off and have some psychobeer which he knew the Witches were enjoying. He was surprised that he cared nothing for those that remained arrayed on the grass. Anyone in this remarkable Alliance Army could have easily killed one of the enemy, and explained it was unavoidable. These people, unable to take an Oath to simply stop being killers had chosen death. They could have it. Despite his words, he could see, Witches and Anti-Princesses making every little scratch and cut healed for those with a black mark. It would give the most time possible to allowed those with a splash of that colour to reconsider.

The Goblins had prepared a slightly different Oath for Nargate's men. 'You will keep or bear no arms. You will never leave your fields and town.' It was bitter, but they took the Oath. Their leader's Oath was harsh. 'You will never approach or live in a Goblin village or town for the remainder of your life.'

'Then I might as well die here.' They were indifferent to that. All his stupidity was sinking in. There was worse than death in battle.

'It's up to you.' said Jackobie who asked him to be returned with his black mark. The once proud leader of the Nargate garrison called them back and he took the specific Oath. He was broken.

The Wizard King's Battlemaster was getting the same impression. He'd been ignored and never even marked with paint. The creature knew he would need to call out for mercy if it wanted any attention. And this was a bitter pill for such a proud and rare creature. All of those with the black mark were all rolled on their side so they could see the HQ and now medical tents come down. Farewells were being said. A contingent of each of the Alliance People would be held back so there would be no rescue. Once the King rode through the amphitheatre, any opportunity to take the

Oath would be at an end. Many Captains and Commandeers from all Peoples watched his departure.

By the time he rode though there was only one. Seren on Brindlefire, Roger on GroundBreaker and Richard on TBA. Grainia came along with Tina holding on like a pillion passenger on a motorbike. One lonely figure. In this case webbed to the grass. Seren urged Richard to leave it to die wrapped densely in web. She knew Richard was already thinking about the next battle and this hateful creature would stop at nothing to stoke resentment in the vanquished and reignite fear of the Alliance Peoples.

But he was the only one. Psychobeer could wear off rapidly when a sudden need for sobriety emerged. One of its many charms. And Ricard had proclaimed and hoped that his army would leave none dead. And that all the captives would be given a fair choice. Fairer than some deserved. Hence Richard felt compelled to say. 'Would you die here?'

The creature said. 'I will take your Oath.'

It was that simple. The Shapeshifter took the Oath.

Then Richard made a serious mistake. 'I know your Oath is worth nothing. The Alliance People will maintain a special corps to ensure you keep it.'

Once freed the creature leapt up and relieved Seren of her bow. 'What Oath. The King proclaimed mine was worth nothing.' The creature moved around at incredible speed. A mere child Goblin at one stage, or a frail, Elder Ogre nearing death. The rapid movement, the confusing shapes and the calls that seemed to come from far away were distractions. It wanted to be close enough to be sure. It wasn't accustomed to the Anti-Princess's bow, so it needed to get closer. Once satisfied, he shot Seren through the heart, and disappeared into the night.

Richard caught her as she slid from her horse. Her expressionless face gave away nothing. Richard said nothing. Tina was beside him within seconds.

'I can do nothing.' She said. 'But the Kings hands have the power to restore life. A one-shot deal though.'

Richard was bending down. 'I don't remember that on the sword.'

'I scrolled over whole sections. Do you know how fucking boring that one is? It was literally written by committee, and everyone wanted their own little narrative. All you need to do is put it close to her face and wave it around a bit.'

Richard was about to do as she instructed but Tina snatched his hand back. 'Not that one. That's the evil one you swapped with that asshole.'

Richard waved his hand, hopefully displaying the right sense of dignity to make sure it worked. The arrow vanished. Seren took a deep breath and sat up to hold Richard in a tight squeeze. 'Father.' She said. Confused. Then embarrassed.

There was an awkward silence.

'Oh. Um. I meant Richard. Hey Richard, what happened. It was all black, and then I saw this light. There were voices. Familiar voices. Calling me forward to leave this life. But I heard your voice. Calling me back.'

'Voices?'

The old Seren was back. 'Voice. Lights.' She looked around smiling 'It was all blackness. I was dead once that asshole shot me.' There was some mood restoring laughter. Richard was laughing with relief.

'That's a one-shot deal Richard. Your Goddess of a Mother didn't want you off healing people willy nilly. That's our job. Use the left hand on *no one.*'

She looked at Richard, still the seductress. 'You know Richard if you're looking for a Queen, you could do a lot worse than me. It would be a casual thing. No one would know that though. I would turn up to the big events and nod my head when you said things, and this would give our wayward daughter here more of an anchor in life.'

Richard smiled. 'I'll give that very serious consideration.' He smiled at both women. 'But first I have to get through what I imagine to be a necessary procession of visiting towns and villages thanking them for their contribution, and I image, being thanked to some degree.'

'How about wild, unrestrained gratitude and admiration Richard.' Said Jackobie

'Do you think so. I'm a figurehead really.'

Roger said. 'With the door it will take a full week. Maybe longer as it may be that some of the *vanquished* would like you to visit. You've released them from thraldom.'

'Tina, could you create a fake me to do this stuff. I have rather a lot on.'

'You know my terms.'

'No.' Said Roger. 'Around you must go. Beautiful daughter and Battlemaster beside you.

'And even more beautiful Queen, on the other side. And I can brew you up some extra special Psychobeer which will make you absolutely love the process. Won't be able to get enough. With a grand finale in the City.'

'Why should I go there?'

'Normal trading of all Peoples has been resumed.' Said Roger. 'People will be making a buck so their thanks will be some of the most…is it rousing.'

'Bring on the beer.' said Richard.

'As long as Grainia and Bosco can be there I'm in.' Richard only then noticed Bosco on Tina's shoulder.

'In the retinue.' Said Richard. Seren groaned.

'We'll be brewing up something special for you Richard. Half the Dwarves and Elves that came through the medical tent wanted their swords and axes read and then written out. The Rat People want to schedule a major reading session on all the weapons they acquired before they go up on their walls. The Coven could now quite literally roll around in Ka-Ching. And we plan to do that when we're done. Naked by the way Seren. Beer will be delivered to you each morning Richard. It will help you be sage when sagacity is called for, or joyous or commanding, Whatever. It knows what it's doing.'

Richard smiled 'There is not one single group that this endeavour couldn't have done without. And it's so true of your Coven.'

'A pleasure my King.' She had reverted to the middle-aged woman she told people was the real her. 'And we are grateful to you Battlemaster Seren.' Said Tina. All the mischief was gone for a moment. Her thanks were real. 'Rule under the Wizard King would have been grim beyond imagination.'

'The gratitude is mutual Tina.' Said Seren.

And celebrations there were. The people of the Alliance, all the Ogres, Rat People, Goblins and Spiders had never won anything before. They were created to lose as far as they knew, maybe after a small victory here or there to keep things interesting. But to win, and to be the merciful, was sweet beyond anything any of them could even imagine. And now dancing in the rain. And some of the vanquished did deliver food, in person, and were invited to engage in the celebrations. And most did.

Richard, Seren and the Commanders and Captains travelled through dozens of towns and villages. The Door made this easier but also more intense. They would finish one visit and flow into the next. Richard thought he needed the special psychobeer but after a day and a half he realised he could relax and be himself. He didn't have to act like a King or anybody else. And from this perspective he really saw how truly awful the lives of these people had become. Even the Rat People had suffered awfully by the merciless rainfall regime. Some Ogres and Goblins said this was the first time in a long time they had seen people light-hearted. There was a growing anger in Richard towards a particular People who had helped to perpetrate this crime and yet lost nothing and promised nothing.

The final visit, a ride through the city was for Richard and his retinue again to be feted. This time for restoring trade which restored many other things. Seren made the procession in a light armour and a stylish helm.'

'Lead these visits on your own if you won't wear some armour.' Said Richard. 'I have other things to do. You can go as my Envoy.' The Goblin Youngers prepared a suit of armour to fit, yet very light. Though it had to fit around the Anti Princess's leathers. They presented it to her before she left. It was more curvatious than she liked. 'Had to make room for the leathers.' Was the Younger's explanation.

In addition, people had been telling the story everywhere that the daring and brilliant Battlemaster was also the Kings daughter, separated by hardships and heartbreak for nearly twenty years. Seren then had to endure being told what an uncanny family likeness there was. She would eventually vent these frustrations at Richard who would say. 'Don't worry. Anyone who knows me would see I could never have a daughter as beautiful and accomplished as you.' This would send her off into broodiness. But this was a minor feature of the tour. Which finally ended with a small Goblin hamlet. They had already begun to have rain, sometimes heavy which helped a few of their crops hang on.

Roger called them together and suggested to Richard a day at a resort would be well spent. But Richard was all business. 'No unfortunately. I would love it, but I need a few days with the Younger Ogres and then I'll need to make a trip back. When I return there should be time. A few weeks at least.'

The two others didn't ask what he meant. Richard now liked to tell people things when he wanted to tell them. A group Younger Ogres always travelling with him now. They would spend at least a few hours a night together. Younger technologists all centralised in what had been the Ogre Headquarters.

Arriving back at the Ogre Town, he'd convened a meeting. This was where he called home, having never lived anywhere else in Tæranon for more than a few days. Some suggested he could occupy the beautiful white marble castle at the far end of the Geopor plain. He laughed and said. 'It will never be occupied. My dream is that both shall be pulled down and spread throughout Tæranon as building materials.' He spent a few hours at the castle at the headwaters of the Nadi, to visit Arnall. And learn more about what he'd been up to.

Later that day and shortly before a meeting he'd arranged to catch up with the entire Younger Technical Team, the Leader of the Pegasus People asked to see him.

Richard didn't want to listen to any excuses. But he came to see him. 'Do you take any responsibility for the suffering and death you've caused to the Villages, Towns, Clusters?'

'We're creatures of the sky. The Dwarves asked for our help with their Project, and we agreed. At that time, we knew nothing of their designs. We were told that all areas would improve from their techniques.'

'Such as your pasture. In good condition is it?'

'The best we have ever enjoyed. We followed your procession and alighted at all the places you passed through and saw the pastures around. We were distraught. We would have never engaged in such crimes. We know we should have looked closer. Pursued our suspicions. We were blinded by the magnificence of our pasture. We work tirelessly now with the Dwarves to reinstate things.'

'Your defence is you were all monumentally stupid and didn't land anywhere except your pastures. You were the fools and playthings of Dwarves. They are towering intellects compared to you.' Said Richard. 'The only thing I ask is that you never trouble me with your presence and your collaborationist bullshit ever again.'

Richard stood to go. The Leader of the Pegasus People said. 'I would give you my wings in exchange for the harm we've done.'

Seren covered her eyes with her hands. Don't play the 'we're going through a process game' with Richard. She thought.

Richard looked back and said. 'Okay.' He disappeared for his meeting. The Leader of the Pegasus was trying to phrase a response which said he was really speaking by way of a symbolic gesture. He offered up his wings metaphorically. Not actually to have his wings chopped off.

But Richard was gone.

Ogres were approaching with very sharp knives. They lifted the wings and had some conversation as to how to do it, and what tools they would need to get through the very considerable amount of bone. And, once they'd cut them, they needed the wherewithal to stem the bleeding. They had observed what the witches did. But witches had spells and incantations. One suggested boiling tar. One said if they break it at the big joining knuckle, only sharp knife would be required, and it might lead to less blood loss. One was sent off to boil the tar. The others started feeling for the connection point to see if they could find the joint and how to snap it. 'Lots of feathers to work around.' Said one. 'We'll have to take them out to see what we're doing. I guess it's like plucking a chicken. Dunk it in boing water don't you.'

'Yes. But to be fair that's a dead chicken.'

'Best get on and pluck them then?'

A member of the Pegasus People had never gone back on their word.

Seren said. 'Wait. Wait until I return.'

Seren caught up with Richard as he entered the workshops. 'You're cutting it fine.' Richard said. 'They haven't started to cut the wings off, have they?'

'No.' She was now catching up with the part she was cast in.

'Good. That would make a hell of a mess. And be entirely unnecessary. It was a symbolic gesture in any event. A metaphor.'

'What part do I play. Hysterical horse lover?'

'It makes me Kingly and you a mediator. The hysterical horse lover goes without saying. Go back and tell them you convinced me to reverse the decision and you will have flying horse rides forever more. Look on the bright side won't you Seren.' There was a trace of annoyance that she failed to look there sometimes.

Later all the leadership of the Army had been assembled. Bertolt had come and even some of the Rat People for what they assumed would be some formal debrief and peace keeping plan. Even Benny made an appearance. 'Not as an Envoy. Here to see a friend of mine before he was a King.' There was a very brief round of congratulations and thanks.

Richard would never be a King. He talked to them as Richard. Roger and Seren were likewise. Seren and Roger as they were when they had first met Richard. Retired as they were from any formal role. Or so they thought. 'I really appreciate you all coming when it may not seem we have much to talk about. We have succeeded in one battle, unfortunately it is inevitable there will be another. I know enough about our Adversary to know that he will build a new army. Those that never took the Oath, Oath breakers and people we may not even know about. He will not let defeat sit as a stain on his ego. We will hear the bell soon. And will have a month to prepare. I'm suggesting that although your stores are low, you continue to train for war. There are a few weapons and protections which are being developed new to our armoury. Weapons such as the medium distance bow, used as a prop in the last battle, will be relied upon heavily. I needn't go into many details here. I'd like you to think about it. I've some business to attend to, but I hope to visit each of you before the Bell tolls or at least soon after.'

At that time the vanquished Elves who made a successful retreat and took no Oath had been walking for days towards the Ogre Head Quarters. They had no horses. The sight of the Trolls dismembering the others had sent them into a frenzy, throwing their riders. Later those also had been caught and cut to pieces and their flesh dried out. They heard of the hundreds of their companions who were made to swear a shameful Oath. They lived in the wilderness, away from the of their brothers who they believed should have chosen death rather than humiliation. One of their towns even hosted a visit from a King who could only win a battle by trickery. They had determined whose death would hurt the King and Alliance the most. It was an easy choice. His daughter and Battlemaster. Horse killer. Saved from an arrow that pierced her heart shot by the Shape Shifter. But not twice they were told.

Richard was flagging. He had reengaged the armies to prepare for battle readiness, some not quite believing, but trusting his judgements of the past. He was quite keen to stop being a King for a while and see Natasha. Show her the new novel idea tattooed on his back. Tell her the improbable story of how they had won a battle.

Elves chose various locations to shoot from. She came from the meeting room with her light armour and helm. Richard insisted she wear it 'for the rest of your life' whenever she was out in the open. One arrow hit her armour harmlessly. The others each sent an arrow though her right eye. She slumped forward immediately, held from falling by Jackobie. Soon there was a large circle of various Peoples looking on as Richard. He looked at his hand. The left hand with stitch marks all around the area above the wrist.

'I understand why Richard. But you don't know what you'll unleash.' Roger was trying to walk a line between warning and the inability of a father to watch his child die. Even if she may not really be a daughter, he had started thinking of her like one.

'I know Roger.' He waved his left hand slowly over her face.

The arrows vanished and her eyes flew open. 'You fool.' Was all she said, looking into his eyes for a second and rolling to get up. She leapt onto Brindlefire, and awkwardly unhitched her sword, breastplate and daggers and cast them aside as if they were burning her.

Richard looked at those surrounding him. 'A costly decision I fear.' He said quietly.

Looking around there was agreement with Gordon who said. 'We would have done likewise.' He changed the subject to divert Richard from the inner turmoil he was feeling. 'Your reminder that another battle is imminent is fitting. An hour of inaction will be an hour lost to preparation for a battle which, I imagine, cannot avoid the clash of arms again.'

Richard nodded sadly. 'Yes. And once such a battle is commenced, our victory will need to be absolute to stop a cycle in which the Wizard King feeds his cravings.'

He said. 'We are working on projects. There is always hope for a peaceful outcome.' He looked around with a resolve new to them.

'Where that hope fails, we'll have built an army of every single one of our Peoples tired of being the playthings of murderers. And we'll confront the greatest murder of all, with the largest army Tæranon has ever seen.' People looked around to see Jackobie speaking.

Richard nodded. 'We've been merciful. If this is rejected, we'll be merciless. There will be no beds for the wounded enemy. There will be *no prisoners*.' Richard could not have imagined himself saying such a thing even a day before. But he got a sense of how profoundly tired all the unfavoured Peoples were. Their rain was restored, but ultimately only at the whim of a power which refused to accept defeat. And so these Peoples were ready to try to finally and completely defeat him, and they needed a King that would lead their army.

'Jackobie is my Battlemaster.' Said Richard. The need for one stinging he heart. 'He'll consult with you, and work with you all on the myriad of things that must be done to prepare. I'll visit the Peoples at times, but the People must give freely, or withhold as they see fit because none of our enemy will survive. There will be techniques of battle and equipment which have never been seen before. As with the last, some of this information will be kept very close, until the time for any one soldier to act is reached.' Richard had never figured himself as a battle strategist, but he had ideas he believed would rip apart the structure of the *head-to-head* battle that his adversary so desired.

He went quietly to Roger. 'Take me home Roger. I don't feel like being a King at the moment.'

As they walked through the door Roger said. 'And here was I thinking we were going to a resort for a drinking session. Now I'll have to go home and help with all those dishes.'

'And so you should. I won't be gone for very long. Perhaps you could organise a small contingent to be there. Save you waiting around.'

'I like waiting. And I don't like dishes. I'll bring over some of my kids and we'll have a campout.'

'Sounds good.' He reached out his hand to Roger and said. 'We won. An extruder and his middleman. Never underestimate the little fellows.'

'We both have to keep selling those things to make a living you know. King and King's Logistics Man are still *very* unremunerated positions. And I fear we've lost our saleswoman.'

'Roger, perhaps you could have a rest for a while. We'll go two star.'

With that Richard faded away. Coming into a toilet now felt very strange. He sat there for a moment to make sure he didn't say anything too outlandish, though anything he could say would be. He came out and opened the laundry door and, seeing it was sometime around the middle of the day, issued forth a tentative. 'I'm back.'

He heard a now familiar voice say. 'Great. My life seems dull, so I want to hear all about yours.'

He came to her and gave her a hug. He had to remind himself though, that he'd been away for weeks, yet for her, only hours. 'We won the battle. Nobody got killed. However Seren, who is sort of my daughter was shot by a Shape Shifter. I brought her back to life with my good hand. But then, unfortunately she was killed again, I know this stretches the credulity somewhat, but I was able to bring her back to life. Unfortunately with my evil hand. Now she's not very nice, although I could never imagine her being truly evil.'

Natasha was unruffled. 'How could that ever stretch the credulity Richard. I was going to have a cup of tea so how about I put on a pot and you can tell me how you fought a battle and no one was killed.'

Watching Natasha get up to prepare the makings of a simple cup of tea was painful. He could only imagine what the actual pain must be like. 'Would my assistance be of...assistance.'

'I thought you'd never ask.'

'Don't you have anyone who...' He said this but immediately felt like he was prying.

'Turn up from time to time. Husband or friends I used to have. I'm an author. Anyone turn up in your life from time to time.'

'I had a girlfriend once. I told her about this book a woman I knew was reading. Fifty Shades of Grey. She left soon after. This departure was also around the time my third book tanked if I were to use Miranda's technical speak. Writing is a solitary habit isn't it. I have an Uncle who turns up in my life occasionally and he used to be the most interesting part of it...now that I think about it.'

'How long are you visiting this time. Another flying visit.'

'It's certain that there will be another battle. Being King and all, I'll need to help with preparations.'

'Why do you come back? Other than to bring me stories so elegantly tattooed on you back. Which I hope you have another.'

'I come back to see you of course. All that King stuff can't hold a candle to a cup of tea with you.' He was about to immediately feel somewhat awkward, but she swept past it.

'I'm honoured and very pleased to be able to compete with Kingly duties. Tell me about the battle, and what you're plan for the next.' He went into some detail about the battle, unable to conceal his immense pride that it as a battle that killed no one. After another cup of tea and looking at his watch, the second half of the visit was very similar to the last one and the one before. He was frantically looking at web pages for about two seconds per page. Most of it was technology but some of it was metallurgy and advanced fabrics and extrusions, wood laminate and ply techniques.

This occurred while his back was being photographed. Natasha said. 'I think whoever's writing this has written a trilogy.'

'These were supposed to be notes, I hadn't really thought of them as a summary of a book.'

'I think your scribes are taking liberties. And we should listen. They live in it. You visit it and I try to imagine it.'

'Once all this over, you could maybe go for a visit in there yourself. I've got lots of friends who would love to show you around.'

'I'd like that. A shame we can't go together.'

'That would take a stroke of genius.' But he thought that genius was not beyond the realms of possibility.

Natasha got up and gave him her first, long frail embrace and then he was back in the lavatory, cramming breakfast cereal into his mouth, and some final internet pages into his brain. The neural net went on. And he was gone.

He arrived back with no one waiting but voices nearby. Someone must have been watching out because there was a whistle and Roger was soon welcoming him, panting from playing a local equivalent of soccer with a dozen or so teenage boys and girls. They all arrived and provided a series of variations on 'It's very nice to meet you Richard, I'm…' and he provided his various responses.

'I'll drop this part of the tribe home and be back in a moment.' Richard noticed Roger giving instruction to one of the older girls about how to use the door.

'Let's go for a beer when you get back.'

Richard hadn't asked the important questions. Had the Bell tolled and how long ago. He wanted to be at a resort, drinking psychobeer and hearing about how they were going on the Ka Ching front.

When Roger arrived back, they stood talking.

'Big uptick in business. Went to the city. Every type of the People there. Christmas is now really just around the corner now. We're rolling in it, metaphorically. Unlike like Tina and her friends who are physically rolling it and bragging about it. But we could at least sit on a little pile without touching the chair, taking turns.'

'In other news?' Richard finally said.

'The Bell tolled under a week ago. Ten days after you left. The preparations on our side of the fence are like a frenzy. A well organised but incredibly intense frenzy. People have had enough. They won, and were merciful, fair and square. This call to arms has drawn out a deep resolution and... fury. They're tired of being cannon fodder in general, but tired of a force that wants a pall of darkness over their lives forever. Teenagers, grandmothers and grandfathers, mothers with babes in arms; all demanding to be a part of the army. I've joined up myself Richard. And don't try to dissuade me. I've consigned hundreds of thousands of these People to their deaths. I'd like to die with them this time. It's like everyone on our side wants the world to change, or they're quite happy for it to end.'

'I'd hoped the Wizard King might have had some trouble raising an army.' Said Richard, though now distracted by other thoughts.

'There are those who weren't there for Part One or successfully deserted, there's Oath Breakers, more than a few of those and whole regions populated by Little People not involved in anybody's business. But they will have to be now. And populations of Humans from the far side of the Black Castle no one had ever heard of before. Including me. The Wizard King created a population never available to Punters. It's caused a bit of an ethical conundrum. There are several hundred humans expressing a desire to fight on our side, but Jackobie doesn't want to break the rules because the other side does. They'll be assigned to the huge logistics effort. Including weapons production. A few being blacksmiths and ready to share their art.'

'Can you remember exactly when the Bell tolled?'

'Today's Wednesday so it would be last Sunday. Around the middle of the day. Why?'

'I need to be somewhere in London for a very important appointment. Hopefully the Youngers can calculate when it tolled to the minute. To the second would be better. I have a feeling it's going to be during the battle which will be extremely inconvenient but that's when the person I'm doing some business with wants to meet. The Peoples don't need me, but they benefit from a figurehead, even if he couldn't fight his way out of paper bag.'

Richard decided to go straight back to the Ogre Town and give the Youngers a download. They were about to lead their horses through the Door when a sharp knife appeared around Richard's throat.

'You two are so predictable.' She said this as two Elves took Roger in hand.

'It hasn't been same without you Seren. You were what made the place worth visiting, that's why I'm leaving early.'

She pulled Richard's head back roughly. 'My instructions are that you have a long walk home. And Roger will come and give us the unfair advantages you enjoyed last time around.'

Roger and his horse were being led through the door. Richard could see it was some complex of yards and stables on the other side. The knife was held hard to his throat, but not quite cutting. 'I've missed you Seren. Would you consider letting me keep TBA? He's a friend. You know.' He noticed she wasn't riding Brindlefire.

'Keep your fucking sentiments to yourself and keep your pathetic nag. You would think a King would ride a better horse. I've convinced the Wizard King to let you live because we're watching the preparation. And we know this time you'll misdirect the energies that are building. Your tricks won't work Richard. Why not go home early and avoid the embarrassment.'

'You overestimate your capacity to convince that man of anything. He needs me this time around. He must be seen to beat me. You might recall I beat him last time. I could have done it any number of alternative Battlemasters. I picked you because you were so desperately in need of a boost to your self-esteem.'

She pushed Richard over and strode through the door while Roger said. 'You're such a bitch now Seren.' He got a very sharp clip across the back of his head with an armoured glove and was told. 'Shut up and drive.'

It turned out Richard was glad for the time he had to think during the ride home. He came up with a lot of ideas. Very unusual ideas. But he believed they would be very effective. And he thought of his secret weapon of last resort. A last hope. He feared it was a ridiculous idea and time wasting. But it was a hope set against a terrible alternative. Once he returned to the Ogre city the greetings were warm. The loss of the door was the subject of brief consternation, but acceptance swiftly.

To respond to this, they built towns near the front and start moving people and stores there much sooner. The volunteers had been flooding in, both to join the battle, and many to support the troops in battle. Hamlets were being build right in the battlefield to supply provisions to the soldiers as they waited for their time to fight. Those who would build and move weapons, stores and equipment had been coming in with no call for recruits. This army was growing organically, and would be the biggest Tæranon had ever seen, by a large margin. Most of the Peoples coming were used to very harsh conditions, so they could travel a long way and make a place to live to satisfy their frugal needs much more easily that less hardy folk. Some people were pulling down their own houses to move them to near the front so they could give accommodation to those preparing to go into battle. Richard could see recruits doing basic training in their hundreds and the same for advanced soldiers. There were so many people insistent on joining the army, many completely unsuitable, there may have been a revolt were they not allowed to do so.

Jackobie took Richard to a series of meeting he'd arranged, some would now need to be delayed without the door, but Bertolt was already in the Ogre city. He had some reservations about how the Spiders should participate this time.

'It's possible the Peoples will be on the field for hours. And the whole battlefield is likely to be torn to pieces. In such a long battle Spiders would need hydration or their web supplies are limited.'

Richard had given that thought. 'I'm suggesting the spiders would again be between the shoulders. The tube would form a loop at the bottom with nutrient rich water. However, this is for their wellbeing during a long battle the same as all our soldier carry water and a little food. But the tube will be much strengthened with new alloys and be nearly impossible to damage. The companions would advise a safe time for the Spider to come out. They would only be delivering a *very* small amount of web to each of the foe. The mouth and nose would be sealed off. The victim could be killed where they lay, but only if it was safe and time permitted it. Otherwise they'd be left to their fate.' Everyone now knew that Richard had cast aside every civil, indeed humane approach to this war.

There was a long pause. 'That's a hard end.' Said Jackobie. 'Could we bind them hand and foot.'

Richard said. 'No. In the previous battle we ensured not one of their enemies was killed. In this battle, we will ensure that *none* survive. *Not one.* I want them to see their compatriots with a killing web over their face. I want them to be terrified which is what they deserve. If we must pursue those that retreat for days, weeks as they flee in ones and twos, so be it. We will find them in their homes and we will kill them there. We will make our intentions about this well known, such that every enemy combatant standing in the ranks knows how we intend to prosecute this battle.'

The other's sat somewhat uncomfortably, including Bertolt, to the degree a spider can.

'Think about the alternatives. Another inconclusive war, another excuse for that evil bastard to raise an army from the same malcontents that didn't accept the outcomes of the first nor a second. If our Peoples win this battle, an uncompromising battle, it will be the last. And the occupant of the Black Castle would become a prisoner. A nasty old fool entrapped there. That's if we can't pull it down.'

Bertolt gave a Spider sigh. Accepting what he'd heard. 'The Rangers will be displeased. Perhaps they could roam in the rock areas bounding the field and, so they can support the army from safety. The mode of death of the enemy will be hard for all of us to accept, although I understand the need for it. Remember Richard, quite a few of our foe will be simple, ordinary peoples who are forced into a service to someone they have no allegiance to. We agree we must do what we must. But it is with a heavy heart.'

Richard nodded sadly, this dimension was not lost on him, but he saw no alternative. 'And it's some of these I hope will flee before their army takes the field.' He started to explain some of his ideas for battlefield strategy, to give them time to digest them and come up with concerns and improvement. He could see Jackobie, an exceptional Battlemaster, but still a young Goblin, turned sixteen only a few days before, was somewhat swamped and in need of time to process things. Richard said as much and headed for the Youngers workshop. There was a tap on his shoulder and a vision of loveliness with a pleasant mixture of smoky sensuality and a perennial sense of fun. 'Before you ask Tina. I've considered your offer, and yes, I want you to be my Queen and we'll tour around in very glamourous clothing and eat nice food in places full of subjects who love us. But it will have to be an exclusive relationship. You and me.'

'Oh. Why did you have to go and spoil it at the end Richard. You know Witches are free spirited. This monogamy fetish you people have. It doesn't work. Look at the statistics. It's a failed experiment. But even though you've left me heartbroken, about what you and I might have shared but can never be…' Richard enjoying this visage of Tina and her engaging personality. He could not help but give her offer second thoughts. But a Queen would complicate things. She was continuing '…based on the crazy zeitgeist at the moment, have come up with a plan whereby we could drop into the battlefield, pick up an injured soldier, and get them to the tents in under a minute.'

'A *very* noble idea Tina but it can't happen.'

'Can't happen? You're only a figurehead you know Richard.' She was now a scolding schoolteacher.

'I know that. However, I assume even Witches can be killed.' She nodded.

'In Battle.' She nodded again.

'Therefore, for each Witch killed how many soldiers will die because the Witch who would have been giving them their expertise and magic, so stylishly, is dead. It's simple arithmetic. There are too few of you to put even one at risk. Hospitals can still be overrun by armies; assassins can be sent to kill those of great value. You will be bearing your share of risk as things are. It's going to be a strange day Tina. The biggest arguments in this army at the moment are about who gets to stand in the front line. If they can't get in the front line, then they want to be in the front rank.'

'And when one of our fighters go down, they still have hope. Simply because the healing of your incredibly glamorous coven. Every one so delightful, witty, charming and with an inherent beauty only the strongest man…or woman…can withstand it. I believe your coven is growing. The Dual Sisterhood initiative. We'll have systems in place to move the injured back as quickly as possible. It will be the highest priority on the battlefield. I can't reveal the detail yet. Even to a goddess.'

'So this is how you get what you want.' Then it was if an idea struck her. 'What about a 'Queen for a Weekend.' Said the seductive Tina. 'I can be monogamous for that long.'

'Now that is something I'll give some serious thought to. We might need to tour the remotest parts of the Realm.' She was already shaking her head as she vanished.

A Younger put the jack into the side of Richard's head which he had again asked for via the LED function. There was again excited chatter about a few technical details. One of the older Youngers said. 'Has Natasha written out the second story.' Silence descended on the workshop.

'Natasha?' Said Richard.

'Oh.' Said a senior Younger. 'A replay of your visit comes with the download. Bit of an irresistible temptation to watch it you know. Especially with our literary collaboration. Sorry.'

Richard smiled. 'It's not like there's anything intimate going on so it's harmless enough for you to watch it.'

'That will start to happen soon, so we'll stop watching from now.' This came from the Younger who had started it all.

'Now setting that aside, there are about twenty high priority technical issues to get the battle strategy supported. If any of them aren't possible in the time allowed, we'll change the strategy to what's possible. This is all in addition to the alternative strategy, which I know you are all most interested in, but it has to be developed with and not before, the battlefield technologies.'

'And one more thing. It's probably academic now that we've lost the door, but I'd like for you to calculate when the Bell tolled, to the second if possible. I have a commitment in London at a specific time and date, and I simply must be there. I want to know how this time relates to the battle.'

Preparations continued at a blistering pace. Masses of supplies and more and more Peoples moved to the proximity of the Battlefield. Richard had time to carefully build a strategy completely unique. Complicated, but he believed, devastating. All the while he had another dice to roll.

Jackobie came to Richard and said he believed he'd uncovered a spy network. Family links to Nargate. Feeding information to a certain individual who had set himself up in a room near the castle decorated all in Black and gold. Some of these spies were probably being compelled because of a threat to their families. Richard was delighted. 'That's great. We'll move them away from the real stuff and trickle out a bunch of plausible but inaccurate information. There is one piece of information I want them to get, overhearing a discussion, ideally between you and Jacinta. You don't need to give all the details at once, we'll spread around. That I need to sign an Agreement with my sister Miranda's employer so that I can take ownership of the briefcase outright. It's a large amount of money. I'll need to give it to him personally. It's an 'off the book's transaction'. My sister's told me it's leaked out that the briefcase is for sale and there's other buyers circling around. Her Boss doesn't know about them, and I need to close the deal which is only around eight hours away in my time.' Richard knew that the Wizard King was well aware of who Miranda was, and that she controlled the briefcase.

Jackobie was reconfirmed as Battlemaster. He installed Gordon as Logistics Commander now that Roger was gone. There was a new appointment of Mustering Commander. Unexpectedly Benny had sought out the King for the role. If this battle failed, so would he. He knew the enemy would simply take his bridge by starving him out. 'There's simply no honour anymore.' He'd say to any who would listen. Benny would arrange a very smooth and rapid muster, or else. The King said there might be a horse or two to turn to jerky. Though Benny had had to build a whole jerky storeroom as it is.

He named Jacinta as his Regent, in addition to being the Commander of the Army. He announced it without consulting her. After some digestion, it was well received. She asked for a meeting, but he put her off for a while to give her time to ruminate. When she eventually got to see him, she launched into a list of her deficiencies.

'I'm not …qualified. I don't know the first thing about how to do such a task and I know too little about all the other Peoples to… interact with them and…represent them.'

Richard liked her. As did most people once they got to know her. She was pragmatic, but personable. In addition to being incredibly large and powerful even though she was some distance from middle age. 'See it as career development opportunity. I think it's best to give an important job to someone who doesn't want to do it.' He paused and smiled. 'I came here only a few months ago Jacinta and knew none of these Peoples. And where I come from, I'm the opposite of a King. I'm no one special at all. So don't worry about your qualifications. I've appointed you for your character. Remember that if you think you need guidance, you either already have what you need but haven't allowed yourself to follow your intuition, or you'll go and get it. I am going to take some chances soon that mean you may be in my chair. For a time, or.' He smiled. 'Permanently. Don't let Tina wear you down with offers of marriage so she can be a Regentess or whatever she decides it would be. Unless you want to.'

'I think my husband would object.'

'There are towns springing up all around the castle of Tær.' The Wizard King still couldn't understand Richard's edict that no one could enter or use the castle. He was frustrated. 'Hundreds. Thousands. Preparing for the battle and you sit idle. Working on strategies, useless if we are swamped with flesh willing to throw itself away for so little, but by sheer weight of numbers tires our soldiers in killing them. Send a hundred men. Burn those towns to the ground. And burn any more that spring up.'

'There are children, babies in those towns. Would you have me burn them alive.' Seren had always been deeply respectful of her new master. But never cowed.

His answer came in a voice that was incredulous. 'Of course you will. Do you think I care what happens to these cast-off beasts of burden? The point of this battle, and the cleansing that follows, is to rid this world of them now that their usefulness has come to an end. If we burn some of these vermin's brats before the battle, it's an advance on the schedule to what will happen after. These creatures are stale old tropes. I am going to conceive new Peoples. After centuries of observation I can conceive an array of new Peoples that will evolve and then in a century perhaps, come again to this field and battle. And again, they may deliver surprises, to which I'm not averse, provided my forces prevail in the end. And note this, you're not to spare any in reserve, all should take to the field. Now use the Door, which is your only notable success to date, and destroy those towns. And do it quickly.'

She was turning away when he said. 'I assume we'll have men, dwarves, elves and those obnoxious little shits such that our forces outnumber them two to one.'

Seren didn't want to say what she thought. Which was that they would be outnumbered five to one. 'The men brought from the South skulk home once a back is turned rather than train. Few of the people who took the Oath will break it. Those that would are not great in number.'

'Your nearly as stupid and useless as that fucking Shape Shifter. Prove me wrong and go out and *motivate* them to join our Army.

A few hours later the hundred men who had been brought by the door to burn the new towns to the ground were burning under a pile of wood. Later, much to Benny's disgust, the horses of the ten men who had been on horseback had their saddlebags filled with ash and sent home. Everyone was training to expect the arrival of the door with troops at any moment from any direction and communicated this with horns. The towns were swelling, and that meant they could easily have a hundred teenagers, grandmothers or permanently disable soldiers on watch and sound the emergency. The Door driver, with no passenger knowing better, including Seren, landed them in one of the least strategic locations. After setting them down Roger said to Seren, who stood watching and the troops filed in. 'What, don't feel like setting fire to a bunch of babies in person today.' He knew these observations could not be completely shrugged off with the pretence of a steely will.

'There's will mix with all the other… filth.' She said the last word after a pause.

'Leave.' She shouted. 'And have a care Roger. I close the noose on your skulking family.'

Roger went to recover the soldiers, but there were no survivors. A hundred men was not an insignificant number in her army. The attacking party had killed four hundred, but Richard would let the Wizard King's spies find that out later. Castigated mercilessly for the failure of an initiative she never had faith in, she was now visiting every large town of the Peoples with an allegiance to the

Wizard King and taking all the children over the age of five to a huge complex being built at the base of the Anor hill behind the castle. Two adults from each town were permitted to oversee the children's welfare.

She returned to the Wizard King being able to boast many hundreds of motivated soldiers, some the most experienced in the ranks.

That night, she walked up beside the man in an Inn a long way from anywhere who said. 'What's a nice girl like you doing in a place like this.' She had not always grasped Richard's idiom.

'I came here once. Met that Shape Shifter. He lost his job you know. And his life.'

'Shame. I'd developed a bit of fondness for the fellow.' Richard looked across and smiled. 'Where does that leave you when the next defeat comes along.'

'There won't be another.'

'Glad to hear it. I've run out of hands to save you.' He held them both up and moved them around like a Minstrel. Richard was slurring his words only slightly. Her spies advised her that he'd been sitting drinking alone for two hours. They didn't know the drinks were Tina specials.

'How did you know I'd come here to find you.'

Richard shrugged. 'Because you're smart. Like your father Luke.'

She shook her here. 'What did you think was going to happen when I got here Richard.'

'I want to work out a deal with your Master.' He knew the more he used the word Master the more annoyed she'd become. 'And you're the *messenger*. And if you'd thought about it at all Seren, capturing the King before the chess game starts isn't what he's made all these elaborate plans for. Even if only to squeeze me for information for a while. It would make your *Master* look weak and on the back foot before the battle even starts.' He said this in a patronising way.

She appeared unruffled. 'I thought I might learn a little from you and then throw you back into the sewerage pit of what has now become a desperate and failing Alliance. Recruiting grandmothers and children yet to reach their teens.' She realised she had in fact miscalculated. Getting any useful intelligence would only anger the Wizard King. A battle with the enemy strategies stolen from the mind of their King would be akin to shooting an arrow before the Horn. And Richard's army would be enraged and contemptuous of such an act of what they would call weakness and treachery.

'Listen carefully. I've had the Youngers develop new functionalities. Very significant functionalities.' The word was unfamiliar to Seren who had only now regained her focus on what Richard was saying.

'What does that ...'

'You don't need to *know* Seren. You're *only* a messenger so *all* you need to do is listen and remember something. Do you think you can manage that?' It was the first time she'd heard Richard dismissive towards anyone. Let alone her.

'Tell him that we've worked out a lot of upgrades. Including things he could bring in and take out, even living things. We can write a message at Tæranon speed, and it's received in the Outside as a text to any phone number. Do I need to writer down some of these words you know nothing about Seren? And there's *a lot* more. All I want is to be left alone. I'll put up the best defence I can with the Alliance. The *best*. But everyone knows we're going to lose. We achieved a miracle last time through a retreat and pursuit strategy, but our Peoples know they'll be decimated in a head-to-head battle, and I see demoralisation as often as I see hope.'

'Here's some of what you wanted to torture out of me Seren. Our forces are going to collapse. The Youngers, in strict confidence, have modelled what a hundred different battles would look like. You'll achieve a breakthrough in the front rank pushing back into the fourth. We'll try to kill as many as we can inside in the salient that you will be stupid enough to allow to form even if I warn you about it. Then we fall back to the real front, and the entire army will make an orderly retreat and save as many as possible. So that's half of our training. Your pathetic spies have seen it. How to retreat without a rout. Marching back while the forward ranks create the opportunity for people to get back to where they live. They are all standing there because they have a slim hope that the Battlemaster of the murdering prick you now bow down to, might mess things up so badly we could somehow win.'

'Face it Seren. All you've ever won is a retreat, never a battle. All of the Peoples and all but the first ranks will drain off protected by Ogres to their homes. The front ranks have volunteered for certain death.'

'In the towns and villages Seren. That's where the nasty surprises will wait for your thugs. Very *nasty surprises* which you know I'm good at and your platinum crusted brain could never even begin to imagine.' He looked at her. Again dismissive. 'They'll pay dearly to get there. We have dozens of strategies. And these are People are more hardy then any of the dilettantes who fight for you. Under duress now I believe. Sorry to be using words you don't under-stand Seren. I keep forgetting you never got any education. You were this mean brat that crawled out of a mine. Then these People have pulled every last piece of agony out of your scum. All you'll ever do is ride through a field of corpses. Dead women, children, the old, the sick the crippled. The garbage you call an army will never get to inflict the atrocities and outrageous you're so eager to oversee, and probably join in on. And then you can go back to being nothing but a *vassal* to your Uncle Seren. He's your Uncle. Remember that.'

'I don't think anyone could blame me. I've will have done my best. Sort of. I have my own happy ending all figured out. I'd like to settle down in that nice little castle with my good friend Arnall, who has disowned you by the way. I don't like it where I live on the Outside. Over here I'll still be a King, even if a minor one. I've got some ideas to make a nice pile of Ka-Ching and I think I could make some good friends to replace the ones you're going to kill. There'll be lots of humans left. And I still have a kick ass sword, plus yours by the way. Which I plan to sell along with the pathetic daggers you carried around. Being the weapons of a Battlemaster, even an unemployed one, at best, they might be work half a life-time in Ka-Ching for those alone. I figure I'd be able to stay at some nice resorts now and then. We could catch up if you're ever allowed off your leash.'

She was angry. 'Why do you think we could ever be friends when you're selling all the friends you've ever had down the drain with some bullshit strategy you know is feeding on the engrained certainty of these inferior beings. You could at least let these creatures die in dignity with a genuine battle plan and not sell them a pathetic lie. And you mock me. I didn't realise what a pathetic specimen of your *ilk* you are. A Punter. And not a very nice one.' Richard was gratified, that for all the insults he'd heaped upon her, this betrayal of his friends she found the most egregious.

'Fuck you Seren.' Richard had been drinking all the time they were talking and was now quite drunk. 'There's no secrets here. I have told these People. All the Captains. Jacinta. Jackobie. I've told them what I've told you. In their case I've described it as a worst-case contingency. A very last resort. They'll be given the Youngers models before the battle. I like the strategy where your Peoples pay the price, one by one as they attempt to start the rape and murder they really want. Then their victory will turn into a pathetic disgrace. You will win a *pyrrhic* victory. I know many of the word I'm using aren't in your vocabulary though Seren. But you get the *gist* of it. I'm telling you all this and you won't be able to do a damn thing about it.'

'There's a free kick for you Seren. A portion of your Army is going to be surrounded and killed with as much cruelty a fundamentally good People can manage. Because if you try a head-to-head battle expecting a part of the front to breach, you can either come at us without much momentum or you don't know where ours will collapse and sucks in part your army into a ring of Peoples that don't care anymore. Go figure that one out. Not a victory for us but it will hold you up long enough to serve my purposes.'

'Get my message to your *Master* Seren. You're a messenger, that's all. You don't know shit about what he and I will be talking about.'

'But I need the Door to be at my disposal at a *specific time* and place to buy the briefcase outright from the Owner. Ten minutes. During the battle unfortunately. After the battle he can assess the functionalities. All I want is a quiet, anonymous life in Tæranon at the head of the Nadi. Take the message back and don't fuck it up.'

He changed the subject. As one does with too much psychobeer under their belt. 'This place brings back memories, well not actual memories for me but I was told all about it. I was in London with a friend. I was such a proud father when I heard you went around the Tavern knifing the Shape Shifters lackeys. You slit the throats of two fellows there, gutted a fellow there and there. And then there was the knife stuck it the ribcage incident. You must admit that was kind of funny.'

'You heard some stories from that night? I'd forgotten most of the details.'

'You might recall that next to every piece of scum you killed, there was a man beside him. These men had daggers drawn behind their back or in their sleeves in case you didn't figure out the Shape Shifter's ruse or missed one of them.' He pointed to a seat along from the bar. 'And then you told that Shape Shifter what a fool he was. His whole kidnap plan turned to shit. And you never needed the team we put together. And why are you riding a black stallion rather than Brindlefire.'

Seren lost her balance. 'She sickened and died.' Then follow up quickly. 'She was just a nag.'

Even with all he'd heard Richard was surprised at this. 'A nag? You must be almost gone Seren. To say something like that about your best friend. TBA, GroundBreaker, Roger, me. We all loved her. Travelled so far with her. Good times you know. Do you have any of those anymore.'

Suddenly Richard had a knife to his throat. 'How could you know I came here on a black steed.'

'One of our men told me as you arrived.'

A knife now came around Seren's throat and another man grabbed her hand a pulled her knife away from Richard's. 'Let's move away from your dad now young lady.'

'He's not my …' A hand went over her mouth.

'Oh. Thank Christ. It's the only way to make her shut up. She is such a bitch now. And she can't move on from the whole paternity thing. Do you think I'm happy about it? Listen to yourself Seren.' He was swaying slightly.

Ten men, hidden for hours, had come forward the moment she drew a blade and took control of the three men guarding the Battlemaster inside and took them outside. They walked her past a pile as the three joined other the other sixteen guards she he'd brought to keep watch outside the Tavern. All with throats slit. 'We'll tell the Rat People where they are.' Said Richard. Seren realised she was now dealing with someone else. Someone ruthless.

Her hands were bound, and she was put on the horse, ankles tied to the stirrups. Richard stood quietly, saying nothing, as the guards walked through to the Ogre City. Once Roger came out, they shared a big hug of greeting and relief. They went through the door and Seren knew where she was. It was a day's ride to the Castle Anon.

'I want her to get back home quickly. The longer she's there the more damage she does. Motivating an army by kidnapping their children eh? No mercy for her when her troops come home.' Richard paused for a while. 'What's Anon like?'

Roger sighed. 'It's a shithole. And I mean the place is a shithole. Everywhere I went anyway, and I did a bit of ferrying people around. As well as all those spies we dropped off in your neck of the woods.'

'Spies eh. Aren't there slaves there too, you know, they do… stuff.'

'Whatever he wants. A lot of people and all kinds of food and anything anyone could want goes in the back door. But only ash ever comes out. Only the Battlemaster can go in through the front door past these Citadel Guards in silly costumes.'

'And how about my first born. What's it like taking her around a bit on these little jaunts.'

'This is going to hurt Richard, but she's a bit of a disappointment.'

'How so?'

'She's a big snob now that she's Battlemaster. Kind of mean, nasty, and anger; she's angry all the time. And about silly little things usually. And the leather's gone. She wears this tacky armour…' He flicked it with his index finger and made a dull metallic sound 'She commissioned it specially, so it gives her curves she doesn't deserve.' He whispered. 'Maybe the Wizard King doesn't want to look at a Bony Battlemaster.'

'I liked the leather. I mean that's why we even bothered to go over and say hello in the first place. What a big mistake that was. Your such an idiot Roger.'

His friend laughed 'She was different then. Gone now forever from what I can tell. But I reunited you with your daughter don't forget.'

'Of course. And if my daughter wants to wear armour with fake curves, I'm going to support it. A father should support his daughter as she goes through, you know, a phase. It'll be implants next I suppose. Ultimately, as an absent father, it's I who must take the blame for what the poor girl's become.'

Breaking her silence, she said. 'Might want to watch your back Roger. He may not be the nice guy you think he is.'

'Kids these days. Never satisfied. Here we bring her a day's ride from her uncle and she's still moaning.' Said Roger.

Richard became more serious. 'Now listen to me young lady. Don't talk to any strangers and pass on the message will you. Sorry about the slap across the face all this is going to earn you.'

'That's not how the relationship works with me.'

Once she was gone Richard said. 'Let's nip off and get a real beer. Tina's brew made me only appear drunk. I need a real drink.' He didn't like what had happened to Seren's guard. He disliked need to be so relentlessly mean and dismissive to her. But this time it was real.

The slap across the face was hard and the sharpness and accuracy of the blow felt practiced. A back door to the Castle flashed though her mind.

'We move our troops laboriously on foot now. Stores, spies, captives, slaves. While he no doubt wanders the lands laughing at making a fool of my Battlemaster.' Seren was aware that unlike what others might think, the Wizard King appeared to be young. In his late twenties. And she knew he could be incredibly charming, and then straight away arrogant and demeaning. Unlike what Roger and Richard might think, there were quarters with chefs, stewards, and housekeepers, and probably others on the lower two floors of the castle. And all, she assumed, came and went. But she couldn't be sure.

He had made his advances early on with charm, and then power. She coolly told him she was a Battlemaster. And some distance and objectivity would be wise. Sometimes he would disappear into a room none could enter. He might be gone for a day or more. She was told week, maybe a month some times. Seren, like anyone exposed to a 'Let it Roll' Punter, now knew where he was going while most believed he travelled his realm in disguise. None knew that he could freeze time Tæranon, often between the Punters so he could spend time in his very humble flat in London.

'The information you were given concerning our pathetic foe is an insight into his thinking. Be it truth or a lie. Our spies will resolve that. Although you've caused a logistics disaster for us, his recapture of the Door without having to beg for it may have outcomes advantageous to me.' He reached out his hand and took hers and squeezed it. 'That slap was impulsive of me. I'm sorry. Are you hurt?' His voice was becoming seductive. A voice that was accustomed to getting what it wanted.

She drew her hand away. 'I'm fine. Thank you for your concern My Lord.' She had come up with My Lord rather than the odious Master others addressed him by. Her response returned him to petulance.

'His Battlemaster is pouring in soldiers, support, and weapons some it's rumoured will be new to our conception of war. All preparing the army for battle. There must be no more mistakes. None. Or your passing will be very different to the swift demise of your predecessor. Now there is one piece of intelligence I need from our spies, in addition to all the many things they should be providing. We know the King will make a journey during the battle. He'll want to minimise the time away, so he'll depart at an exact time. I need to know what that time is, to the second. They must find that out for me. I want you to arrange to meet him. Tell him his proposition is of considerable interest to me. Her and I will meet once he has secured the briefcase *after* the battle. And that his pathetic small kingdom on the Nadi will be immune to harm. Now go. And return with only good news in the future.'

Soldiers were filling her ranks, but more slowly than the opposition and now they had to walk or ride for days. And many arrived at the front reluctantly. Turned into Oath Breakers by the foulest of means. But a large army would take the field.

And finally, only days before the battle she was able to give the Wizard King what he wanted. A time, to the second, when Richard would disappear into the portal. It was passed on by a sister of a Nargate Goblin who now lived at the Ogre HQ with her husband. She got a job cleaning up in a Youngers workshop. She said they made a device to measure from the second when the Bell tolled. The Goblin, as with the Battlemaster, didn't know what a second was.

She sent an envoy advising she wanted to meet with Richard. He appeared in the Geopor plain at midnight, well inside the enemy territory so Seren had only a little distance to travel. She knew he would send Roger away. Not wanting to share this particular message. 'My Lord is interested in the proposition. He will make a time to meet in the castle at headwaters of Nadi after the battle.' Seren was ready to have to listen to observations about the irony of her being born there, but Richard simply said. 'Good.' He rode a few hundred yards and vanished.

The Wizard King of the Invincible Hand could finally give some qualified praise. 'I see the army growing, and I'm pleased with how they are training and arranged. An improvement on the Shapeshifter so don't take every word of mine as one of discouragement. Go. Prepare for war. Win.'

She couldn't stop Roger's observations floating though her mind. 'What happens to a Battlemaster after the war is won?'

Richard sat around a large table with Jackobie, his Commanders and Captains. In addition to the leaders of the Spider People, Witches, Rat People and Benny.

Richard launched in without preliminaries and introductions. They were grateful for it. Some of the Peoples went overboard with that sort of thing. 'This is the list of both battle priorities and techniques. The overall strategy will be apparent once we've run thorough them. Get ready, it's going to *seem* complicated.'

'One: Any of our People injured or killed will be recovered from the battlefield and passed back to waiting Ogres who will lope them directly to the hospital tents. Everyone is to understand that this policy will lead to more of our Peoples to be killed, by the very act of coming into the battlefield and removing them.' Everyone supported this without question.

'Two: The front rank of soldiers ten deep must never fail. Running troops from the second rank will be available to backfill a space left by a casualty within *a few seconds*. As their comrades step forward to fill the space'

'Three:' Richard motioned the group to watch the Battlemaster. No one had seen that he had a device strapped to his wrist which was a small crossbow. He lifted it and shot twenty darts in quick succession at the wall in front of the group. They penetrated the wood, burying their small, sharp bronze heads. 'These operate by squeezing a trigger to load and fire the dart in one action. There are twenty in a rack and racks can be replaced in fifteen seconds. Our front line will double in density during an initial charge with Dartsmen laying between the legs of the front rank soldiers. They will exhaust their darts, we will have two rack each only, then fall back as the two armies clash.'

'Four. Mid-Range Bowmen will operate paired with a crouching Ogre in random locations in the first two ranks. The Bowmen will be lifted above the army, take aim and shoot. Fifty bowmen will arise from locations difficult to remember. The highest value targets will be selected although this may cost some bowmen their lives.'

'Five Corridors. There will be gaps in our front ranks however this will not be apparent at their charge. Two Goblins holding shields will step sideways into the ranks at a Captain's call leaving an empty corridor. New shields for the front rank are built with a second shield joined at a right angle. This means the shield provides protection at the front and to the side. This maintains the front line of shields and creates corridors at intervals. The enemy will run into a corridor of shields and be pushed in by the weight of their army behind. The Goblins holding the shields will put a sword though a slot and leave it on hooks. Those caught in a corridor will mainly be killed by spiders, waiting in heavily fortified shoulder chambers which they will only come to when it's safe. They will be sending out web through holes. The webs will be cast over the nose and mouth of the enemy. Ogres with very heavy-duty helms will emerge from the end of the corridor and recover our dead or injured. The corridor will close briefly, and swords withdrawn.'

'Six: Iron Clubs.' Richard walked over to an iron club which in his world would be like a stubby, oversized baseball bat. He tried to lift it and could barely get it off the table. 'Jacinta?' The Ogress came over and picked up the solid club and held it with two fingers. Richard smiled. 'Once our injured are recovered the corridors will open briefly. Ogres will be running at full speed by the time they *enter* the corridor. The enemy still alive will probably all be trampled. As the Ogre leaves the corridor, the will begin to swing the club in wide arcs smashing all before them. Three such Ogres will come out of each corridor and will run in an arrow formation. Their objective is to smash their way *right through* the entire army all the way to the rear. The rank and file are not expecting them and so will be unprepared. We want Ogres to gather and grow in number at the rear of the enemy force. We expect heavy losses of these volunteers. The surviving Ogres will form squads which will ensure every enemy deserting or those in retreat are killed.'

Richard continued straight on: 'Seven: Marching Back.' Some of the leadership were getting tired and confused only listening to how the battle was to be conducted. Richard could see this, and he and Jackobie knew it would be a natural reaction to their battle plans. 'I know it's complicated for a battleground. And I'll be going through this several times, however each soldier on the field has only *one* task. Only one. And the People who manage the first two ranks will have had intensive training, locked down in training halls into which only the Battlemaster has access to. Marching back the length of the corridor occurs immediately the Ogres leave and it's closed. Then the first rank marches back the length of the corridor. We will fight on clean turf. The enemy always fighting over their dead upon churned earth.'

'Eight. Long Range Bowmen. These Goblin Bowmen will have taken position early in the morning in cliff areas they will need ropes to access. Their contributions can't occur unless we move our army back in the first manoeuvres. They will shoot at will.'

'Nine: In the case of the enemy retreating in a slow defence, our front ranks will march forward quickly but hold the line. Except half the Ogres will pass through our front rank and smash their way to join those already at the rear. If their retreat becomes a rout, half our army will make a pursuit, calling a target to make the destruction of their army efficient. Not one will remain alive on the field and any attempts at surrender must be ignored. Any that flee will each individually be the quarry of the fastest Lopers and brought down with rocks to the head. There is only one enemy combatant who will not be harmed.'

'If our army is called to retreat the first four ranks will close up and carry out defensive measures only. They will be backfilled immediately and take any losses necessary to allow supporting Peoples, the injured and the main army to reach safety through the Door into which thousands would pass through long before the enemy could reach them.'

Jacinta spoke for all, except Benny and the Rat People represented by Jonathan. 'Though always cast as heartless, soulless even, our natural inclination is not to kill the unarmed, injured, those surrendering or fleeing. I know this has been decided but it's disquieting to many.'

Richard was firm. 'Although I have the title of a King, I would never expect you to do something you don't believe is right. I'm uncomfortable with it, but here are my reasons. If the enemy is forewarned of our policy on this, many will desert before the battle, as I believe is happening right now for this very reason. Hence some of these people have already escaped to safety.

If there are injured on the field, they could still arise and strike at us and we must fight around them. We could bind them with spider's web however our object if our safety and victory not theirs. A swift death where time permits may be the most merciful then what they will return to as deserters. We know some of those fleeing the last battle suffered tortures which left them pleading for death.'

'Nothing and no one will ever enter or leave again. He will grow old in it as his supplies and servants dwindling. To achieve this, we must be sure that there is no force to challenge our garrison and no need for us to rearm and fight such a force. Remember that his army is ready, mostly volunteers, to sweep through every town and village you live in. And yet all we will do is to clear the field of our enemies. We'll hurt only those intent on hurting us or our families. We'll take nothing but the war trophies of enemies.' Richard looked at the head Rat. 'And Jonathan, we're not going to eat the fallen.'

'It was almost a deal breaker for us.' He whispered to Benny. The Rat Leader bemused as to why a dead enemy should not be eaten rather than left to rot. But half the weapons of the fallen would be a massive haul and would decorate every wall the Rat people had. 'We'll have to negotiate with those Ka-Ching hungry Witches for a bulk deal on readings.'

Jacinta broke in on the Rat's aside. 'There are dire risks which justify a harshness we would usually not contemplate. We will do it.'

This assured Richard of his choice of Regent as Jacinta lent her support to the approach.

He now tried to allay their fears about complexity. He went though it three more times until they tired of the explanations and Jacinta had to say. 'We get it Richard.'

Richard wrapped things up. 'Now that you know this, each of you will all be surrounded by five guards at all times, and you will discuss improvements and clarifications only in this room as a group. Our secrets must live to the first minute of battle. Our enemy must come in heedless of darts and all the other defences. And there is one more hope. A tiny hope. If it comes it will come at the end of Jackobie's speech. It will be strange, but you must embrace it quickly.'

This, as so many parts of the briefing, was new and unexpected. They looked to Jackobie for an explanation, but he shrugged in a way that conveyed. 'Not allowed to say and I wish I hadn't been given the job'.

Roger sat opposite Richard. He looked at the King in a way he hoped would be uncompromising. He had overseen logistics for the first war, yet their relationship hadn't changed at all. He only saw less of Richard. Richard appreciated this was the first time Roger was asking for something, ever since he'd consigned Richard to the life of a plastics extruder.

'You must realise you're too important, not only to the Alliance, but all Tæranon. To me. The Portal, and the huge strategic value of the Door. How could you expect me to agree?'

'Richard, I've consigned tens of thousands over the centuries to an unpleasant death. I dealt with representatives for each People who trained them for that purpose. I never really got to know the Peoples. Certainly these. Now I realise what I've been a party to, I'd like to die with them for a change. I have sons and daughters who can run the Portal and the Door as well as I can. It must be in the blood because others can't.'

Richard thought for a time. 'You can be on the first line of the first rank. It assembles nearly *two hours* before the battle. What the first ranks do during that time will be of significant strategic value. It will favour us and cause our enemy to make difficult decisions. You'll suggest to at least the rank and file of our enemy how poorly equipped we are and the lack of depth in the army. The first rank is full of lottery winners there are so many wanting to go to battle. Most entirely unsuitable for it.'

'Everyone had been assigned a rank, towards the back but some have pleaded their case to be at the front. There will be no forces protecting villages and towns this time. We've got every grand-mother and baby we have on this roll of the dice. And we're trying to load it.' Richard smiled. Hoping his uncle would be pleased with his attempt to be a King. 'And we have our man on the Door.'

'Being in the front row will not be a permanent position. Our first two will be exhausted from standing in the sun. If we have to cart some away from heat exhaustion so much the better. These ranks will be completing the first Marching Back manoeuvres which are essential to our plan's success. Twenty minutes from the Horn, the first three ranks will start changing out with fresh troops through the Door. The modern weapons and shields we have, that you don't know about and our very best fighters, hydrated and rested, will come forward and refill while the first two ranks go to recover and then be ready to become the final ranks of the army. Those behind the first two will have been sitting and resting in formation, supplied with food and water until called. Ranks will only stand to fight on a Captains call when five ahead are engaged. The enemy will meet with rested troops in every rank they face.'

On the day Roger was in position, at the front line of a cast of strange characters readying for a huge battle. Looking down the line he saw grandmothers, child Goblins, an aged Rat Person, his coat all grey, a huge Ogre, playing a rock game while he waited with only a childlike grasp of the common tongue. Roger looked to a woman five across with a baby strapped to her back and smiled.

'They're mustering hours in advance of the Horn. Must be quite an army to place into ranks for such an early assembly.' Said a voice from a man looking out the window.

'Let them perish in the sun. They'll be easier to slaughter.' Seren said this with growing confidence, her methods had drawn in a thousand experienced troops in addition to so many others willing or compelled to fight. She had thought of strategies to counter Richard's overconfidence in what he said was an inevitable result of a charge and planned local collapse in his front.

'I want them to see the best of our army. Caparisoned and made of a mix of Peoples who will flood over them with the unique strength each possess.' There was a pregnant pause.

Seren disliked the idea intensely but knew the difference between a suggestion and a command. 'I'll send out our third rank and have the others prepare for an earlier muster but remain resting under cover. Our third rank is as well to look at, and only slightly less deadly than the first.' Whom I'll preserve until half an hour before.' Seren would take only so much interference in her business. She then realised if she sent out only one rank it would look ridiculous. This decision was galling. She would send out her ranks five to ten. It immediately put her specific plans for each rank into disorder which she would need to correct in the field before the Horn. Her opponents were renowned to be poor fighters head on, but they were tough, and standing in the sun would drain them less. The first small ploy of Richard's. She decided to disregard his tone and returned to remonstrate with him on this point and hold muster until her schedule as Battlemaster. She received a clear message. 'Are they moving out. I see nothing.'

She saw a long tapering tube with a glass at its end pointed out of the window the like of which she'd never seen before. He'd shown her once. An excuse to lay a casual hand on her thigh. It brought things far away up close. It was uncanny. She would try again to avoid the deployment of her troops upsetting of her plans. 'These creatures are stupid but tough. This is a ploy of their King. He grasps at his few advantages.'

'Is my army not tough? Get them out there.'

'As you wish.' Her voice became as hard as it ever had. 'A single rank would look ill and achieve the reverse of your aims. I'll send out five.'

'Very Well.' Came the reply. As if the whole endeavour was hers. If she failed, this would be one of the many inadequacies he would point out before punishments was exacted.

She led out the ranks. Very slowly and with the soldiers with a double issue of water. They came to their line, looking across the gap of a four hundred yards at the opposition. The fifth rank of the Wizard King's army was still magnificent to behold. A kaleidoscope of colours in the Knights surcoats, Elven shades of green and brown, Dwarves in coloured clothes and hats and the Little People still in their awful clashing green pants and red tunic. They were her least favourite soldiers and they looked at her with unalloyed disgust.

Looking across she saw the state of the army facing her on the other side. It wasn't the tradition, but it broke no rule for her to cross the line and ride up and down the enemy troops as if on an inspection of her own troops. 'What a rabble. I was Battlemaster when you had to skulk away to win a battle and I know you can do better than this line up of pathetic losers. Another doomed ploy of a King bereft of a real army. You think our troops will feel compassion for you?' She laughed. 'Don't expect any.'

'Hello Seren.' She turned the horse quickly at the familiar voice.

'And what are you doing here. I thought the King would at least value what you can do, and probably only that.'

Roger said. 'Our King values everyone. As you can't deny that from *our* last victory. No Seren. The King came under immense pressure from ordinary people. People who are tired or your Master and the mouthpieces he talks though, one of which you've become. There was a lottery for the first rank. See that beautiful woman five spaces along. That's my wife of nearly three centuries.'

'March Back.' A call came.

The first two ranks turned and walked back two hundred yards into the empty space in front of the third rank and turned forward.

Seren breathed out what sounded like a low growl and said. 'Richard.' Under her breath. Her force would have to run further. It would be more difficult to keep the mix of Elves and Knights on horseback and Dwarf, the men, and Little People in the line they'd trained for. The Enemy would have more time standing unmolested to shoot with the longer distance bowmen her spies advised her of. Making her concentrated flights of Elven arrows, which her Lord insisted on despite her resistance, pointless as they would fall short. Her forces would now have to shoot on the run during a charge. Which they could gain no more momentum from than that achieved in the traditional gap. What plagued her most was the pathetic endurance of the Dwarves and Little People. The Dwarves regale the disinterested listener with stories of their incredible walking prowess. But those little legs mean they can't run for shit, she thought.

Returning to her line, reluctantly Seren called 'Slow March.' There was a ripple of unease that this would break the few rules of battle, no attack before the Horn. 'Swords sheathed, weapons down.' She sent a messenger to ride to the Castle. Before the messenger left one arrived. 'Muster the Army.' She advised him of her advance. And rode up and down the line to make sure there was not one move of aggression. One stupid knight however, lowered his jousting stick so far it caught in the turf and lifted him from his saddle to a mess of armour on the grass. Seren had no idea a Knight had brought a jousting stick. Surely even they weren't so stupid. In the enemy rank it had been noticed. Now it was the subject of hilarity rippling down her opponents ranks as the story was told, and no doubt embellished. A ten-year-old Goblin boy chased the discomfited Knight's horse, running terrified in the dead ground. He caught it, quietened it down, and brought it to the Page Boy of the Knight, who expressed his thanks. Seren could only look on darkly at the embarrassment. The comedy had stopped the Slow March forward which, after a short time, was resumed until she reformed at the approximate traditional distance between the armies.

She rode across and said to Roger. 'The ground falls even more steeply behind you now. To our advantage. But it will also allow you to see a real army marching out to crush you from higher ground.'

Roger laughed. 'If you want to see a real army, see if you can get your pathetic show pony to walk up that cutting.' He pointed to a road leading to one of the many quarries where small lodes of obsidian had long since been mined out.

'March Back.' The booming voice of an Ogre came again.

Roger turned with the first two ranks and began to walk two hundred yards, then turned to face the enemy.

Seren was furious as she saw her large army walking out to muster. Now there would be an awkward maneuverer to reorder the ranks. Curiosity got the better of her and she walked her horse, which she hadn't bothered to name, along the narrow cutting a third of the way up the escarpment to the old quarry. She gasped. The massive valley was starting to fill all the way up to the castle, and more were coming. There were sheds and tents everywhere all around the castle and even among the ranks. Centres for provisioning for the soldiers. There was a large space behind the first two ranks. They would continue to fall back.

She came down and a small group walked forward to the middle of the dead ground. She knew most of them. They all wore armour, except for Jonathon. Benny was even there in light armour. The armour of Jacinta was purely ceremonial. No Ogre needed it except for a helm. Her armour was beautiful, with exquisite patterns and she, for all her pragmatism, found it hard to hide the pleasure it gave her. Many wore surcoats with what Seren assumed to be probably the newly designed the coat of arms for those People.

'Change out First Rank' called Jacinta. Her voice booming. They had decided to demonstrate the new front ranks since the Wizard King had mustered early. Seren saw a movement of people, starting from the first row as they turned to jog down a narrow corridor which appeared in the ranks. A much denser formation of Goblins took the field. Soldiers carrying strange shields ran forward. They came out of the door operated by Roger's fifty-year-old daughter behind the fourth second rank. The door would deliver fresh troops to the backfill ranks as forward ranks depleted. Seren studied the unusual shields. It was a shield that had two sides on a right angle. Within a few minutes the entire front line had disappeared.

The shields concealed the bearer head to toe, even an ogre crouching low was hidden.

She spoke to those who had not long before been friends. 'Our forces are about to crush you. If I had friendship remaining, which I do not, I would plead with you to retreat from the most powerful army in the history of Tæranon.' Though Seren's voice had to give grudging respect for what she'd seen. And the realisation she'd been completely deceived by Richard. And she could not deny it had had the effect of making her overconfident in her preparations. Even if only slightly.

'We don't need to boast Seren as you must have to be compelled to do, as it's not in your nature.' Said Jacinta. 'Could you please pace your horse to the left.'

'You command me Jacinta?'

Jacinta repeated pleasantly. 'Please move to the left Seren. Just a little.'

A deluge of Fat Slag shit fell on the imperious Battlemaster. It was foul and slightly acidic. The chuckling sound of a Fat Slag, very high up, was heard retreating into the distance. Seren was squeezing and scaping the revolting liquid off her face and armour. Starting with her eyes.

Tina materialised. 'Not an act of war, rather a ghastly mistake. I left my broom at home you see, and I ordered a lift on that fucking money gouging excuse for a bird to go and get it. When it saw a battle was about to start, it scared the shit out if it.' She dematerialised, the briefly rematerialized. 'We've set up a new program

227

Seren. 'Witch for An Afternoon'. Only Battlemasters need apply.'
She dematerialised.

Seren was gagging. 'By pure co-incidence we brought you several
damp towels.' Said Jacinta 'Would you like a bit of help to get it
off.' The towels were laid across her horse's neck.

'Fuck your towels.' she pushed them off. 'If you want to hear laughter you wait until I'm laughing while you're slow roasted.'

Back at her line and unable to avoid the stench and humiliation, a
Page Boy came and retrieved the towels to clean her armour and
sooth her burning skin.

Jacinta called, in an unbelievably loud voice. 'Army! Warn
the enemy.'

What might have been now ten thousand creatures started to shout
and stamp.

No Prisoners

No Survivors

No Mercy

We Fight to the Last

This call continued like a rolling thunder as people found their
voices. The words may have reached the Black Castle. Every one
of the People in Seren's army knew from the tenor of the voices,
this was no ruse to weaken their morale. This was the reality of the

battle looming, and of what they had hitherto thought to be merciful King.

Those with the Ogre Commander retired and it was only Jacinta left facing forward. Seren had seen out to the corner of her recovering eye, the long bowmen high up among the rocks of the escarpment. Impossible to get to from above or below. They must have been lowered on ropes. From that range they would be able to strike her charging front line as they crashed into the shield wall the enemy had erected. An enemy that had always charged in every battle they had ever fought except the last.

Jacinta called across to her. 'We know you're still in there Seren.' Then she turned and called. 'March Back!' The wall maintained a perfect line and the shields all lightly swept the turf as they walked back. There was no gap between ranks on this final march. If Seren marched forward the long bowmen would be aiming at a perfect angle into her front ranks immediately the Horn sounded. She knew they would not march back further. They were at the location perfect for their front line and eventually would fill the entire capacity of the valley. She knew there would be more waiting to come through the Door. Her Army began to muster behind her.

Her troops in ranks five to ten had been in formation for over an hour. She called to reorder the ranks. Her Army was tightly packed between the escarpment and the river at the narrowest point in the battlefield. What was supposed to be nn intentional disadvantage to the Alliance People. Two third of the width of where the armies usually met. Seren's reordering process was not edifying to watch as they had never planned or trained to reorder once mustered. The Knights continually made an awful mess of the process. The

Wizard King wanted to spread the different Peoples of his army across the front ranks. She wished she listened to her instincts and put all the Knights at the back. In the tight space she now had to create and extra rank.

Suddenly there was a loud noise coming from above both armies. It came from a small rock promontory on the top of the escarpment and originated from Jackobie standing there. His voice was amplified to the extent that those in the final ranks in both Armies could hear it. 'Can everybody hear me?' Yet another innovation brought from where Richard lived and improved on by the Youngers were speakers all along the escarpment.

'War.' Said Jackobie clearly. 'What is it good for? Absolutely nothing.' He didn't know why Richard insisted on this being the first line, because all he got to help prepare the rest of his talk were some notes. So Jackobie said what he wanted to say. 'Are we here because we despise our families? We wish to deny our husbands or wives our love and affection. Our sons and daughters. Still babies for some of us. Do we value being here more than contributing to the needs of our loved ones. Our pride and concern for our next generation. Our co-operation and contribution which is our due to our communities. Do we care so little for them that we would come here. Risking our lives, but their lives also.'

'Or are we here because we covet what our enemies have. We want to steal their lands, their water, what they own. Their money. Take them as slaves. A chattel. To be bought sold or killed at will. To make whole towns and villages to do our bidding.'

'Or are we here for the love of killing. The Glory. To sweep through and slay enemies. Burning their homes.'

Down on the field Benny leaned across to Jonathan. 'Is there something wrong with that?'

'Not sure that I like where this is going.' Replied Jonathan.

They picked up on what Jackobie was saying. 'Do we really believe our enemies are only worthless things. Conceived only to crush them beneath our feet and hooves. Peruse them to their pathetic homes and kill women, children, the old ones.'

'Or are we all here at the behest of a Power. A Power that knows how to divide. To sow hate. Stimulate the desire to take arms. Teach us that our enemies are worthless vermin. Worthy only of death. Can it ever be changed?' Jackobie was running out of things to say. Richard said he'd be there by now.

Richard had been working frantically with the Youngers in the secret production rooms for sixteen hours a day, two days prior to the battle. He had come out only occasionally to work with the leaders of the Peoples. They had added innovations that to the battle plan. An Ogre would be beside each of the Goblins in the first line, leaning together to take the fists impact of the charge. And they would also slide out a fifteen-foot pike between each of the shields in the wall a moment before the enemy charge hit their line. Richard responded that these were excellent ideas. Then said. 'I hope we won't need them.' And disappeared into the production rooms. It was rumoured he had been essential to the project, partly because a plastics extruder was required. His Captains wondered what could be achieved in battle through the pursuit of his trade. But no one could think of a time he had worried about anything but them.

He was now considerably behind schedule. They had not made as many as they would like so they would have to give most of them to the enemy, while it would need to look like they were distributing throughout his army also. They were to be loaded into sacks for the Lopers. They were fragile and he belatedly realised they would have to layer them in wadding. Loading would take hours and they didn't have that much time.

Richard had heard stories from Roger about the difficulty he had working with Magic Unicorns. He decided he would take any help he could get and thought it was worth a try. After all. They were magic. 'I wish there a was a bunch of magical unicorns here to help us.' A hooved fetlock came around his shoulder and a beautiful, horned equine face looked at him.

'Sooo what's the job here compadre? Me and my pals have other things we'd like to be doing. Y'know?

'You really came?' Was all Richard could manage.

The horse face conveyed the impression he was talking to an idiot. 'Hey Larry. This guy doesn't understand the 'Magic' part of Magic Unicorns.'

'What a chump.' Came the answer for another Unicorn.

'You called us in. Now what's the deal. I have, what I hope, will be a hot date. But here I am wasting my time.'

'How did you get here so fast.'

'We heard what you said a week ago. A Punter has to *very* specifically say they wish a magical unicorn would turn up. Hardly ever happens. So not to put too fine a point on it mister; what the fuck do you want. We're magical, but we're not very nice. If that prick who built this place hadn't smeared a layer of nice over us, we'd be evil Unicorns. But we can't live according to our true nature.'

There were many comments. Mainly along the lines of. 'Hey Boss, you were really scaping that veneer away there.'

Richard still saw the job as hopeless 'We need to get those things packed safety and take them to the space between two large armies. We've made about a thousand of them. We've only loaded one tenth.

The piles disappeared into the saddle bags that materialised on the Unicorns. Richard was about to say something when the lead Unicorn said. 'Magic remember? Now tell us where to go and we're out of here.'

'Sure.' Said Richard. 'I also thought something would be nice for when you arrive.' Richard was catching up with their temperament, but also saw an opportunity for their arrival to lighten things up.

There was equine shock. 'No. No way. That doesn't come in the terms of the *Wish you were Here*' deal.' Yet it happened because Richard could adjust the settings. They hated him for it.

While Jackobie was finishing his speech Richard appeared with Unicorns sporting rainbow coats. He thought they would fly from the Ogre Town however they instantly appeared above the battle-field and strode though the air to the ground.

'And don't worry, we're not going to let you foul up the distribution of whatever the hell these things are.' Immediately the white plastic and glass objects were in the hands of the Wizard King's army and one between four in the front ranks in Richards army. Richard thought the Unicorns would leave, being so perennially irritable. But the situation had piqued their interest.

'Okay everybody. It's me again.' His speech had ended shortly before and so he started on a fresh subject. His voice was clear, not shouting, it was a conversional tone, everywhere. 'I'll work you through the...ah...functionalities of this...device.' Most people had no ideas what those words meant, including Jackobie, but they generally knew what he was talking about. 'If you press that round button at the bottom, the glass window thing will light up and you'll see a list of things called a menu in the Common Language. If you tap the top one...' People were tapping and immediately and there were expressions of wonder throughout the field. There were rapid movements of the tablets to show others.

'Like a mirror isn't it. But if your press that button, you'll hear a sound, and it will take a picture. That means it saves that exact place that the mirror was showing you, and you can go back to it any time you want. You can hold the thing away as far as you can reach and take a picture with your friends and family or get some-one else to take it.'

One of the tablets had materialised in Seren hands. She had been shouting for the devices to be cast down and stamped on. About ten People nearby in the army followed her instructions. She cast her's away. It was caught by a nimble Little Person before it hit the ground.

'But here's the interesting part, if you tap on GO BACK, which is always there, then tap on the next thing on the list. It's going to ask you to write or say your name and the Town you come from. But all this information is kept, you know, really private. Then you can tap in or say someone else's name. The first message to them is always 'Hello' and press Send. If you're, like, popular, you might get lots of Hellos. I only got one from my mother.' Jackobie was offering up some light-hearted banter, even though it was true. There were thousands of 'dings' and his voice was swamped with the kinds Ohs and Ahs such as those universal at fireworks displays. Some didn't need to wait to be told how to attach a picture and send it to a growing list of 'friends'. There were messages flying back and forward with groups of different friends in dignified pictures, or sometimes silly poses with different friends or with their horse.

'Now as a …product launch initiative…' Richard loved writing this stuff for Jackobie. 'If anyone connects with a real fiend across the line, you each get a twentieth of a Ka-Ching. And that's a real physical Ka Ching, not the ones in the games on the tablet I'll show you in a minute.' Richard had taken out a line of credit with the Witches. Not hundreds but certainly a surprising number of voices were calling out the various equivalents of. 'Yeah. *Unpronounceable name*, it's me. It's me. I'm back in the fourth rank. I've climbed up on a friend's shoulders and I'm waving a red handkerchief. A twentieth of a Ka Ching. Not to be sneezed at.' There were many clandestine friendships formed between Peoples, often due to trade of items only available from specialists among those People. The Little People had no such friendships to show for, which they experienced a strange embarrassment about.

Not much more instruction was required, though there were three more functionalities, including a range of games where the pretend Ka Ching could be won, for every Wizard King vanquished. But Jackobie had to finish on his favourite. 'Now those that want to know more, there's a tab on the menu saying 'Share Video' this is where you put a video, which is a moving picture you can take, up in a place where anybody can watch it. As an example, Richard, I mean the King, brought all these moving pictures of a creature called a cat from, I guess where the Punters live. We don't get them here, but they're doing all kinds of crazy things. Even the little tiny 'kittens'. But you could put anything you want up there. Your child's first steps. Things like that.'

Soon the valley was filled with laughter and 'Isn't that so cute.' And people were using the Share link to send a specific video to friends. Richard was now fifty Ka Ching out of pocket. If it kept going at this pace he was going to have to make Tina his Queen and get his extrusion products cranking after the battle. He would start off with Queen for a Weekend. His mind was wandering to the idea of having this as a permanent initiative. But how would Natasha respond?

Jackobie's voice on the loudspeaker cut through his musings. 'And you know what the most important thing in our lives is. It's not war. It's not cat videos. It's...' The timing was critical. Roger was ready with the Door open when Jackobie said a particular word which had been calculated to the second.

Jackobie called out, causing some distortion. 'It's CHILDREN.' He obliterated the Horn to join battle. Then children came pouring though the widened archway of the Door. Hundreds of them. All those held hostage by Seren. But more. Children from every People who chose to join in. Next came Oath Keepers, unarmed who'd pleaded to go in, to convince those who broke their Oath not to fight. They could tell their friends they would be pardoned because they'd been compelled. The space between the armies was soon full of them, but the children were encouraged to run down the ranks, calling to a father or a mother, or a brother. They might be directed down or to the left or right by a friend. Soldiers were sharing the tablets with children who soon took control of them.

A lone rider, on a painted horse, unarmed but for a sword not drawn since his demonstration to the Nargate Garrison Commander, began to ride slowly into the centre of the enemy line. People made way, many knowing who he was. His clothes were that of a lowly craftsman. Seren was pinned against the escarpment screaming at her army to drop the devices and join battle. She was ignored.

Only part way into the ranks Richard recognised someone he'd seen on his first day in Tæranon. It was the Page Boy of the Knight they'd met who'd gone in the wrong direction. The Knight had a broken Jousting stick and armour which was no longer burnished on patches. Richard said. 'Hi.' In his usual way. The Knight pulled up his visor and Richard continued. 'Hope you're okay.' The Knight nodded.

In an unexpectedly clear and loud voice the Knight called out. 'Make Way. Make Way for the King!'

All the People on the field made way creating a wedge as Richard walked through. Some were suspicious or confused. But most said something like. 'Hail the King.' or 'Thank you for returning our children.' Most said nothing. Looking at inevitability and wondering where this would leave them. There were also small groups of men far to the left and right, each similarly dressed in what Richard thought were somewhat ostentatious costumes. Verging on silly. They were moving through the crowd and keeping pace with him. He thought he recognised some of them, but he couldn't remember where.

Things had gone more quickly than expected. But Roger knew the Door must be ready for him at the exact second he needed to leave. He believed the Wizard King would want to steal the Briefcase more than ever now and lock Richard out and Tæranon down. Brian Cummins would give himself some time to lick his wounds and start again. Richard would be gone from the scene forever. As would everyone close to him. Or he may even have a reset button. A recent anxiety only Richard had contemplated.

He saw a figure on a black horse shouting. 'Are none of you soldier enough to strike down our enemy.' Eventually she rode up beside him.

'Looks like that's your job Seren.' He said. 'How will you dispatch me, the gauche sword you have now, or those rather tacky obsidian daggers? No comparison to what you carried as a free woman. But I can see you're a little anxious. I know why. A lot of these People feel the same way. *There goes the Old Boss. And here comes the New Boss. Same as the Old Boss. So don't be fooled again.'*

'You speak in riddles.' However by her words and gestures she conveyed the fact that she would never be able to kill him. 'Finish this phase of the war on the steps of the Citadel and give your pathetic speech of victory. The battle will run again and again until the forces designed by fate prevail.'

He smiled. 'And there is the core of the lie you believe. As you know, the Wizard King is a Punter the same as I am. Yes, he has some attributes which appear to be magic. He appears to be powerful. But it's all trickery.' Richard laughed. 'I met him Seren. I was in the toilet, and he offered me a cup of tea.' Richard had to reflect on how boring things were where he came from. 'If you met him on a London street you would pass him by and see nothing unusual. An ordinary man among thousands. And an old one. And think about this Seren, he's sitting in his house in a big city Outside of Tæranon where Punters come from. On the toilet. That right. He's sitting on the toilet. I am also by the way. I mean what kind of dignified Wizard King is doing that day in and day out. All this Wizardry is bullshit Seren.'

This was certainly all scratching on Seren's mind. It made her angry at herself for listening to heresy. 'If you want to see real Power, try to pass the Citadel Guard. Anyone other than the Battlemaster will turn to ash. Only all the Guard Challengers descendants, deliberately spread by the Wizard King to the four winds, can ever breach the Citadel. A hundred years is nothing to him Richard. He'll be patient, no matter what you think victory looks like.'

Richard reached the steps and left TBA to an Elf who introduced himself only as an Oath Keeper. Richard saw Benny and was briefly concerned as to how he was going to generate some major compensation to the Trolls and the Rat People for the training they did and the inconvenience of showing up. And the expectations he'd allowed them to develop. He had a few ideas. He reached the wide platform between most of the steps to the Citadel, with only a few left to climb.

Seren turned to Richard to further reinforce the futility of any kind of interaction with her Lord. Richard took the opportunity to say 'Lord' was a much better choice of words. A Younger appear from the door and said 'Soon'. A string of people entered the Citadel. Seren looked at them and knew who they were. Richard now also knew. They were the men in slightly silly costumes that had been shadowing him since leaving the middle of the field. She drew her sword and was turning to run after them when daggers plunged into her from every direction. Representatives of the Dwarves, the Elves, and the men from the South each landed a vicious dagger blow. And the last, the Head of the Little People reached up and slit her throat. 'You would take our children hostage and force us to break an Oath. Take what's owed.'

Richard caught her, bleeding from the wounds, in his arms. The murderers melted away. Seren's eyes were closed. Roger appeared from the door. 'You have an appoint to keep in...' Roger was at his side.

'I'd still rather have her around as that insufferable bitch then not around at all.' Richard said to him. He didn't care about the briefcase now.

240

There was a sound beside him, but more a vibration as the entire staircase caught a huge weight. and he looked up. 'Hi Richard.' It was Andy.

'Oh. Hello Andy.' Richard didn't know how to react with Seren dead in arms. 'Didn't expect to see you here.'

'It's that magic thing you don't seem to be able to grasp Richard. Heard about this a little while back. Anyway, we decided not to be so aloof anymore. We've had enough of this asshole, so we thought we'd help. Bugger the rules. And, as you know Richard, you've changed our lives in good ways. And me in particular. I'm in demand as a home renovations guy and I have a beautiful beer garden.'

'That's nice Andy.' He said. The he wanted to say. '*Is this the best time for this conversation.*'

'You know about Dragon's breath Richard. I can use it only one time. I've been saving mine these centuries gone in case one of my own kind might need it. But you've been a real friend Richard.'

'You can bring her back to life?' Said Richard to the Dragon. 'It's stretching the credulity a bit.'

Andy needed to get this done. 'You know this doesn't work when she goes all stiff and starts to smell. Out in the hot sun here.' They nodded. He leaned in close to her and said. 'Dragon breath. Nothing purer in all the land.' He breathed softly on her face.

Seren coughed. They were all unsure which Seren they would get back. 'Oh Fuck. My God. Did someone fart in my face?' After more coughing she looked around and said. 'Again?' She said at Andy. 'Sorry about that Andy. And thank you. Thank you. I know you only have only one of those to hand out.'

She immediately turned to Richard. 'Did you bring one of my old daggers because you're hopelessly nostalgic.'

'I saw it more as hopefulness, which you'll notice has been proven correct.'

'Give it to me. There's not much time.' She took it and ran up the last flight of stairs.

A Younger was at Richard's shoulder tapping insistently. In thirty-three of those 'seconds' you have to leave to do what you wanted to do.'

Richard ran to the Door, with a thank you to Andy as he passed by. The door was set to the portal. He was through five seconds ahead of schedule.

Meanwhile Jackobie's voice was heard, amplified again. 'Hi everybody. I have a message for all of you. The bad Battlemaster has come back to life and she's back to how she was. Not evil anymore. So please don't kill her, you know, *again*. She's one of the good People now. And guess what? We all are.'

Seren had arrived where the Citadel Guardians stood in a half circle, a man's width between their shoulders around a pair of ornate doors in the same shape behind them. The Wizard King, to his credit, had always left a path for his own defeat, however difficult and unlikely. It was part of the great narrative he'd conceived. And it could always be reversed.

Travelling with Richard and Roger had given Seren the opportunity to complete the puzzle she had been brooding over for years. She had been creating connections that made the people she met ask questions of their Elders. Their Elders knew the secret and had the costumes hidden in fear of immediate execution if they were found. And with the loss of only one costume, and the one with the bloodline to wear it, would come the loss of the only real opportunity to permanently defeat the Wizard King. Or so they were led to believe.

For the first time ever ten men stood facing the Citadel Guardsmen. Others had tried. They were ash before passing the Guard. When Seren, not yet renounced by the Wizard King as Battlemaster arrived, the ten passed through unharmed. Each carried a dagger. Their quarry was already walking towards the door none one entered. The battle should have been joined at the signal Horn half an hour ago. He had decided Richard's need to be in London to purchase the briefcase was the best opportunity to take it from him. He had planned arrive ahead of him, to ensure all was in place. He'd been watching events on the battlefield and to control the second briefcase now became imperative. He had planned that his brief absence early on would not be missed because his Battlemaster controlled the battle which he expected to last hours and he could replay it at any time he wanted.

But there was an unimaginably strange turn of events on the battlefield. His Battlemaster killed. The Citadel Challengers pointlessly assembling now that she was dead. His guards would give them no access. It had all been fascinating. He respected the resurrection of the Challengers and the turn of fortune for his enemies. But his briefcase had the ultimate response. Unlike Richard's briefcase his had a red button under a Perspex cover one had to slide and then lift on a hinge. It said RESET. He would miss all the nuance of such an evolved world. But a new world contained so many possibilities. He was also disappointed to lose the Upgrades Richard had developed, but now he knew all he had to do was to cultivate the Youngers to develop them again. He arrived at his portal satisfied with the outcomes.

Seren now knew there was a portal inside and ran to the Wizard King, or more accurately, Brian Cummins. He turned around to see Seren, who was supposed to be either dead or working for him, arrive at the Door's threshold and drive her dagger between his ribs. Then Ten Citadel Challenges landed dagger blows all over his body. The impossible combination he had put in place to make his story interesting. He slid backwards and through the door with the momentum from so many dagger blows. He vanished.

They came out to find ash where the Guardsmen had been.

All the Peoples on the field and beyond felt a subtle ripple pass through them. It made them feel no one would ever control their freewill again. It felt good.

Seren came out with a group of ten men. Now Roger remembered who they were. The Lifeguard, and the Armoury Manager, the Gardener. Seren felt relieved of years of the need to search Tæranon to fulfil a shrouded mission. 'I didn't understand what I was doing during all that broodiness and confusion about my mystical undertaking, but this was why.'

'You perceived these men as those fated to take on the Guardsmen.' Roger said.

'Yeah.' She shrugged. 'With some trial and error.'

Jacinta had been primed to the fact that she would need to say some words from the steps as Richard's Regent. A title she was unsure of. Very briefly she said. 'Our King could say many lofty and righteous things, but he told me that you're all intelligent People, ultimately with good in your hearts. There are two words most of us have craved and they are all we really need to hear.' She paused. 'It's over.'

A cheer rose. She thought it would be brief. But then it grew and grew until it was a mighty roar. As she had found many times before, Richard had shown more faith in people than they had in themselves.

She was now all business. 'The Door will be returning all People with their horses to their Towns and Villages. The Little People won a lottery to go first. If you could form groups based on where you live everyone can be home before nightfall. If People miss their home trip, we'll do a run at the end for anyone left behind. We've asked stores to be brought from both ends to bring up food and drink to circulate throughout while you wait. Feel free to try another cultures food.' The amazing voice amplifier went quiet.

Richard came to himself in the toilet. A sensation he was getting more and more accustomed to as time went by. Out of the Laundry door he saw it was late at night, Natasha having left only the dim light of the oven rangehood on. He was quietly creeping out to the cab Terry had arranged. He'd texted his uncle using the new TærTalker invented by the Youngers.

'Leaving me so soon. I was looking forward to the next instalment.' Richard gave a start. She was in her wheelchair sitting back from the kitchen table, knitting. 'Knitting used to seem boring but between and this and writing the hours get soaked up.'

'Hi.' He walked over and gave her a hello kiss on the cheek. His first ever. 'I've got to see a man about a briefcase. I'll be back here as soon as I can.'

'You're welcome any time.' There was a beeping on the street. As he left the room she said. 'Who won the war?'

He looked back at her with a boyish pleasure. 'Everyone.'

Meanwhile, two men were waiting near the front of Richard's flat for a meeting that never started.

Brian Cummings had arrived back in a room which had a toilet, but his was inclusive of a routinely scheduled bidet function, automatic flush mechanism and a padded seat. It was a pleasant place to return to, not like the rest of his accommodations. He was a Wizard King in Tæranon living on the aged pension in a rented flat in London. Hence his toilet was his only indulgence. His spies had told him the timing of Richard's trip, and he'd made sure he arrived in advance of the meeting by an hour. He'd paid the kind of people who take care of such things to take possession of the briefcase as soon as the boss of the publishing house had left Richard's flat. After waiting for a while, giving Richard the chance to return to Tæranon and participate in the celebrations, visitors of the unpleasant kind would let themselves in. The flat would be thoroughly burgled and trashed. For a Punter, if the neural cap was removed, after the usual length of time for a visit, the bells would start sounding in their head and send them insane. He could never return to the Outside as he had no portal. He'd be trapped in his mind with the bells and with People who knew nothing about him after the Reset which was about to happen. If the men found he hadn't yet returned to Tæranon, they would help him on his way.

Arriving back Cummins was feeling strange. He knew his world would be falling to pieces now that the Citadel was breached. He also knew he'd been very badly injured before he left, but he was confident this didn't return with him to the Outside. He had trouble concentrating to slide down the Perspex cover so it could be then lifted on the hinges. He'd never pressed RESET and had made sure he didn't do so by accident. That was as far as he got before he slumped dead over the briefcase.

Richard, like Cummins, arrived an hour ahead of the time he fed to The Wizard King's spies. He was relieved to see Terry was already waiting outside Cummins flat. 'It's nice that it's you needing some help from your old Uncle for a change. What's the job.'

'There's a chap going to come out of that flat soon and get into a cab. Unfortunately, he's tremendously cruel to his cat. We need to... save the cat. We might need to open the door somehow and find him. There's a chance though it may not be there. But there may be something in there that I should really take and get repaired.'

'Crystal clear. We wait for this cove to scarper. Save a cat, or not. Get the dodgy equipment and scarper ourselves.' Richard loved being with Terry. 'I've had to save a few horses recently. Needed to save them from running so fast. Horses can get hurt if they run too fast. They can get depressed if they run too slow, so I can help with that too. I'm kind-hearted at…heart. You've been hard to get hold of Richard. We needed a trusty lad who can drive fast if the need arises.'

'I've been busy.'

His assumption was that Cummins would leave home to be at Richard's flat for the meeting and break in as soon as he thought Richard had departed to Tæranon. But Cummins didn't leave. Richard realised what a fool he'd been. Cummins wasn't going to get his hands dirty when he knew Richard wanted to keep the brief-case. He was the kind of Wizard King who got others to do un-pleasant things for him. And he was old. He would have some hard men going in after Miranda's boss left. Of course her boss would never come. Richard was doing the same thing front of Cummins flat. Waiting for no one. He quickly arrived at a Plan B. He ex-plained his predicament to Terry who was straight on the phone. 'Jobber. A couple of lads waiting in front of a flat…' Richard gave Terry the address '…Find out who they are and sling 'em a few bob to go home eh.'

'Thanks Uncle Terry. Do you think we could go and knock on the door and get Cummins to come with you to inspect it on some...pretext?'

'Right up my alley. I've got him distracted while you get the broken piece of shit you might as well chuck in the bin or have a little tinker with.'

'I guess this time of night it's difficult to come up with...'

'Easy done. What's that mob? Respect the Cruelty of Animals. Or is it Renovate Cruel Animals. Anyway, there have been some complaints. Unhappy cat. I do the night shift for the Cruelty Police. How would my lawyer say it? *'The onus is on him to prove there are no unhappy cats in his abode'.*'

'Sounds perfect. If you could leave the door open and keep him in the kitchen that would allow me to recover the...piece of junk.' Richard was both excited and terrified.

Having knocked on the door several times, Terry said. 'Look at your watch and time me Richard.' He started to look down and was about to tell his uncle he didn't wear a watch when Terry said 'We're in. I'll go on a cat in distress tour, and you go and find the junk.'

Richard walked into the bathroom. Surprised, only briefly, at the opulent décor. His focus quickly switched Cummings lying, apparently dead, slumped over the briefcase. Richard hadn't seen what went on in the Citadel after Seren had left. He noticed was the bidet and auto flush functions, and he wanted them.

Terry was beside him. 'Same as Elvis. Died on the shitter. And what a shitter. He's draped all over your piece of junk?' Richard nodded, absorbing all this while he heard Terry talking on the phone.

'Yeah. Full clean up. Missing Person. Never seen again.' There's was a voice on the phone for some time. 'That's a lot of lolly. My price went up ten times if you want any help from me again Jobber.' There was a pause. 'That's fair.'

Terry was putting plastic gloves on. 'Used to be ginger we shoved up their ass to help them trot along a bit quicker. Now we have a secret recipe. Stewards can never figure it out. Still gotta shove it up there though. Hence these gloves are extra-long. No cat to save so assuming this is the piece of junk let's hit the frog and toe.' Terry carefully removed the briefcase and gave it to Richard in a towel. 'First we'll had a little geeze about. Never hurts.' Richard was already worrying about how much it was costing Terry to pay to make Cummins a Missing Person. Terry's wander through the flat led him to an old display cabinet. It had some Royal Doulton figurines in it. The dust distribution suggested a few had disappeared from the display over time.

'Poor old bugger was running out of dosh.' Terry took them out and photographed them one by one. They went and looked at the fridge and pantry while Terry was waiting for a response. 'This old prick was as poor as a church mouse. Living on baked beans and those Asian noodle things.'

Even though it was nine at night there was a response on Terry's phone in minutes. He whistled. 'At least thirty big ones for these stupid looking things.' He made a call. 'Jobber. Display cabinet needs to go missing also. China people worth quite a quid in there. Handle with care. Get them valued, I already have. Fence them and we split the proceeds. You'll be well ahead.'

They got in the cab and Terry noticed Richard wasn't going back to his flat. 'Girlfriend at last Richard.'

'Kind of.'

'Kind of a good start lad.'

'I'll drop the cash to her place shall I.'

'Terry you can't imagine what this means to me. What you've done. Please keep it.'

He laughed. 'Since you said please. But I want to be the first man you'll call when you have another a cat rescue mission.'

'You'll always be the only man Uncle Terry.' They gave each other a hug in front of Natasha's flat. Richard, out of interest, was trying to count the number of crimes he could be implicated in.

He felt like a total bastard. 'Natasha I've got to go unfortunately. I'll be back for longer next time. I need to help tidy up a few things after the war. I nominated an Ogre, Jacinta, as Regent. Lovely lady. Doesn't realise her potential and I want to go back and give her some support. And... could I borrow a screwdriver?'

'Of course.' She pointed to a drawer. 'No tattoo's this time.'

'No. It was all King stuff this time and ripping off the iPad. My daughter was killed, *again*, but fortunately a Dragon breathed on her and brought her back. And the good version. I think.' Richards said this while carefully lifting the central control panel out of the Wizard King's briefcase. He saw the RESET button. Halfway exposed from its two layers of accidental initiation protection and closed it up. He studied the innards of the case very carefully as he had the outer panel.

'What's that now.' Natasha mused. 'Three times she's been brought back to life. Stretching the credulity a bit don't you think.'

'That's exactly what I said. But what do you do?' As he put it back together, he said mainly to himself. 'I have to have both of in the loo and Youngers want them both on.'

He dashed over and leaned down and gave a kiss and a hug. 'I miss you when I'm in there.'

'Me too.' she said.

Within a moment of kissing Natasha goodbye, he was standing in front of Roger.

'Hi Roger. Sorry to make you wait.'

'My King.'

'Don't ever start that. I'm back to being a humble extruder now.'

'People want a figurehead King Richard.'

Richard shrugged. 'No big deal really. I wish you didn't have to wait around or at least be able to wait where they sold psychobeer.'

'More camp outs. Trying to do my job as a dad. My daughter can also wait here and leave me home to do the dishes and wash the clothes for a change.' Richard heard children playing.

'How's all the war stuff.'

'All wrapped up. If people could not accept sweet reason they would be dealing directly with an irritated Ogress. Stroke of Human Resources genius on your part to put her in charge. Went to the People and asked who was willing to give their dead or dying horse or old nags no one wanted to the Trolls. Trolls said horse jerky is now so well supplied they've set a universal price to cross bridges all over Tæranon, and you pay at one side only. The Rat People can clean the shit out of any Town or Village in Tæranon in safety. Any village that has no cemeteries and no rituals be-liefs about dead bodies were thrown in to sweeten the deal. Now you have a People who found the war a disappointment are now making huge improvements to municipal hygiene. There are also drop off points for worn out weapons. Happy Rat People are quite an asset to society.

The Witches have been forced to cut their prices a little because the heritage of a weapons is less of an urgent priority. But now that every border is open, they're flying all over the place reading them. And healing the odd wound and broken bone free if people go and collect all the weird stuff they need to drop into a cauldron. Because they now sell all sorts of potions that aren't placebos at retail prices. And that's going to be a big earner for them as time goes by. Bosco and Tina are now formally in a non-exclusive casual relationship.'

'Hence who needs a Figurehead?'

'The instinctive nature of People. And they'd like you to be a reminder of the source of their good fortune. Anyway, something tells me you're going to be disappearing quite a bit now. Oh, and do you know those devices you handed out on the battleground all started to get weird patterns on the screen then died. People have thrown them all away. Jackobie said he'd forgotten to mention they were only ever an example of *'planned obsolescence'.'*

Richard smiled. 'Good. Something like that would spoil Tæranon.' Though the Youngers all had good quality iPads with dozens of apps. When they downloaded the photographs of the Master briefcase there was an immediate frenzy of excitement.

For a few days he visited the Leaders of the People and receiving thanks and asked them what a figurehead King should be. It came down to attending some ceremonies at various Peoples traditional celebrations. And being the final arbiter to resolve tensions between Peoples where the usual processes weren't working. All understood there might be a royal Hiatus and Jacinta was broadly accepted as Regent.

Unfortunately, Seren was not welcome for some of these visits as she had been in the wake of the previous victory. No matter how much the malign influence the Wizard King was explained to them, there was little forgiveness in some quarters.

Her opaque mystic purpose was gone now. Completed as a footnote to the success of the other initiatives. She didn't mention what things would be like if they hadn't rid the land of the Wizard King with those dagger blows before he disappeared through the portal. Apart from the Youngers, she was the only one to find out about the condition of Cummins. And Richard also told her about the RESET button, and how things would be back to original setting as on a chess board, all unawares had it not been for her and her… Challengers. He told her that even if no one else knew, she had the most important and lasting role in the battle. All the Guardsmen Challengers had gone back to overseeing swimming pool safety, resort gardens, cellars, and armoury cloakrooms. Richard wanted to ensure they received some accolades. They weren't interested. He offered a pile of Ka Ching donated by grateful merchant in Younameit. Each one declined his offer. Seren helped with the no-yes-thankyou process, and they accepted the Ka Ching.

Richard told her in confidence that the Youngers thought that using the Master Briefcase they might be able to send someone back to Natasha's London flat where he was sitting.

'When do we go?'

'Oh. It's too dangerous for…for you.'

'You're considering it for somebody else but I'm not a candidate because you want me to hang around here and be what?'

'Alive would be nice. I've lost you an unprecedented three times you know.'

'I'm *yours* Richard to lose. But suit yourself. I'll wait my turn. Naturally, I'll be letting anyone you choose to take that you really don't care what happens to them, they're just a guinea pig to prove it up until you take me, which is what you really want to do.'

Richard knew when he was going to lose a fight. In this case via endless nagging and complaining. And possibly a return to broodiness. He was on his sixth psychobeer with Seren and Roger not long before leaving. Elves and Dwarves passed by. Some they knew. The Elves were supercilious, but much less so. The Dwarves, barely pompous anymore. Just proud and happy. It's like the passing of the Wizard King amplified the best and dampened the worst of all the People. But not to the extent they were boring.

It was during this session in the resort that Richard remembered a promise he'd made. He wished a small group of Rainbow Unicorns to appear at the next table. Beers materialising out of nowhere. 'Hey asshole. You can see what our coats have been stuck like since you fucked off immediately after the battle. The battle *we* won for you. You thought humiliating us at home might be a fitting reward?'

'Terribly sorry.' He wished they had the most beautiful coats *they* had ever dreamed of and immediately there was a beautiful range. Richard noticed there was a Painted Horse, Appaloosa, Palomino, and Draught Horse which none had before. They had been the same boring white all unicorns were in Tæranon.

'Wow guy. That's a very cool upgrade. It's been... like a secret desire of mine because we can't change our coats. We're not that magical. Now the other thing. We want to be evil. Just like we are deep down. Get rid of this thin covering of fucking niceness. We're all sick of it.'

Richard made a wish that they had integrated personalities. There was good and evil. Nice and nasty. Pleasant and unpleasant. At degrees based on the situation, and how they felt.

'You fucker. That wasn't what we…' There was a pause and a tone of revelation '… Lenny do you feel more, I don't know; integrated.'

'I think that's what I'd say Boss. See I'd like to go and take a big dump on this guy's doorstep.' He nodded towards Richard. 'I know we all would. But *now*, the thing is, for the first time I know I *could* go and do that if I wanted. Knowing I can do stuff if I want to, then balancing the other stuff, like he gave me the coat I always I dreamed of, and we felt kind of good being the ones who won the whole war for all these saps… overall, I think, why bother taking that crap.'

They all drained their glasses and started fade. 'There could be worse Kings.' Said the representative Unicorn. Then he snapped back into sharp focus momentarily. His head swung across and looked at Richard in the eye. 'Don't call us again.' He vanished.

'Going to be a long time away this time Richard?' Said Roger. While Seren feigned disinterest.

He stared into his glass. 'Most of the people I've loved meeting in Tæranon. Working together to achieve so many amazing things. They'll be old by the time I come back.' No one disturbed his silence. 'But I've got something I want to do. At least try to do. I keep leaving someone behind I want to get to know better.'

'I think it's time to do what *you* want Richard. I've met hundreds and hundreds of Punters. And there's no one like you. I don't believe in fate Richard because that man with the Master Briefcase intended to always get what he wanted. And would have. But we've had good luck. Good luck you came along when you did.'

Richard had left the Master Briefcase turned on and the Youngers had been able to view the pictures from Richard's mind and build a replica in Tæranon.

For the first time ever, two people faded though the portal. Both materialised at the location where the Slave and the and Master Briefcase leaned against the opposite walls of a loo.

'What the Fuck.' And this was the most serious *'What the Fuck'* tone of voice Seren had ever used. Richard realised he'd not re-minded her of the mechanism by which people entered and exited Tæranon. More particularly the physical arrangements. And he'd expected her to materialise standing up next to him. Though he didn't know why.

'Richard. Am I sitting on your lap? And you're naked. You're fuck-ing naked.'

He was trying to explain the processes and that he wasn't exactly naked, he just had…

She was spinning the faux brass door handle so hard it was doing nothing. 'What kind of weird little room is this.'

'Just turn it gently for God's sake and it'll open.' He tried to in-troduce some *Just grow up will you'* into his voice but he knew he should have given her a more detailed warning. Part of his mind was relieved she'd made it, another grateful he hadn't invited an Ogre. But that was never going to happen. The Youngers, wise as usual, said that sending nonhumanoid People would ultimately draw attention to the Briefcases and they would be tracked down and destroyed. They recommend that Seren be the only visitor.

By the time Richard had his trousers up and adjusted the boxes to the setting the Younger's had recommended, Seren was sitting at a table with Natasha. 'On his lap. Naked. And I thought… what kind of place is this? But you seem normal. You know he drones on and on and on about you. So much that I thought, I'm going to dislike this person because he just doesn't know when to shut up.'

'It's the same over here. It's Seren this and Seren that. I hardly know anything about anyone else in Tæranon. He just dashes in and out, tells me a few stories about you. It seems you die and come back to life each time he visits there.'

'It's all been just lights and voices for me half the time.'

Richard sat down with the two women who had been looking forward to ganging up on him. But it didn't last long. Seren said she was over her initial traumatic experience. It was early afternoon. She was offered tea or beer. 'Do you need to ask?'

Richard was just in the process of explaining that there no equivalent to Psychobeer while she had taken a confident swig as a stranger in a new land. 'O fuck. O fuck. What is that. Whatever it is it's not beer. It's some kind of animal urine with bubbles. What I do with this. Can I pour this vile shit out of a window? Is that what you people do? Am I being rude? Can I rinse my mouth in that water tub?'

Natasha and Richard were laughing. 'You're not being rude Seren. It's probably just off.' Said Natasha. But then Richard had some and ran to the sink and spat it out. 'Oh. That's appalling.'

Natasha was mortified that she'd offered friends a beer that was off. Richard had left it on the table. It was almost out of her reach and Seren noticed how difficult Natasha found it to move. Seren passed the beer. Natasha took an exploratory sip. 'It's fine. Just like it's supposed to be.'

Richard hadn't had a beer since his visits to Tæranon. 'It's the psychobeer. I think it somehow ruins all other beers for you, except Andy's apparently. But we may be able to find some among the hundreds of beers available.'

'They have hundreds of beers here. For God's sake why. Even the number Andy makes is a bit overboard, though I'd never tell him that to his face.'

'Here there are all these different countries that make different beers and people, I suppose they have more time on their hands and more money... Ka Ching... than in times gone so by they can afford to have all these different beers.' Richard knew he was going to have to go through a lot of background information just to answer questions. He changed the subject and cast around for ideas for something which would be a fitting celebration for the first, and possibly last, visitor from Tæranon. He whispered an idea to Natasha who smiled and said it was a fantastic way to introduce Seren to the new world.

'I'll see if there's any vacancies for sunset. Be a hell of a cab fare but it'll be worth it.' Richard said.

'I have a car Richard. And I'm still driving it even thought I probably shouldn't be.'

Within an hour Richard had installed Seren in the front seat, partly as a courtesy to a guest but also, he only now fully realised just how tall she was. He could see a moment of anxiety pass across her eyes. Once on the road Seren nearly unbuckled her seatbelt, planning to leap from the car, but they assured her it was safe. She was looking at cars all around her, and people. Sometimes stopped at lights, sometimes whizzing along.

'How many people are here?'

'Just in this city. About twenty-five million. If you took Younameit in Tæranon, there would need to be five thousand of those in a big squeezed up group to compare with London. It's going to take us just over an hour to get where we're going.'

'It takes so long because of speed limits and traffic.' Said Natasha. 'How many miles could you ride in a day?'

Seren shrugged. 'Maybe Forty miles. That was on Brindlefire anyway.' Her voice trailed off a little.

'In twelve hours, this car could do a thousand miles with no traffic.'

'But where would you get to if you went so far.'

'Punter Land is big.' That was Seren's name for the Outside. 'We never usually want to travel that far in a day. We don't travel that far ever usually unless it's for a holiday or moving house.'

'You have to go so far away for a holiday. And you take your house to a place so far away?' Natasha pointed to a double decker London bus to distract her. As they drove Seren said. 'Why can't you walk anymore.' Natasha had come to the garage in a wheelchair and climbed into the car with some help from Richard.

Natasha said. 'I have cancer Seren. I've been in denial until recently as to how far advanced it is. I spent a long-time having treatments, but they can make you sicker than the cancer sometimes. So, I'm just waiting around for the end.'

Richards's hand came from the back and squeezed Natasha's arm. He hadn't thought about it in such brutal terms.

'That's all a bit shit.' Said Seren. 'In Tæranon, somebody kills you, or maybe you get badly injured, or you die of old age. What kind of crap world is this?'

'I think the same thing every morning when I wake up Seren. But there have been lots of good times in my life. I'm making and effort to remember them. One of those good times has been meeting you.'

Seren changed the subject. But only slightly. 'Do people get killed riding in these roaring wagons. And where *the fuck* are all these people going.'

Richard took over the explanations. 'Hardly any. And like I said, there's millions of people, and they're going somewhere to do something. Just like we are. Going to work, picking up their children, going to some appointment or other. Going to watch a sporting match. I'll take you into the city tomorrow and you'll get a sense of the place. There's a big sort of Ferris wheel and you can look over the whole city. Helps you get an idea of its size.'

'What's a Ferris wheel?'

'Best if I show you tomorrow. When I arrived in Tæranon everything was so strange to me. It will feel the same to you, but you'll
start to understand and relate to this world, to the extent you want
to, soon enough.' While they were talking, Natasha had taken them
though a gate and they were driving toward a beautiful display of
hot air balloons. It was only when Seren got out of the car that
she could see the scale of the colourful balloons. She just stood
and stared.

She didn't say anything. She was mesmerised by them, just following as Richard was pushing the wheelchair. A voice broke through
and she heard she was being spoken to by a somewhat tentative
young man. She had been watching the balloons. All she imagined
they were for was to watch them go up to see how beautiful they
were from below and then pulled them back down. 'Ah, Miss. You
can't really take a sword on the balloon. Come to think of it, probably not allowed to have a sword in the compound. Probably not
allowed to have a sword most places really.' Richard had suggested
she leave in the car, but Seren felt naked without a sword. Even
when they had been too ridiculously big to wield.

'You can go and....'

'It's a prop sword, but we understand your concern. It's very valuable, and my friend would need to know it was in good hands.'
Said Richard.

'I can hold onto it.'

'Seren. He seems like a trustworthy fellow.'

She nodded and smiled at him. 'He'll be a dead fellow if anything happens to that sword.'

He smiled. Giving her as much assurance as he could. She was six feet five, dressed in the most amazing leather costume he'd ever seen, and he knew she had daggers in scabbards behind her back, but he decided to just let that one go.

Walking along she said. 'What a stupid place this is. It's not right for *me* to have a sword, but *he's* allowed to carry it around.' She looked around. They'd gone through a little door. 'What's going on?' She hadn't suspected that people flew in them.

'We're going up in the air.' Said Natasha.

Seren dropped to the floor of the basket. 'Are we inside one of those things?'

'We're in a basket connected to the balloon. And the balloon rises and falls when I pull this lever.' Said the pilot. 'I have people from time to time who find this type of flying strange. But I absolutely guarantee, that if you stand up and look around, for *one* minute, you're going to love it.' It didn't always work out that way, but he always tried it. He held out his hand. He was a large, jovial man who exuded confidence and a desire for people he took ballooning to love it. And indeed, within one minute she was loving it and overflowing with questions. The man was unused to so many questions and those about what the small things moving on black lines were, what kind of people lived in the villages they could see, did they use the balloons to control the rain and why couldn't people carry swords.

This last question he thought about a while and said. 'I think it's because if you let one person carry a sword, lots of people will want to and so when people get angry, they've all got a sword right there with them. It's going to be worse than if no one had a sword. If nobody has a sword, it's a bit safer for everyone.'

Seren could mount a few arguments to the contrary but overall she thought the idea was a good one. 'I think that's intelligent. I come from a place where everybody has a sword or some kind of weapon already, so it wouldn't work there, but I think in Punter Land it's a good idea. As long as I can keep *mine*.'

That night Seren fell asleep eventually. The sounds were different. She was accustomed to the quiet of the wilderness, or the sounds of a village or town around her or an Inn. But here she could hear the roaring wagons, just now and again, at various distances. And things in the kitchen were humming occasionally. She slept though. And she was a little anxious the next day. Seren was not accustomed to much anxiety. Even when fighting for her life. But millions of people. And Richard convinced her to leave the sword at home. She wondered if she could just take the scabbard. But he advised against it. The daggers nestled flush with the back of the suit, and she initially agreed to wear a soft leather jacket which was a poor fit, and she took off laughing as soon as she got out of the cab.

She was filled with wonder. They rode on the top of a red bus which she found amazing. They looked at landmarks and crowded streets that she found amazing. She rode a giant wheel and saw more amazing things. Going in between these places she noticed the people, and many noticed her. Seren was a magnificent human being. She was walking through crowds in a leather suit, the style of which no one had ever seen. Though not intended to be sensual and the closest comparison would be like high-end bespoke motorcycle leathers, not all accurately divined her reasons for dressing that way. She strode along with remarkable assurance and didn't mind being noticed. Initially.

Meanwhile, she was noticing them. 'These people are all the same. All humans. But even for humans they dress much the same. No one says hello which is just rude. And they're all obsessed with whatever those little machines are, like the Youngers made. It's like they're alone. All walking alone. Maybe two sometimes.' Seren laughed. 'And I can see some of them look at me as if *I'm* strange.'

But occasionally it was less pleasant. She got looks, some of curiosity some disparaging. And comments expressing a range of observations. And soon propositions from young men passing by. 'These people are rude Richard. And prejudiced like the Little People.' Richard had tried to warn her about crowds in Punter Land but her only point of reference was Younameit City.

'Some are curious Seren, and some are afraid of things they've never seen before. Try if you can recall the first time you saw a Goblin or an Ogre or a Troll, like Benny. Maybe you felt anxious and insecure until you knew how to manage the relationship on your terms. They have felt that way too.'

'There's a good reason you're a King Richard. I can now take enjoyment from our walks among crowds.' He hadn't suggested her solution to the problem. Someone would call out and she would call back. 'I know why you're doing that now. It's because you're unaccustomed to anything new.' She would substitute 'you're afraid of me and that's the correct response.' Or when propositioned. 'I don't want to have sex with that person. That should be obvious.'

They had been walking down a long flight of stairs, Seren unready for escalators. They came to what was the first tunnel she'd been in since the mines, which Richard hadn't thought about. That unhappy recollection was swept away by the most amazing contraption she had ever seen as it flew past at impossible speeds only a few feet from where she stood. And then one slowed down and people came pouring out and Richard led her into the thing and people kept coming and coming until everyone was squeezed up against each other. It was fascinating, frightening, and she hated it. Everything in this place had been about having people crowded close together.

Richard realised this a little belatedly. 'I should have taken you to Hyde Park. We'll do that tomorrow. Much more open space…for London at least. Or maybe we'll go to a horse-riding place, and you can get in the saddle in the English countryside. I wonder if I can ride a horse now over here. I have the beer issue so maybe I can.'

'You're not coming with me anywhere anymore. You want to be with Natasha. You need to be with her. I can navigate this place. How hard can it be? Like you say I'll go and hire a horse and go riding. I can go in those big red roaring wagons and see, what did you say, Museums and Galleries. And get a giant metal snake to some villages by the ocean. Which I assume have resorts like we do.'

'Sort of…or… sort of not really.'

Seren was disdainful. 'What's the point of having an ocean?'

Advised of her decision to go solo from then on Natasha was firm. 'Before you set off on your own, we're going shopping. Where going to get some clothes that still say 'Seren' but don't create constant unwanted attention, and whether you believe it or not, danger. And you're going to do it because I'm dying, and you have to be sympathetic.'

Seren laughed. 'You don't know me well at all. But I can see the sense in what you say.'

Richard felt it essential that he come along to push the wheelchair. Until Seren said 'Fuck off King. I can push the rolling chair. You sit here and do…Richard stuff.'

And he did.

Natasha was convinced faded jeans, a leather jacket, dark glasses, and a band T Shirt, in this case The Clash, would allow her to still be like she was, but draw slightly less attention. Natasha knew it screamed nineties but that's all she had experience of for this kind of thing. 'You're magnificent Seren, so still expect quite a bit of attention from men.'

'I'm accustomed to that. Being magnificent that is.'

'What I've suggested you wear is dated so you might be behind the latest fashion. Keep an eye on what other young women are wearing and use the money, Ka Ching, you have to get some things you like better.'

She laughed. 'I only found out about fashion yesterday and I already don't care about it. I miss my leathers, but I understand why I have to look like this.' There were limits though. 'Is there a place to alter the jacket so I can have my daggers with me.'

'I'll get an address.' Said Natasha.

Seren had a surprisingly low-key presence in their lives for the next week. She spent some time with Richard and Natasha when she was home but wanted to give them space to focus on each other. At another Richard was at meetings and Natasha was writing 'what the young Ogres wrote'. Seren commenced a brief love affair with television and then computers but after a few days of each said. 'I wish I could ride a horse instead of looking at them in a little box.' She arrived home at three in the morning on one occasion to find Richard and Natasha looking at her in a parental kind of way. They knew not to say anything, or they'd get an entirely reasonable and devastating rebuke. Richard went off to bed in case there was a need for 'girl talk'. Seren told Natasha. 'This man took me to a club specially for night-time. The drinks were an unbelievable amount of Ka-Ching but all these men kept buying them for me. And it went on and on. The spirits here aren't so bad once you get used to them. They talked a load of shit and kept buying me drinks. In the end they were all crawling around on the floor, so I came home. Andy's spirits are still better.'

'You can certainly hold it, but I hope it doesn't affect you. If you drink enough spirits here, it can give you what we call a hangover. You get an excruciating headache, and you throw up.' Said Natasha.

Seren threw her head back and laughed. 'These people here in the Punter Land do suffer so many afflictions.' She looked at Natasha. 'Oh… was that a bit insensitive?'

'That's alright.' Natasha gave a slightly wicked smile. 'I'll be there holding your head over the toilet bowl in the morning' And she was. Seren said she'd never been so violently ill. 'Why do people put poison in their spirits. I've never had this before. I've only seen people affected this way when they eat rotting food. The stupid assholes.'

'The great thing about hangovers is they don't last too long provided you …ah…get rid of the poison and keep hydrated. You'll be fine for the weekend. Richard's going to take you to Ireland. He wants you to see somewhere a little like Tæranon.' Natasha had resorted to National Geographic and some documentaries, to show her how diverse humans were. To Seren they were still all much the same except for different colours which meant nothing.

She said she'd like to go and meet some of these different coloured people living in less boring places. When Natasha told her it was a long way she shrugged and said. 'That roaring wagon of yours can go a thousand miles. In one day.' Natasha explained that the people in the pictures were usually thousands and thousands of miles away and there were all kinds or passports, visas, borders, and oceans to consider. Natasha realised Seren would probably need to have any identification even to get on a ferry to Ireland. She felt stupid and now fully realised realised how limited the amount of things Seren could experience was.

Natasha told her to have a shower and she might want to sleep the hangover off. Seren found the showers in Punter Land one of the highlights of the place. A vast improvement to the bags of warm water you had to pay for in Tæranon. Richard and Natasha thought they should mention a forty-five-minute shower was a bit long, but they decided to get to some of the hard truths of modern life later.

Natasha was wheeling past the guest bedroom to get some yarn from her embarrassingly large stockpile in a cupboard now filled with the stuff. She heard a sound probably Arnall had only ever heard. Seren was crying. She got up from the chair and knocked, but then walked in and sat beside Seren at the end of the bed.

'Are you okay.'

'Yes.'

'You're not upset?'

'No.'

Natasha decided not to say anything. Seren would tell her if she wanted to and would resent being pushed. She was sure Seren wasn't one to share how she felt unless she decided to.

'I 'hired' a horse for a ridiculous amount of local Ka-Ching. It was the stupidest horse I've ever met. I had to tell the nag every little thing with my reins and my heels. And they said I could ride any-where. They said it was some 'paddock' which meant grass and some forests trails. I saw what the horse could do, which wasn't much, and we came up to a fence. I went in another direction through a few trees as if it was a real forest, and a fence across the road with a locked gate. I rode right around the perimeter. In Tæranon places are fenced *in*. You ride anywhere. I took the witless animal back. They complained I rode their horse too fast. I said their useless nag was only fit for Troll jerky.'

'There aren't many open spaces around here anymore.' Said Natasha. 'It's changed even since I was a little girl. There are some big National Parks in the north, but they don't allow horses. There are large moors where you can ride a long way from fences. But it's hundreds of miles away and the horses would be the same as the one you hired.'

'The men here. The people. A man called out to me and I was curious, so I went over and asked him why he called out. I asked him what he wanted. His answer it was so…mean.' This was the cause some laughter in an otherwise sombre mood 'He must have misconstrued my interest. A roaring wagon with flashing lights arrived as I left.' She was quiet, as if embarrassed at some weakness. 'Men in Tæranon, they like to have fun, but they're…sweet.'

'The people calling out in some of the places you visited aren't necessarily the best to judge men Seren. And there are women that don't want a man who's sweet. At least temporarily. But think of Richard. He's a sweet man, but not weak and there are thousands that are like that. Still, women in Punter Land have a saying. 'A good man is hard to find.' And I think there is some truth in that, for one reason or another. And it might be true to some extent in Tæranon.' Seren nodded a little.

Natasha touched Seren's cheek lightly, so they were looking directly at each other. 'Seren. Stop talking about the symptoms. I think we both know what's really wrong.'

Now she was crying again. 'I don't like here. There are some good things, but I like Tæranon better. Richard went to so much trouble to bring me here and show me around, and now taking me to an

Ireland for a weekend. When I know he'd rather be with you. And the friends I have. Not so many since I took thousands of children hostage, but I still have a few. They're getting older and older. When I arrive back they'll be doing other things, have other friends and I'll have no real place in their lives and no purpose anymore. Unless I choose to be a witch. In every minute that passes their lives fly by.'

Natasha smiled. She decided not to be curious about the thousands of children taken hostage. She'd ask Richard about that later. 'Go and put those remarkable leathers on and get your daggers and sword ready.' Natasha tried to get up, but she couldn't. It made her so angry, but she tried not to show it.

Powerful arms picked her up and put her lightly in the chair. 'I'm sorry this has happened to you Natasha.' Seren said simply.

Natasha smiled and said. 'Thanks Seren. Me too.'

She knew that Richard would be only moments away because he always arrived home to casually check that she had taken her medication. He would also offer to drive her somewhere nice; a park to sit at or a café to have cup of coffee or a glass of wine, which she could only drink so diluted it was dispiriting. He arrived back and gave her a kiss and said. 'I think I might have a lawyer who has identified a very shaky precedent.'

Natasha didn't know what he was talking about. She was looking down the passage to see Seren. Leathers, sword, and daggers like the day she arrived. Richard saw Seren as she was meant to be.

'Magnificent.' Said Natasha. 'This girl needs to go home Richard.'

'I suppose a farewell dinner's out of the question.' He said. A little sad.

'No. It needs to be now.' Natasha pulled herself upright. Seren gave her such a tender hug. Richard's was more robust.

She put on the neural network skullcap on the Master case. Richard assured her she didn't need to sit on the toilet. The Youngers had explained the materialisation and dematerialisation program they'd developed, but it was too complicated to understand. Natasha had noticed in her pantry a great number of bottles and containers of things were only half full or completely empty when Seren arrived 'Thanks for bringing me here Richard.' She shrugged. 'It's just I hate it.'

'Don't worry about that. Roger will get a week's notice you're coming. And …Oh…the Tina thing. I forgot to tell you something. I mean I'm not supposed to tell you something. I thought I'd have more time to explain…apologise really. The Youngers… Tina got to them. I have nothing to do with it. I'm only a figurehead as you know.'

'And?' Seren's voice slid right past suspicion one word.

'They thought it would be kind of funny.'

Seren could feel the skull cap charging up. 'They'll be waiting. Your sword and daggers will transfer no problems. But ah... your leathers will stay with us. Kind of a memento of your visit.' He said this wincing. 'Tina's arranged a welcome back party. Bye.'

A look fury populated her face she lifted a pointing finger. 'You better be making this up Richard.' And she vanished.

'That's so weird. Seren simply disappearing like that.' Said Natasha.

'I wanted to avoid a sad farewell which she might try to pretend to participate in, which would be awkward. Tina and Roger will be there to meet her. So will her sword, daggers, and leathers. Right where they're supposed to be.' He was now businesslike. 'Now, I've made a time for a meeting with your Oncologist tomorrow.'

'He's going to try to make me do the same things again that I've said I won't and…'

There was a note of Kingly authority from Richard. 'Let me explain. I've been meeting with a lawyer who specialises in medical law. She has an option for us Natasha. She has done a great deal of research and met with a few colleagues.' Then he revealed he had been working a process for Natasha to consider going into an induced coma and coming to live in Tæranon with him for the time she had remaining. The suffering would be at an end and if there were treatments, and she could have them in a coma. it might keep her oncologist happy. If she went into remission she could come back to Punter Land.

'Not much chance of that I'd say.'

'Yes. But even the time you…have would be quite a bit longer in Tæranon.' Richard had been preparing in case there was the possibilities of a successful meeting by removing all the perishables from his flat and preparing to put it up for rent. If Natasha agreed to the arrangements, he would stay in her flat and be on the loo five hours out of every six. When he was up, he'd eat nutritious food and exercise nearly all that time to stave off muscle atrophy but also go and quickly do whatever business needed doing and pay bills and say hello to neighbours as if he lived there.

She would be in a private hospital cared for twenty-four hours a day with her neural skull cap on and the briefcase under her bed. If she wanted to leave Tæranon, it would be a simple matter of going through the portal.

The Oncologist didn't see it the same way as Richard's lawyer had with her precedents. 'It's a big decision and a big medical risk. And it is usually...' he was a little annoyed here, '...for people who have explored other options and nothing succeeds. It's a risk to me as much as it is to you Natasha. Surely you can see that.' He looked askance at Richard as someone trying to pressure Natasha into something even though he couldn't image why. 'Are your next of kin aware of this?'

'Richard is my Power of Attorney and you can give me any treatment you like when I'm... in the coma.' Said Natasha.

'It doesn't work that way Natasha, though I do admit there are a few things we could do.'

'Doctor Manning, I understand you don't trust me. Because yes, I have suggested this path to Natasha. But I see her in terrible pain every day and we have an option to share a life together when we are both in a particular state due to an interface with a machine.' It didn't sound so good saying that to a doctor. 'I know that sounds implausible but if you went there you'd understand.'

'If I went there?'

'Doctor Manning, you could go there right now. It would only be for ten or fifteens seconds here.'

The Doctor tried not to be overtly sarcastic when he said. 'How about... no. I'll pass.'

'I've done it lots of times. It's completely safe and then you'll know why I can be with Natasha ten hours out of every twelve.'

Manning couldn't deny the sincerity in Richard's voice. Without further prompting Richard pulled out the skullcap from the brief-case and handed it to the Doctor. 'God knows what our neurologist would think of this garage manufactured machinery.' He had put the neural net on in a kind of playful way, about to say he'd have to be crazy to take this kind of risk. But Richard hit Let It Roll with the LED instruction to return him in ten seconds. Somewhat longer in Tæranon. He was standing in a grassy field.

There was a man sitting on a chair a few yards away with his face in his hands. He was moaning. He looked up and said. 'Who are you?'

Manning looked around. If he'd come through some kind of Door it was gone now. 'Who are you?' He said to Roger. He saw a woman standing frozen nearby clad in a spectacular leather outfit looking like she was about to lose a very considerable temper.

Neither made an introduction. 'Is Richard coming. Is he still going to come back? He needs to hurry.' Said Roger.

'You seem to be in a great deal of pain, Mister…we need to get you to…' Manning was back at his desk. Richard was beside him to stop him from falling and took the offending piece of equipment from his head.

'That wasn't proper.' He looked at Richard. 'There's a man there saying you need to come back urgently. There's a woman frozen in state of …anger. The man's suffering. As a doctor I feel compelled to help him. But… does he exist?'

'You only saw the portal area. There are towns, villages, one city and beautiful landscapes and I'm the…' Richard thought saying he was the King would be too implausible. '…Emissary from the Outside World.'

There was an incredibly long pause. It became uncomfortable for Richard and Natasha. But Manning made decisions after as much deliberation as he believed they needed. 'Based on the fact you will have those treatments we're able to administer. You would be put into an induced coma provisionally. If there's the slightest indication that your well-being would be better served by being conscious my decision will be reversed.'

Instead of allowing Natasha to get in with a thankyou Richard was saying. 'Thank you so much doctor. Best hospital in London.' Natasha had heard nothing of this. She didn't have that kind of money.

'Our care here is more than adequate Richard and I'll be visiting regularly to review Natasha's well-being.' He sighed. 'That was an interesting experience. The man seemed in some kind of pain in anticipation of your return.'

'It's Roger. Can we prepare Natasha and, you know, send her off now?'

'I don't even know how to answer...yes I do. The answer is no. We have tests too run. All of this isn't as simple as you apparently believe.'

'How long Doctor.' Natasha cut through the wrangling between the two men. Her eyes, so strong, were pleading.

The doctor sighed and shook his head. 'Come back this evening.' Richard was about to say something, but the Doctor warned him off with a glance.

'This means a lot to me Bart. Do whatever treatments you want. I'm happy to be a lab rat if you want one.'

He laughed. 'Excellent. I'll have the paperwork drawn up.'

Richard was a little agitated. 'And evening would be...?'

'When I *tell you* it's evening.'

None of this dampened the sincerity of Richard's thanks and handshake. In the car Natasha said. 'Things are too slow for you but it's all at light speed for everyone else Richard. Including me.'

'Sorry. It's because you haven't...'

'Got long to live. Yes, I know. And I know what you're doing is trying to make the time I have left amazing. So, I'll join you at light speed.'

'Amazing and no longer painful Natasha. I think.' Richard advised that his rent money could go to medical costs to keep her in a good room and keeping her house in order if she was cured, which was still possible, or if she wanted to come home.

It did seem like light speed when Natasha was laying down in a single room, by then the next morning, When things took a little longer than expected. All sorts of things hooked up to her. Including the neural skullcap which Bart Manning had to fight others on the medical staff to allow. This he found ironic given his earlier scepticism. Richard wasn't there, which felt strange. He was strapped to a toilet seat in her flat. Intending to upgrade to the Cummins version. She worried that when she got to this place he wasn't going to be there, or she would still be sick. Richard said the Young Ogres had been working on that, which, now that she thought about it, didn't give her a lot of confidence. She didn't know if she was saying goodbye to people or if she would see them soon. Was all this a ruse so Richard so he could take her flat? And why was Miranda walking through the door?

'Sorry the last time we met I was such a bitch. I'm only like that at work. I think.'

'You weren't a bitch Miranda, you were being honest. You don't let people down very gently of course. But that's not always a bad thing. Why are you here?' Natasha was letting anxiety get the better of her. Was this the time for a discussion about a book.

Miranda smiled. 'Yes. I do want to talk briefly about the book.' Miranda anticipated her response. 'Plus Richard has told me what to do and I'll press the button at a specific time, to the second. Richard will already be there.'

Although Richard had told her this, it was somehow comforting to hear if from her. Miranda never even stretched the truth, though she sometimes put spikes all over it.

'On the book front. We like it. It's no best seller but it's a bit of a curiosity and initial reviews are warm rather than lukewarm. We need an author. I believe it's a collaboration. People don't like it when there's two authors. Neither do I. Dissonance you know.'

Natasha didn't agree but didn't want to argue about it right now. She didn't care if the book tanked or not. It hardly mattered now. She had an idea 'The author is Seren.' She cast around for a second name. Something to do with Seren. 'It's Seren Brindlefire. No that's stupid. Seren Brindle.'

Miranda shrugged. 'As good as any other of these made-up authors names.' Miranda reached out to take her hand.

'Goodbye Miranda.

'Not farewell?'

'No, it's goodbye from me, but I hope things are good for you.' Miranda nodded. The nurses made their preparations. She waited and watched as Natasha lost consciousness. Miranda waited a bit loner and looked at her watch. Did she really need to wait to the exact time? She had places to be, and she wasn't fond of hospitals.

Richard had already typed a long message on and LED screen. She smiled at Natasha and pressed 'Let it Roll' as instructed. A minute or so ahead of schedule. Patience was something she believed was the opposite of a virtue. Natasha disappeared into a new world.

Miranda had been the cause of an unexpected anxiety for Richard late in the afternoon after the meeting with Manning. He'd been called in to see his sister who broke the news that there were authors who wanted to use the machine.

Richard told her a summary version of his story. Miranda wasn't big on sympathy or patience. Yet on this occasion she breathed in deeply. 'I think it's relevant there are a few people threatening lawsuits because of alleged side effects from that damn thing. I could let all these would-be users know that and then draft up some ridiculous disclaimer for them to sign. Hoping no one would.'

'Could I by it.'

'They don't want to sell it Richard. But I could tell them you have anger management issue and threw it in the Thames when it made your tenuous grip on creative writing even more tenuous.'

'Well thank you.'

'But the company will need to be compensated.' She was fishing for a number.

'Five thousand.' He suggested.

'Richard how can you come up with such a ridiculous offer. Because you're my brother you think you can trot out something like that.

It's five hundred quid and not a penny less. And we're going to take it out of your current royalties which should pay it off...sometime around when the next ice age hits.'

She stood up and gave him a hug. There was nothing more of substance to discuss so it was time for him to go. 'Let me know about this cycle of getting back every day. We could catch up. Have a coffee.'

'I'd love that.'

The morning of Natasha's procedure, twelve hours behind his schedule, he was in the flat getting ready to strap in so he was in Tæranon at least an hour before Natasha arrived. He was cleaning out the toilet with the various liquids and air fresheners for the purpose After a final flush he was turning to sit down and there was a knock on the door. He thought he'd ignore it. It was insistent. He worried it could be something to do with Natasha.

It was the police. 'Good morning Mr Campbell. I'm Officer Dowsett and this is Officer Reece. We've come to ask you a few questions about a Missing Person.' She held up pictures of a much younger of Cummins. Richard tried to have a sly look at the clock.

'We spoke with his last known employer, that he worked for. The same place that makes books...from the ones you write.' Emma was from Essex and was trying, reluctantly, to sound official.

'I never met anyone of that name.' *Except as a Wizard King which doesn't count.* Thought Richard.

Emma pursued the line of questioning. Her partner was a little on edge. Because *they weren't Detectives and had no reason to be there*. 'Do you know what's strange Mister Campbell?' Said Emma.

'No…what's strange.' Said Richard

'He hired two men to come into your flat, do you harm, steal anything they wanted as long as they stole a briefcase you had.' Emma had heard about these two men and their association with Cummins from the man who fenced some Royal Daulton figurines. Then she looked at Richard, frowned and changed the subject. 'Haven't I met you before.'

'Maybe?'

'You were what might have been a lookout man for what may have been an illegal gambling establishment although when we visited the next day found it was a warehouse full of shit plastic toys from China.' Richard was on the verge of trembling as she continued. 'Now where was I. Oh. Can you remember where you were. The night these hired men were going to burgle your flat, and possibly bludgeon you to death?'

It would be easy make something up. But they might talk to his Uncle. Stay as close to the truth as possible he'd always heard. But he couldn't. 'I was with my Uncle Terry. We thought it would be nice to visit the local of a friend of his. But we heard a cat in distress. It was giving off a terrible din. Meowing up a storm. It was stuck in a drain, but we got it out using a jacket for protection. It all claws and teeth having a red hot go at us. We were going to take it to a cat shelter. But the creature took off. Had a bad limp though.' She had been taking notes as he spoke.

Emma looked up to see her partner on the phone. 'Mister Campbell, we interviewed your uncle about the same incident.' She let this sink in. 'And that's exactly what your uncle said. Almost word for word. Limp and all.'

Brendan said. 'Emma. Some human remains found in a park in the city.' *Where we're supposed to be.* 'We've got to go and do crowd control.'

She was briefly irritated by this. 'We'll have to stay back while those lay about Detectives go and peck some shit into a computer.' She turned smiling at Richard. She had an engaging smile, especially when she was enjoying herself. Finishing the notes, she said 'I see. That all sounds completely plausible Mister Campbell. Unlikely we'll have further questions. Thanks for your time.' She tore out the page from her notebook and handed it over. 'You might as well keep this.'

'Thank you…um…Officers. Have a good day.'

When they returned to the car, Brendan driving somewhat faster than he normally would, the two constables had a big laugh. 'Do you really think that bloke's related to Terry.' Said Brendan.

'Has been for years.' She laughed. 'I heard about these two blokes hired to do him a mischief until Jobber called them off. Thought I'd go and listen to whatever rubbish story he came up with and have a laugh at Terry's expense.' Brendan smiled. But worried about who Emma associated with.

Richard looked at the piece of paper she'd handed over. There were doodles all around the edges. It simply read. *'What an absolute load of bollocks.'*

He looked at his watch. He had a minute before Miranda was going to send Natasha across.

But Natasha had arrived before him. It was like a grassy moor with the occasional outcrop of black rock. There was no evidence of a Door she might have come through. There was a man on a chair with his face in his hands. Seren was frozen like a statue pointing at no one, caught with the same 'this better be a joke Richard' look on her face.

'You're Roger?'

'Yes. Sorry I can't talk. Need to concentrate. Is Richard coming soon?'

'Yes.' She said. Suddenly distracted. She felt well. For the first time in years she was free of the constant unwelcome pain which had been an unwanted companion that had grown more and more un-pleasant as time passed. She was standing easily and looked down to see she was wearing a beautiful emerald coloured dress that swept the grass with fine brocade down the front. But that wasn't the biggest surprise. The hand she brought up to touch the fabric was young. Late twenties maybe.

Richard arrived. He came out facing Roger who was sitting in pain and ran to him asking what he could do. Roger sat up and breathed out. Then fell off his chair. He sat up on the grass. 'Oh, that was awful. Apparently, the Dark Wizard could do it through the Master

Briefcase so he could come in and out with no change in Tæranon time and always return to the existing narrative.' Roger said this between slow, deep breaths. 'The Youngers built a Master briefcase here but said they couldn't figure out how to make it work without a 'rider'. As the Portal and Door Master, I was the only one.' He took a few more deep breaths and blew them out quickly. 'Feeling better already. You seem to be ignoring someone Richard.'

Richard immediately turned around. He saw a woman who was almost a stranger given her youth and vigour and swept her up into a big hug and said 'Welcome to Tæranon. And you're so young and beautiful.'

'I wasn't beautiful before?' Natasha laughed. 'I know what you mean. I'm more beautiful. Partly because of this amazing dress. I feel like some Middle Age princess.'

'You might be in for a promotion.' Said Roger

'Why's Seren still frozen.' Richard asked

'Thought it would be fun if I let her out when we are all standing around making the same stupid pose she's making. I had time to think about it. It's not easy to disorient Seren, so I thought this would be a good opportunity.' While Roger was saying this, they could both see Richard looking at his hands and feeling his mid-section. Same middle-aged man with the 'slight' paunch he'd had when he'd hit Let It Roll.

Natasha came up beside him and gave him a squeeze. She was still trying to navigate things Roger was calling to the others to stand around making the same imperious gesture Seren was. He unfroze her and she was briefly disoriented. 'I'm glad there's no Witches. You're young Natasha. That's great. We can party.'

Natasha gave Seren a huge hug. 'I'm so glad to be here and see you again. You fit right in here now that you're home. Of course, any… ah…partying I do will be with Richard.'

Seren threw her head back and laughed as only she could do. She leaned in quickly to Natasha she said. 'We'll talk later.'

At that moment Jackobie came from around a ridge of black rock leading four horses behind his white mare. Seeing her first Goblin was a shock. However, once she was engaged in a conversation with a genial young man it quickly faded One of the horses follow-ing was GroundBreaker, there was TBA and two other horses. One horse with a magnificent brindled pattern no one had ever seen the like of. It had large tan brindles over a white coat. Jackobie also led out a beautifully marked Appaloosa. Its disposition was very much more relaxed and easy-going than that of the larger brindled horse.

Jackobie motioned Roger across for a word in his ear. The Youngers had made an adjustment to the Master briefcase and thought it would be funny to let Richard think he would be stuck at the same age as ever. Richard was transformed to about the same age as Natasha.

Initially the two ladies didn't notice. Seren was somewhat in awe of the horse being drawn up to her. She said without the slightest exaggeration. 'That's the most beautiful coat I've ever seen.' The horse immediately knew who he would be carrying about and came in for a good nuzzle. The nuzzle was just hard enough that it might have knocked over a lesser person. Seren stretched up and said something into the horse's ear. Very likely a death threat in horse. The horse was happy. He knew where he stood.

Natasha was looking admiringly at her beautiful horse and looking down occasionally at the fine brocade of her dress. Richard finally drew attention to himself. She was immediately in his arms telling him this whole thing was better then she had ever hoped for.

'Come on you guys. Psychobeer awaits. What do you think Roger? Let's ride for a few hours and then slip right through that Door.' Seren was master of ceremonies.

'I could not think of a better way to celebrate the return of the King. And there's more diverse patronage there these days.'

'First. I want to see what this little baby can do.' Seren was suddenly streaking away on a horse built to love speed or any other kind of travel through wilderness. She was back in a few moments. 'Makes that thing I rode on in Punter Land look like a donkey.' After another short spurt away she was back. 'You know Richard, this blows the whole father-daughter thing right out of the water doesn't it.'

'Would you like an older brother.'

'That could work.'

'And what does that make me,' Said Natasha.

'You're my Sister-in-Law of course. And Queen.' Said Seren 'There. I've saved you pair months of manoeuvring.'

Richard laughed. Not displeased by the fact that, according to Seren, he was now married.

She was galloping in circles around them like an excited child which in this case she would have no problem being compared to.

'Did you think Seren was your daughter.' Said Natasha.

'I was never quite sure, but I wanted her to be.'

He had the familiar sensation of another rider suddenly sitting on his horse's rump.

Seren said. 'Me too.' And she was gone.

www.ingramcontent.com/pod-product-compliance
Lightning Source LLC
Chambersburg PA
CBHW070656180626
46817CB00006B/2391